GIVE LOVE A CHAI

COMMON THREADS BOOK #2

NANXI WEN

WWW.SMARTYPANTSROMANCE.COM

COPYRIGHT

This book is a work of fiction. Names, characters, places, rants, facts, contrivances, and incidents are either the product of the author's questionable imagination or are used factitiously. Any resemblance to actual persons, living or dead or undead, events, locales is entirely coincidental if not somewhat disturbing/concerning.

Made in the United States of America

Print Edition:
978-1-949202-75-5

AUTHOR'S NOTE

CONTENT WARNING

When I started writing this book, one of my goals was to ensure that the characters are relatable. Some parts of the book are very much fictional, but many parts are grounded in experiences that I've had, or my friends or family have had, including events, habits, places, etc. Some of these experiences are hopefully light and funny, and some are not.

With that, I want to call out that this book contains sensitive topics that may be triggering for some of you, such as pregnancy and miscarriage. I have tried to treat the experiences with care. A huge thank you to my sensitive readers who provided thoughtful feedback. Anything that I got wrong is on me, and I apologize in advance.

Thank you,

Nanxi

CHAPTER ONE

TIA

November 1, 2009 (never sent)
~~*Dear*~~ *Andrew,*
I hate you. I hate you. I hate you. Where did you go?
Hatefully not yours,
Ting

I really needed to pee. The more I thought about how much I needed to pee, the more I had to. I started to fidget in the small driver seat of my rental car. As if I wasn't already a complete weirdo, sitting in a tiny lime green Beetle (the only car left at the rental place), wearing sunglasses and a hat to hide my face even though it was cloudy outside.

I squinted at my empty tea cup and debated peeing there, instead of getting out of the car. Knowing myself though, I would make a giant mess. Or get arrested for mooning. Probably both.

Somehow, I doubted the police would understand why I was stalking a townhouse in downtown Chicago for hours on a Saturday in mid-October. In fact, that would guarantee a mugshot for me.

Taking a giant breath, I opened the car and nearly fell on my face. Four hours and thirty-six minutes of being squished in a car had lulled my legs to sleep. Luckily for me, the street was pretty quiet, and only a judgy five-year-old had seen me flailing to regain my balance.

Or, unluckily me? The little Judge Judy wannabe tugged on his mom's hand. "Mommy, what's she doing? Why is she walking weird? Mommy, Mommy, Mommmmmy!"

Wringing out the pins and needles in my legs, I shot the poor kid a death stare. He stared back, confused. "Mommy, why is she making that face? Did she go poop? Does she have a diaper like baby George? Mommy?"

Okay, so my death stare needed some work. The poor mom threw me an apologetic smile and hustled her kid along. I was almost jealous of them, going to wherever they were going.

I shook out the last of the inertia from my legs. As if I were taking steps for the first time after an injury, I forced my legs to move toward the red door in front of me.

I knew *he* was inside. I had seen him go out earlier for a run, in casual shorts and a long-sleeved shirt. Forty-five minutes later, he'd returned, sweat curling his black hair around his neck and making his shirt cling to a body that obviously had never taken a cheat day. I had seen a tantalizing glimpse of toned abs as he stretched his arms over his head, before I covered my eyes in guilt.

Unless he had climbed out a back window or run away via a basement tunnel, I was ninety-nine percent sure that he was still inside. The remaining one percent still couldn't believe that he was this close.

Wincing, I knocked on the door, the sound so jarring that I whispered "*Shhh*" to the inanimate object. After a quick heartbeat, my courage completely failed me, and I turned to flee. When the door flung open behind me, I jumped like a startled rabbit.

"Ting?"

His voice was deeper. That was my first thought after my brain started working again. Something forbidden and forcefully buried responded to that baritone. A rush of emotions overwhelmed me, like a physical force so strong I had to close my eyes to try to fight it off. I didn't have the time or the desire or the strength to wade through the tidal wave now. I *couldn't* get lost in him and lose myself.

Again.

His footsteps sounded behind me, coming closer. Was it too late to run away?

"Ting?" he repeated. His voice was right behind me. If I leaned back, I would fall against his chest. Not that I wanted to, of course. *Liar.*

I turned around cautiously, preparing myself. His chest was broader than I remembered. We had both gained a few pounds since I had last seen him ten years ago, but whereas mine had gone to my booty, his was clearly all muscle. My gaze traced up his chest to his neck, searching for the left dimple. Andrew let me peruse him slowly, holding himself unnaturally still, waiting for me to say something.

Memories upon memories of Andrew blurred into the man in front of me. Nine-year-old Andrew teaching me to fish, and when I hadn't caught anything after four Saturday mornings, announcing that he would catch enough fish to feed me. Andrew brushing away my question when I asked about the hole in his sneakers. Teenage Andrew flashing a private smile for me in the hallways between classes, encouraging me during my awkward teenage years. He had once been my lifeline and the source of all of my adventures.

Yet, here he stood—almost a stranger. Except for the familiar, piercing gray eyes that looked too deep within me and rarely gave anything away.

When my gaze finally reached his face, I could see his eyes widen before quickly slamming into neutral. I couldn't help letting out a small gasp, as every part of me was screaming to run. Run home to Boston, run home to my safe apartment with the weighted blankets and pints of Ben & Jerry's, run away from this man who had defined my past. Despite the warnings in my head, my traitorous legs took a step toward him.

A second step.

Stupid legs, ignoring my head, that delivered me to him until there was no air between us. Despite the chilly autumn day, heat radiated from him to my greedy body.

Because it would be too much even for me to just stand there and breathe his warmth in, I gave him a quick squeeze around the waist and jumped back. "Hi, Andrew, hi!" I waved cheerily, as if a day had separated us instead of ten years.

Ten years, one month, twelve days, and a few hours, but who was counting?

Head tilted slightly to one side and brows furrowed, Andrew asked, "This is a surprise. What are you doing here? How do you know where I live?"

"From a friend who knew a friend," I responded vaguely to his second question. I didn't admit that this friend of a friend of a friend was a private detective that I had hired. Because nothing screamed "run away" than knowing your ex hired a professional to track you down.

As for his first question—what was I doing here? When I had left ten years ago, I had promised myself that he was not going to be part of my life anymore. I thought I had taken steps, painful steps, to extract myself from him.

Yet here I was—one shocking phone call, lots of freaking out, an impulsive plane ride, a car ride, and a few hours of stalking his door later.

Which reminded me. "Um, can I use your bathroom?"

Whatever he expected me to say, that was not it. He glared at me for a few seconds to see if I was serious. Thankfully, before I had to start hopping up and down, Andrew gestured toward his still-open door. I did not wait for him to follow before sprinting inside.

A few minutes later, I had run out of excuses to hide in his bathroom. I could only wash my hands for so long before he became suspicious, if he wasn't already. Sighing, I finger-combed my straight black hair and pulled it into a low ponytail. Brown eyes stared back at me, looking huge in the reflection. I had been too much of a mess to put on makeup that morning before I headed to the airport. Not that I was trying to make an impression.

I didn't care what Andrew Parker thought.

Not anymore.

Still, I put on some lip balm before I could think too much about why and opened the door. Andrew sat by the little island in his kitchen, hands gripping a beer.

Huh.

I had never seen him drink alcohol before. Unlike pretty much everyone that I knew, he had been very intentional about not engaging in underage drinking. It made me sad to think about all of the changes that I missed, moments that I had expected to be part of if he hadn't pushed me away.

Now, I was getting angry. I held on to that anger. Anger was easy. Anger had carried me through the first few months after he had betrayed me, especially when I was railing against the world in those awful days in the hospital.

Oblivious to my anger, he looked up. "You still smell like those fruity Lip Smackers you used to love, Ting." His gray eyes roamed over me. A single dimple flashed at me, as his lips tugged to one side.

I couldn't believe he still remembered my fondness for Lip Smackers. I had been using them since I first immigrated to the United States from China and discovered them in the aisle of some supermarket. I was the only person over the age of ten that still used them, but I was loyal to what I liked. Unlike Mr. Cool in front of me. "I don't go by Ting anymore. It's Tia now."

"When did you decide that?" Andrew asked, unfurling himself to standing. His six feet two inches of muscles towered over me. The large kitchen suddenly felt small. Andrew the man had a presence that overwhelmed me in a way that Andrew the boy had never.

"Almost ten years ago when I needed a fresh start. I wanted a name that helped me to fit in," I said, daring him to say anything.

His only response was the tightening of his shoulders. I couldn't tell if he was reacting to my dig about a fresh start, or to me changing my name after years of him encouraging me to keep my given name. When we first met twenty years ago, we had bonded over not fitting in. As much as he told me "screw them" when our classmates made fun of my foreign-sounding name, my faint accent, or squinted their eyes while saying "konnichiwa" despite my protests that I was from China, I had cared too much. My name was the part of me that was the easiest to change.

"Okay, Tia," he started, letting my name roll over his tongue, as if testing how it felt. "Why are you here?"

I looked into his face, so achingly familiar that I could have drawn his features from memory. I let myself feel the full weight of sadness, bitterness, and regret wash over me. Andrew Parker was my past, an anchor that I hadn't even realized was holding me back. I needed to move forward now.

In a voice that sounded stronger than I felt, I said, "I want a divorce."

CHAPTER TWO

ANDREW

September 19, 2008
Dear Ting Ting,
I miss having my best friend around every day. There—I shared my feelings. Now, you can't complain that I never tell you what I think.
I went to a party yesterday, and I've been eating lunch and dinner with some of the guys in my dorm. It's freeing not having anyone know about my dad. I can't wait until you're at college with me next year. I can feel it, next year will be our year.
Yours,
Andrew

Fuck. What?

After weeks spent traveling for work, I had been looking forward to a weekend of nothing. Some working out. Some vegging in front of the TV. Lots of takeout and sleep. I was not expecting to see Ting, um, Tia, trying to run away from my door. Or standing in my kitchen, smelling like piña colada, and looking smoking hot.

Demanding a divorce.

Ten years ago, she had been cute in an approachable way. Today, she was all *woman—*

curvy, full pouty lips, and smooth-skinned. Despite how much she had changed, she still blushed easily. Right now, her face was flush with color, and I was very curious to see how far the blush extended. She had all of my attention. By all, I mean *all* parts of me were aware of her.

"Andrew, I need you to sign these papers." Tia waved a stack of documents in my face. "Now."

I shook my head in confusion. Tia must have mistook the gesture to mean that I refused to sign, because she started to look pissed. "Look, Andrew, you owe it to me. I mean, you were happy to do it the first time. Why—"

Out of years of habit, my hands reached for hers. Bad idea. She dropped the papers in shock, leaving just her warm hands in mine. Her fingers were soft, yet I also knew they were strong from years of playing the piano. Her awkward hug earlier had caught me by surprise. It was so quick and separated by so many layers of clothing that I didn't have time to respond. This time though, her bare hands in mine did something to me. I wanted to pull her closer. I wanted to see if her lips would taste as sweet as before.

I was a fool.

My Ting—damn—*Tia* was asking for a divorce. Wait, what the … "Aren't we already divorced?"

At my words, she snapped and yanked her hands away. My hands felt the loss.

"No!" She glared at me in accusation, as if I had done something sneaky. "There was some sort of filing error that my new lawyer just told me about. I was … distracted during the whole process before. I must have missed something. It was a busy time."

Tia looked guilty. She may have grown and changed in ways that I didn't fully understand, but she still sucked at hiding her feelings. Even though she tried to hold my gaze, her face was bright red, and her hands fidgeted with nonexistent dust on her jeans. I didn't blame her for being distracted or too busy all those years ago. Hell, I had buried myself in school, my part-time job, anything that came my way, just so I wouldn't go mad thinking about her.

Besides, it was my fault that I didn't even confirm the divorce. When she texted, "It's done," I had no reason to question her then. Our marriage was over.

Except, I guess, not.

"What do we do now?"

My question was met with more waving of those damn papers. I grabbed the stack from her and skimmed through. Typical divorce verbiage, except this was about me. My name was on the contract. The most significant relationship of my life was classified as: Irretrievable Breakdown of Marriage. I finally understood why my clients often ignored my suggestion to stay objective.

While I skimmed, Tia asked, "Do you need a lawyer? I can refer you to some in Chicago. My lawyer has a bunch of people he knows in the area. Do you want the list? Do you want to call some of them? I bet one of them works weekends. Or maybe you could leave a message—"

"I'm a lawyer," I said simply.

"Really?" Surprise laced the word.

"Really. Not as much of a delinquent as you expected?" I asked, trying to infuse amusement into my voice. It surprised me how much her disbelief stung.

If tomatoes could sunburn, that was Tia. She looked down and said to her socks, "I never thought that. I didn't laugh when you said you were thinking about college. I made you flashcards for the SATs and dragged you to college fairs. Remember?"

I remembered.

She may have thought that she left. I knew the truth. Even as my heart beat for her, I had pushed her away. Who would want to be with the son of a criminal who had nothing to offer? I couldn't even fulfill her request to open up. Because what if Tia had discovered that there was nothing inside, or worse, she saw signs of the same rottenness as in my dad?

As much as I had moved on with my life, I hadn't been able to get rid of my memories of her. Nor had I wanted to at first. Call me a glutton for pain, but memories of her had kept me awake for years after she had run away. Memories and regret.

I ran my hand through my hair, trying to pull myself from such dark thoughts. Instead of dwelling on how far apart we had drifted, I forced myself to choke out, "I remember. I was going to win the Wimbledon while you became a world-famous artist, and we would live with our six kids and five rescue dogs."

I expected her to laugh, as she had howled with laughter whenever we had joked about this as kids. The dream was ludicrous—my mom couldn't have afforded tennis lessons for me, and Tia had never graduated beyond drawing stick figures.

Instead, a flash of pain crossed her expressive face, and her eyes squeezed shut for a moment. I forced myself to stand still, to not rush to wrap her into my arms. When she finally looked up at me, the depth of anguish in her eyes knocked the breath out of me. Had I ever seen her hurt this much before? The last time we were in front of each other, she had been accusing, confused … but not sad.

Screw it.

I pulled Tia into my arms. She smelled the same—fruity, like her silly Lip Smackers. She felt *amazing*. There were curves that I couldn't help react to. More than that, there was also a sense of relief in holding her again. It was as if my body had been on alert for years, but now felt safe enough to finally let out that deep breath it had been holding for so long. The unexpected peace made no sense, because part of me was not relaxed.

By instinct, because it couldn't be by her choice, Tia's arms came up to wrap themselves around my neck. Just like before, she stood on tiptoes to get closer, her cheek resting on my chest. I didn't know how much time passed, as we stood there, in my bright bare kitchen, and held on.

In my tumultuous past, Tia had offered herself as a safe place for me. I had craved her warmth, optimism, and acceptance of me, even as I had acted like a selfish bastard in holding back. That craving roared back. I acknowledged the truth—I missed her.

She's here. Show her you've changed. This was our second chance. We were still married for now. This time, I would be worthy of her.

CHAPTER THREE

TIA

November 26, 2009 (never sent)
Andrew,
It's Thanksgiving. I can't find anything this year to be thankful about.
My mom made duck and stuffed it with rice and chestnuts. After ten years in the US, she's still not sold on turkey. I wonder if my parents regret uprooting their lives to come to America for me to have a better life? I doubt she expected me to fail so spectacularly.
Ting

I snuggled into the unique warmth of Andrew. He might have changed. I might have changed. However, this hug took me back to feelings that I had shoved away into the dark corners of my brain. The weekends that I snuck out to visit him in college, while telling my parents that I was at friends' houses—to just see him, to touch him—he had hugged me just like this, as if we hadn't seen each other in months instead of days.

I had missed him, I realized. Not his body, though that was magnificent. I had missed the essence of Andrew. The way that he had held me as if I were fragile. The way he hesitated before letting me go after each embrace as if he wasn't sure if that would be our last. The solace he gave me throughout our childhood when things didn't go my way, the sense of peace that he provided by letting me be myself. I almost cried with relief at the familiarity and intensity of being in his arms again.

It had been too long since I felt this needed and appreciated for myself.

Just like that, I snapped out of it. As in the past, I misconstrued gestures for more. The hug meant nothing to him. I needed to remember that. Why care about someone who didn't believe in love? Who closed himself to the possibility of happiness?

Sensing the change, Andrew's arms fell to his sides, a defiant glint in his eyes, as if daring me to deny the electrifying spark between us.

More than anything, I was furious with myself. I felt as if I had betrayed my younger self who had shed all of those tears. No, *wasted* all those tears on someone who never wanted them.

Yanking back, I scrambled for the papers Andrew had laid on the kitchen table and shoved them against his chest. I didn't get out of my comfy bed while it was still dark outside, to fly halfway around the country just to fall into a puddle at his feet. No, I had a mission, and I wasn't leaving until he signed. I glared at him impatiently, until he sat down with a shrug at his kitchen table, head bent over the papers, a pen twirling in his fingers.

"Okay, okay, let me take a closer look first before I sign anything." Andrew's voice drifted over.

Standing awkwardly in his kitchen, I looked around surreptitiously. It was clean and uncluttered, as expected. Having grown up with a single mother who worked two jobs, Andrew had never understood why I liked buying things that had no practical purpose. What was the point of candles that smelled like cucumber melon? Why did I have cheesy holiday mugs when regular mugs could be used the entire year? No matter how many times I explained that drinking tea from a giant Santa mug in December was better, he would laugh and shake his head.

His kitchen and townhouse definitely reflected that minimalist streak. There was nothing on the counter except for a simple coffee pot and … huh … a candle? A soy, apple-pie-scented candle that clearly wasn't meant to be used as a backup in case of electric outages.

I looked over at Andrew, fully expecting him to have sprouted a narwhal tusk. Nope, he was still concentrating on the papers, a frown marring his tusk-free forehead, as he made notes in the margins.

"Are you done? I haven't got all day," I asked.

"I'm thorough. It's my *own* divorce contract."

I left him to the contract and instead glanced around more carefully. I had so many questions about his current life, but I also didn't want him to know that I was curious. He was a potent mix of familiarity and mystery, and I had no desire to be caught.

On second glance around his home, I saw more out-of-place touches: the small magnets from foreign cities on his fridge, the crotchet throw on the couch in the living room, a couple of framed photos scattered around. The one nearest to me, I was pretty sure was of him and his mom. The one on the bookcase was too small for me to see clearly.

I squinted. Definitely him with a female—I could just make out the long hair. Definitely not Andrew's mom. This woman's hair was blonde.

Bitterness washed over me. I had no right to feel anything about who he was taking pictures with or who decorated his home. I was the last person to judge him for having someone in his life. I was just surprised, that's all. Not jealous. Not at all.

"You could get closer."

Startled, I responded so very elegantly with, "Huh?" Very smooth. I mentally smacked my forehead.

Andrew stood up and walked toward me. His walk was no longer gangly and full of restless energy. It was confident, and it suited this grown-up version of Andrew too well.

He nodded to the living room. "Whatever you're squinting at, you could move closer. Technically, since we're still married, it is *our* house."

I ignored the flutter at hearing him say "our" and blurted out, "Does your girlfriend know you are married?"

Confusion crossed his features for a moment, before his eyes landed on the bookcase. A smile broke out, making him look almost boyish. "Jealous, Ting Ting?"

"No! And don't call me that. It's a childish nickname."

His smile widened.

"Whatever, I *don't* care. I just want to make sure this"—I pointed to the papers that he was still holding on to—"isn't an issue for whoever *she* is."

Andrew sobered at the mention of the divorce papers. He nodded toward the picture frame. "She's a friend."

"A friend you have a framed photo of?"

"Just a friend—nothing more," he repeated, not quite holding my eyes.

"Where are the pictures of your other friends?"

"I don't go around taking pictures of my friends when we're hanging out."

I knew I sounded like a jealous wife. I couldn't help it. I had to know what she was to him. "Yet, there's a picture of this *friend*."

Andrew ran a hand through his hair. "Charlie thought my house was too bare. She took a selfie of us, printed it out, and put it there. That's it. She's a friend who thought I sucked at decorating."

Ouch. She had a name. This Charlie was clearly important to Andrew, no matter how hard he was protesting. I wished that I hadn't asked. I wished that I didn't know that there was someone in Andrew's life who bought decorations for him. Did she make the throw on the couch? For them to snuggle in? Though I had no right, I felt queasy and it had nothing to do with drinking too much tea and skipping lunch.

What had I expected when I saw Andrew again? It had been ten years, and the man was single. If I had fallen for the awkward, chip-on-his-shoulder boy, why wouldn't there be a line out the door of women attracted to this confident, extremely easy-on-the-eyes man?

It was just unexpected, I told myself. Except it shouldn't have been.

In the three days since my lawyer had shocked me with the news that I was still married, I had thrown myself into tracking Andrew down and working with my lawyer to get new divorce papers drafted. The longer that I was still married, the easier it would be for someone to find out. I hadn't had any time to think about what I might find when I actually saw Andrew. After all, I had spent much of the past ten years actively *not* thinking about him.

"Sorry, Andrew, I didn't mean to pry," I said, trying to get us back on stable footing. "I was just curious. It's none of my business. You can do whatever you want. It's not like we were married."

He chuckled at my lame attempt at a joke. "If you wanted to pry, I would have told you that I am single—no girlfriend, no wife." He held up his left hand, wriggling his bare ring finger.

On instinct, I touched my own left hand. Except for a scar from a bike fall when I was a kid, my hand was smooth, unadorned. I sidestepped Andrew's searching look. "Does everything look all right to you? I'm told they are pretty standard divorce papers."

"Except the part where I have to also sign an NDA not to talk about the marriage or divorce," he pointed out.

Nervousness bubbled inside of me. *What if Andrew talked about this?* My life was perfect. I couldn't have gossip about the past break that image.

I tried for casual, hiding my panic. "It's the past. I just want to make sure that it stays in the past. So, can you sign them?"

"No," Andrew said, walking over to his fridge. "Are you hungry?"

I stared at him in confusion, before running to grab his sleeve. "Wait, what?"

One hand on the fridge door, Andrew looked down at where I was gripping his shirt. As if his eyes were glued to that point of contact. He didn't look up as he shook his head slowly.

What the—? "Explain yourself. Why won't you sign? You signed ten years ago. What's different now?"

"I'm not a teenager anymore that can be forced to sign—"

"Forced?" I was livid now. Willing myself to lower my hands to my side, I clenched them until I could feel my nails digging into my palms. "Who forced you? Was it the same person who forced you to bring a random chick to our home?"

"I told you then, and I'm telling you now—she was a friend. She was having some issues at home, and she didn't know anyone else who could help," Andrew said evenly.

"Right, and you let her sleep in our bed. Our bed, Andrew!" I shouted. I hoped his walls were thick. Actually, I couldn't have cared less if his neighbors heard. Let them find out how shitty of a husband he'd been. Couldn't even last a few months, before he got bored.

"But I wasn't in the bed with her, was I? I was on the couch, waiting for you to come home," Andrew said. His voice was calm, but I could hear the frustration mounting.

"So you said." I mirrored his frustration. This was the same strain of argument that we had years ago. I would accuse him of not letting me in. He would clam up. I would yell that he wasn't trying. He would pull back even further.

"Who was she? If you weren't so secretive—"

He shut down, just like he had years ago. "She's just a friend, Ting Ting."

That sentence triggered a memory that I had tried to keep buried. Ten years ago, it had been weird to find a strange person in our bedroom. I hadn't been suspicious at first. After all, as Andrew said, he was dressed and in the living room. I would have believed him if he hadn't been so defensive. If he hadn't dismissed my questions with, "She's just a friend, Ting Ting."

No other explanations of who she was or where she had come from, just that she was a friend. He expected me to believe him blindly when he had so little faith in us, in my ability to handle the truth. The lack of further explanation drew unnecessary walls between us, and in that moment, I had finally realized that our marriage was over. If he couldn't or wouldn't tell me what was happening in this situation, where was the hope for us?

Just a friend. Just a friend.

I gasped in realization and marched over to his bookcase. *Charlie*. She looked a little older in the picture, but it was definitely the same girl. She was still stunning: long blonde hair, large blue eyes. She looked happy in the photo. Bitterly, I noted the wide smile on Andrew's face as he stood next to her in the photo.

My heart broke. I didn't think it was possible for my heart to break twice. The first time, I had burst. The anger had been fiery hot, scalding me, leaving me covered in fog that I had almost lost myself in. This time, I felt cold. And fragile. As if any small movements or words could shatter me into pieces that could easily be crushed.

I couldn't tell if the pain that was hovering was from ten years ago or this moment. I just knew that I needed to keep myself together in front of Andrew. He couldn't see me fall apart.

"Charlie? I didn't even know her name until today," I whispered, looking back at Andrew.

He was closer than I had expected, as if he had tried to bridge the distance. *Impossible, Andrew doesn't compromise. I'm seeing things.* He didn't move. I didn't move. We simply stared at each other.

I broke the silence first. "I wish you had fought for us, as much as you're fighting to protect Charlie."

"Have you forgotten?" His eyebrows shot up, incredulity on his face. "Charlie was just an excuse for you to leave. You had a foot out of the door as soon as we got married. You were too embarrassed to tell your friends or your parents that you had gotten married until your parents showed up at our door. I asked you to give us a real chance, and you served me with papers. You didn't even tell me to my face. I had to hear the news from your dad."

"I wasn't in a, um, good place to face you. It seemed easier at the time. I'm sorry for not telling you in person." I had known then that it was shitty to do, but I hadn't been strong enough, emotionally or physically, to look him in the eyes directly. It was pure self-preservation that had made me accept my dad's offer to make the whole mess go away.

He raised his eyebrow, mocking my words.

I continued, "You think I didn't fight for you? I ran away with you to Vegas of all places. I deferred Harvard to be closer to you. I tried, as much as I could at eighteen. It was hard fighting with my family when I'd always been held up as an obedient daughter. And you were running hot and cold all the time. Half the time, you seemed to regret us. How could I make any inroads?"

"Tia … I didn't … I don't …" He opened his mouth a couple times to continue, and each time, stopped himself.

My voice so low it was almost a whisper, I pleaded for our younger selves. "Andrew, why didn't you let me in?"

"I never wanted you to give up your family or your dreams, especially not for me. I had nothing. No money. No family net to catch us. How could we have survived?" he said in a defeated tone. "What were we thinking?"

"Clearly, we weren't. Teenage hormones and all," I joked sadly.

He cracked a tiny smile, as he walked closer to me until he stood just inches in front of me. In a carefully modulated voice, he said, "I've thought about you. I've wondered what you were like now."

"You thought about me?" I squeaked.

Nodding, he replied, "Haven't you ever wondered about me? Maybe this non-divorce is a sign." He looked confused at his own words.

"We were just fighting," I said slowly, equally confused. "Plus, it's not like we ended on roses and rainbows last time either."

Leaning in closer until only a breath separated our faces, he said, his voice dropping, "It wasn't always so bad. We were best friends for years, and I'll tell you a secret."

His voice was doing funny things to me. It weaved a net of tingly feelings all around me.

"I didn't hate kissing you. Or touching you."

My breath caught. We were so close now, sharing the heated air between us. I wanted to lean in to this web that we were drawing around each other. His hands came up to rest on my shoulders, gliding upward. One thumb stroked my cheek, as a part of me practically purred at his touch.

No, no, no. Big mistake.

His eyes, so dark they were like the sky during a thunderstorm and just as tumultuous, held me in place. It wasn't necessary. I couldn't have moved. I was caught.

My hands reached for his black hair, reveling in touching him, as he closed his eyes in pleasure.

What was wrong with my body? I was overly warm, despite it being the middle of October. And, what was wrong with my mind, that I was letting … maybe even wishing for *something* to happen? Hoping I wouldn't regret this and knowing I probably would, I closed my eyes and leaned in slightly.

When he applied light pressure on the back of my neck, I swayed … an inch … another inch … until I could feel his breath against me. A whispered hello.

In a husky voice, Andrew said, his words caressing me, "I missed you."

"No!" Panicked, I pushed him away. *Oh no, no, no!* Whatever spell I was under, it was broken with his confession. I was fully back to reality. What in the world was I doing? With him, of all people?

I looked at Andrew. His hair was tousled. I groaned internally, knowing that my hands had been playing with those strands just moments ago. His eyes were still looking at me tenderly, if a bit confused by my outburst.

I hadn't felt this bone-deep passion and *craving* for anyone … not since Andrew. And that scared me.

The full weight of what I had almost done came crashing down on me, suffocating me with guilt and self-disgust. Where had my brain, my sense of self, my self-control been? I wasn't a lust-driven teenager anymore, so I had nothing and no one to blame but my own stupidity.

I was the worst person to lead him on. Especially, when I was not in a position to be having a dinner date or starting a new relationship, or continuing an old relationship, whatever it was that we were in. Remorse filled me. It was too late to take my actions back.

"I can't do this, Andrew," I whispered, shaking my head, steeling myself from the hurt that I saw in his eyes. "This was a mistake. I'm sorry."

Not waiting for his reaction, I ran away.

CHAPTER FOUR

ANDREW

October 14, 2008
Dear Ting,
I'm keeping my promise and writing you another letter. I still think email would be faster, but here you go.
Where do your parents think you're going when you visit? Whatever it is, I'm glad you're coming this weekend. I put in extra hours at work this week, so I don't have to work this weekend. We can do whatever you want—I'll even go see that ridiculous rom-com that you mentioned on the phone.
Yours,
Andrew

I took a deep breath, checked the nameplate by the door and knocked. It had been almost two weeks since I had last seen Tia. I gripped the bag in my hand tighter —the contents were pretty lame excuses for a visit, but I was grasping at anything.

When Tia fled my house, I had been too shocked to react. By the time I pulled myself out of the clouds, she was already speeding away in her ridiculous, lime green Beetle as if she was running from some villain in a James Bond movie. Unfortunately for me, Tia had cast me as the villain.

In the years that we had separated, I had consciously forced myself not to google her. I had avoided going back to our hometown in Colorado, because everything there was a painful reminder. It was easier to pretend that we hadn't been married. After seeing her again, my mind was stuck on the possibility of something between us.

Two weeks after she had shown up on my doorstep, I finally gave into my curiosity. It was with some trepidation I typed "Tia Wang" into Google. Quickly, I ruled out Tia Wang the Australian figure skater and Tia Wang the cruise ship singer easily. The Ting Ting that I knew was clumsy and had a singing voice that, for the sake of all ears, should be kept far away from microphones.

After an hour of reading about a dozen Tia Wangs, I clicked on a link for the MIT computational science staff site. Her smiling face popped up above an article about her joining the department as an assistant professor, specializing in using natural language processing and machine learning platforms to predict healthcare interventions. I didn't know what the hell that meant, but MIT plus professor sounded big. I beamed with pride.

So what if a tiny part of me would have loved to have been by her side, cheering her on as she achieved success? There wasn't much I could do about the past.

I was wholly focused on the present and seeing if there was even a chance for us. If only she answered my calls. Or opened the door to her office.

I knocked again. No response.

This group of offices was in a newer yet crowded wing of the MIT campus. Behind me, students rushed through the hallway. I was about to start banging on the door, just in case she couldn't hear me above the noise, when the door opened abruptly.

"Hold on, please, I'm just wrapping up with some students and—"

Shocked brown eyes stared into mine. Tia looked different from when she showed up at my house. No longer in jeans and a fitted sweater, she was all professional today. Damn, she looked good in that pink top and tight skirt. She had probably meant to look conservative, but with that almost-kiss still on my mind, my brain went somewhere not appropriate for public hallways.

Pulling my brain out of the gutter, I said, "Hi. Miss me?"

With a look of panic, her eyes darted behind me before she dragged me inside her small office. Two very confused students stopped in the middle of typing notes on their laptops to stare at me. Hands waving, Tia turned to the students. “C’mon, you must be late for your next class.”

One of the students blurted out, “Professor, we don’t have any more classes for the day.”

“Yes, well, I’m sure you have lots of homework,” Tia replied, gesturing to the door.

The other student said, “Actually, we don’t. Ryan and I just finished up everything in the library before coming to your office.”

“Go on. Out. Now. I’ll see you tomorrow in class.” Tia shoved their laptops at them and all but pushed them out of the office.

Closing the door behind them, she turned back to me. She looked cute when she was frustrated. I grinned at her like a fool. Being around her again was, I don’t know, weirdly comfortable yet exciting.

Hands on her hips, Tia hissed at me, “What. Are. You. Doing. Here?”

Oh man. Clearly, she wasn’t as thrilled to see me. I wiped the smile from my face and opened up my duffel bag. “You forgot your coat when you ran away. And your shoes.”

Groaning, Tia covered her face with her hands. “Ugh. I looked ridiculous at the airport. You should have heard the TSA folks and flight attendants telling me that I still had time to go back to security to grab my shoes. They sell the most ridiculous things at the airport, like twenty different kinds of shot glasses. Why don’t they sell useful things, like shoes?”

I chuckled. I had missed her self-deprecating humor. When she smiled tentatively at me, it felt as if we were still best friends. More than anything, I had missed having Tia as my friend. She had a knack for making light out of situations.

“Andrew, you know you could have just shipped these back to me,” she began, walking around her desk to sit down in her chair. “You didn’t have to personally deliver them.”

I frowned at the physical distance she was deliberately putting between us. “I know. I wanted to see you again, and you refused to answer my calls. That moment in Chicago felt unfinished.”

Red colored her cheeks, and she looked down at her hands. "I thought we wrapped it up pretty well," she said, twirling a pen frantically around her fingers. "I expressed my wishes, and left, giving you some time to read the document carefully before signing. I was going to have my lawyer check with you soon."

In disbelief, I sat down in the chair facing her. "Did you miss the part where I suggested we try again before signing? Who knows, it might be different this time. What do we have to lose?"

"You're not serious, right?" Her eyes widened as her hands nervously stacked papers on her crowded desk.

This conversation was not going the way that I had hoped. It wasn't as if I'd expected her to hop into my arms in delight. Okay, maybe I had.

Seeing Tia again, experiencing feelings for her that had been buried—yeah, that scared the shit out of me. I assumed that she felt the same seismic shift as I did when we touched, the same sparks when we talked. I had flown to Boston, hoping her curiosity was stronger than her fears of repeating the past.

Now, I wasn't sure I had read the situation correctly. She had freaked out, but maybe not for the reasons that I had assumed. Fuck. I hated, fucking *hated*, making a fool out of myself and here I was, looking like an ass.

Stalling for time, I asked the one question that had been bugging me since I saw Tia outside my house. "Why did you come find me now? We thought we had been divorced for ten years. What prompted you to dig into this?"

Tia looked around her office, a frown marring her beautiful face. A pit opened up in my stomach. She looked as uncomfortable and guilty as I had ever seen her.

I followed up, needing to know. "Did you show up in Chicago just to serve me divorce papers? Was that the only reason?"

Say no. Say you were curious about me too. I was surprised at how much I cared about her answer.

"I'm sorry, Andrew," Tia said, her voice wavering, her eyes finally meeting mine. Her brown eyes were large and apologetic. "I'm getting—"

"Hey, Tia!"

Both of us whirled around at the newcomer. If the newcomer was surprised to see us, he hid it quickly. Then again, Clayton Davenport had always been unfailingly polite and unflappable. That mantra was likely tattooed into his blue blood by some ancestor.

"Andrew, how's it going?" Clayton reached out his hand, his smile friendly.

Without thinking, my hand shook his. I noted the horrified expression on Tia's face. A poker player, my Tia was not. She stood up and shook her head in alarm, while backing away from us in her tiny, cluttered office.

Thump.

Tia smacked into the window behind her desk. Startled, she jumped sideways. Right into a very full coat stand.

"Tia!" Clayton's voice called out as I leaped over some plant to try to get to her. For a comical second, Tia's arms flailed, and she was suspended in air, teetering in some horrific ballerina pose.

Thud. Ba-dum. "Oof!" *Thud.* "Ow!"

Leaning over the heap that was Tia, I offered my hand to help her. Swatting it away, Tia pushed off the offending coat stand. Sprawled on the floor, her dark hair coming out of a bun underneath a fallen hat, she looked more like a student after a drunken night of revelry than a respected professor.

"How … how do you two know each other?" she asked accusingly, using an umbrella to help her stand.

Cross off hungover student. She looked like an avenging Mary Poppins, waving that umbrella wildly between Clayton and me. Clearly, Tia Poppins did not appreciate the humor of the situation, as she jabbed me in the chest. It wasn't as if I was laughing at her.

Not much.

Just a tiny facial tic.

While I was rubbing my chest—you try being poked with something sharp—Clayton shook off his shock and hurried over to Tia. Stopping him with a wave of her umbrella, she pointed at me. "Do you know *him*? Why did you shake his hand?"

Clayton looked back at me, as if expecting to see some horrible monster judging by the vehemence in her voice. He said evenly, "Andrew? We went to law school together and were associates at the same firm in New York right after graduation."

Shocked eyes met mine. Frowning, Tia asked, "The same law firm that you and Pippa used to work at? You went to Yale Law?"

Annoyed at her surprise, I said, "Geez, thanks for the vote of confidence, Tia. Guess they do accept mere mortals whose names are not on buildings." Wincing, I turned to Clayton. "Sorry, man."

He shrugged and joked easily, "How else would people know you were rich if your name wasn't on some stodgy, old building?"

It was an unintentional reminder of how wide the gap had been between me and my classmates. I had a full-ride scholarship, supplemented by working a couple of side jobs. On the other hand, my classmates came from families who funded scholarships. I was the potato next to a basket of heirloom-whatever-grapes champagne was made out of.

"But I've visited Pippa at your firm, and I never saw you there," Tia said to me.

"I was probably holed away on a case," I said in an effort to mask my shock. One, I was stunned that my Tia hobnobbed with these heirloom champagne grapes. Two, my mind couldn't wrap around the fact that Tia had visited my former office. I wasn't close to Clayton or Pippa. Still, we had known one another for years, and now, to hear that they knew Tia—it blew me away.

So close. What would I have done if I had seen her? Would she have run away, or run to me? Would I have wanted her to run to me?

Clayton stepped forward.

"Oh shit," I whispered under my breath, realization twisting me upside down.

"What are you doing in Boston? I thought you had moved out to Chicago," Clayton asked, oblivious to my torment. As if it was the most natural thing in the world, he draped an arm around *not-my* Tia's shoulders.

"Here for some business," I replied robotically.

Of course. *Him*.

He was exactly the kind of guy Tia's parents wanted her to be with. Upstanding, dependable, too boring for skeletons. For fuck's sake, his family had come to America on the Mayflower. He was the blue-blooded American prince that Tia's immigrant parents had never made a secret of wanting her to end up with. And he was so nice that I couldn't despise him.

Law firms were notoriously competitive, churning out associates and pitting them against each other to see who floated to the top. Everybody played office politics, except for me and Clayton. I didn't know how, even if I had cared enough to try to butter up to a partner or sabotage another associate. And Clayton had enough old-money confidence and connections that he didn't need to. We didn't meet for beers outside of work or play golf, but I had grown to grudgingly respect his professionalism and intelligence. Which was not helpful in this situation.

Fuck. They must be serious, if she needed a divorce. I should have known that *the* girl from my past wouldn't just show up at my front door, ready to magically erase our years apart. There had been a hundred clues that I had missed. Asking for a divorce? Running away? The nervousness and anxiety?

Stupid me. I should have seen this coming. People like me did not get second chances.

Clayton must have finished whatever he was saying, as he was looking at me. Was it my turn to exchange silly pleasantries? What was I supposed to say, "Congrats, good luck with my wife?"

I glanced over at Tia. She stared at the floor, as if she was trying to disappear into it. I willed her to reassure me. To smile in that way that said everything was going to be okay, that this was a joke, and that we'd laugh about it later. Instead, she stayed silent.

Clayton asked, "How do you know each other?"

"We were best friends growing up," I answered at the same time as Tia said, "Acquaintances."

If Clayton was confused by the conflicting answers, he ignored it. He asked, "So you two grew up together in Colorado? How nice that you stayed in touch."

"Ha, funny story," I began, itching to wipe the friendly smile from his face. "Tia showed up—"

"Andrew!" cried out Tia in alarm. "I don't think Clayton has time right now for stories of our childhood."

"Actually, I took the rest of the afternoon off," said Clayton. "I'd love to hear stories about you growing up."

Miserable, Tia pleaded, "Maybe later? Let's grab some food before my next class starts. I'm starving."

Clayton smiled warmly at Tia and nodded. Looking at me, he asked, "How long are you in Boston? We're throwing a small party this Saturday to celebrate the engagement. If you're free, you should stop by."

Still in denial, and still an idiot, I asked, "Whose engagement?"

"Mine." With that one quietly whispered word from Tia, my mind went blank.

CHAPTER FIVE

TIA

November 28, 2009 (never sent)
Andrew,
You probably guessed this already, but I hate running with a passion. There is no part of running that I enjoy. It does not clear my head, I don't look cute in sweats, and it's deathly boring. I only joined track because you were on the team. That and my parents were convinced that I needed to do some sort of sports to get into college.
You were fast. State champ your senior year!
When I left, why didn't you run after me? You could have caught me. I was ready with excuses for you, if you had run after me.
Ting

This was what I got for going to see Andrew in Chicago. For trying to bottle up my guilt for the past two weeks. Even though no physical lines had been crossed, it didn't feel that way. Not when I had thought about Andrew nonstop since.

At this time of the day, I could get to the airport in twenty minutes and be on my way to some place far away. Without cell service. Or Wi-Fi. I could hunker down in some cute cottage until Andrew got bored and signed those stupid papers. It wasn't really hiding from my problems per se, just removing myself from the situation until it resolved itself.

My heart was ready to give out from all of the stops and starts. Back in college, I had tried Red Bull for the first time right before a final. Bad choice. Instead of helping me focus, I spent the entire two hours during the test wondering if my heart palpitations were going to lead to a heart attack.

Once again I was worried for my cardiovascular health. Only instead of Red Bull, it was Andrew giving me heart palpitations. His reentry into my life. His presence in my tiny office. Him and Clayton in my tiny office. *Ai ya ya, Clayton.*

Of course they would know each other. I had been a fool to rely on the impenetrable wall that I had painstakingly crafted between my past life and my current one.

Of course, ever-so-nice Clayton was now inviting my soon-to-be ex-husband to our engagement party.

Of course Andrew was confused. I was still his wife, at least in name. I couldn't even claim ignorance on the marriage, as I was the one who had told him that we were still married. I felt an overwhelming need for him to *not* hate me.

When Andrew looked at me again, his eyes were shuttered. He looked, but I wasn't sure if he saw me anymore. When we were younger, people thought he was cold, aloof, hard. But to me, when I looked closely enough, his eyes would show what he didn't say. Now, those beautiful, expressive eyes were dull.

There was a bleakness in how he carried himself, a half breath deflated. I understood. I was completely deflated and defeated by this whole situation. There was a reason why I had moved on. The past was too thorny, and I had no place in my life for complications.

Sounding far away, yet too close, Andrew finally responded to Clayton's invitation. "Sure, just text me the time and place. My number hasn't changed since New York."

Ai ya ya. As if this encounter wasn't awkward enough, I could look forward to an engagement party with Clayton's very proper parents, my very prim parents, our friends, my fiancé, and my husband. A whole night of fun!

I gave a half-hearted wave of goodbye as Andrew left my office, more out of politeness than anything else. Taking a deep breath, I turned around to face my fiancé.

Clayton looked down at his Patek Philippe watch and pointed toward the door. "You still got time before your next class. You want to try the new burger food truck outside?"

I peered at him, trying to see the questions that he must have. What hidden meanings were behind his suggestion of food trucks? Would burgers loosen my tongue enough to spill the secrets of my past? Was the glance at his watch a not-so-subtle reminder of his Kennedy-esque wealth and family connections? Could he read the guilt all over my face?

"You okay, Tia?" He peered back at me, his lips curved up in a teasing smile. "Should we get some food? I don't know about you, but breakfast was a long time ago."

Huh.

I guess he really did just want to get burgers? His gaze was curious, but there was no censure. *Yet*, I reminded myself. Clayton didn't know who Andrew was. Well, he did. Or rather does know him. Just not all the ways we were connected. In the past! Andrew and I were connected in the past. Not connected now. Very painfully disconnected now.

Ai ya ya. I shook my head a little to get my brain started again. Seeing Andrew had charged my brain and fried it all at the same time. Seeing Andrew and Clayton together had spun that charged, fried brain into a muddle. Not a puddle, mind you, because I hoped that my brain was still solidly inside my head. Just a solid, charged, fried mess of thoughts that were banging against my skull.

By this time, Clayton was starting to look worried. Before I could get out of my mental muddle, he grabbed my coat, draped it over me and pushed me gently out of the door. "C'mon, Tia, you look like you need some fresh air and food."

Whether it was something he was born with or a lifetime spent being dragged on the campaign trail for his father, Clayton had this instinct for making people feel comfortable. He may not know exactly why I was out of sorts, but he sensed enough to keep up a stream of small talk while I devoured my burger. Nothing that I really needed to respond to—a little bit about his day, a bill that his father was trying to pass in the senate, some funny videos that his brother had sent.

He was right. I did need fresh air, food, and normalcy. Sitting on a bench with a cheeseburger and a bucket of greasy fries, I felt human again. My brain had upgraded to a functioning muddle. I could do stuff … like talk to my fiancé.

"Small world, huh? You and Andrew knowing each other."

My heart sank with guilt, as I thought about what to say. Two weeks after the almost-kiss, I still couldn't reconcile what had happened. *I* didn't do things like fly halfway across the country to see a guy. I had never been tempted by someone else when I was in a relationship.

Yet here I was, still tempted by the possibility of Andrew and me. Was he right? Have we matured enough that we could have more good than bad? Because the good —the sense of rightness and utter joy in being around him—those were highs that I hadn't achieved with Clayton, no matter how much I tried.

Clayton is the right choice. I had to keep reminding myself. No one would question why I chose Clayton. If I were really honest with myself, part of his appeal to me was his universal appeal. I would never have to fight with my friends or parents to accept him. *If everyone agreed that getting engaged to him was a coup, then, they can't all be wrong, right?*

We weren't in some movie where Clayton was the evil guy standing between soul-mates. This was real life. I was ready to be Mrs. Clayton Davenport, and if that meant brunches at the country club with his golf buddies and their wives, wearing argyle and pearls, then so be it. Well, maybe not the argyle part. But yes to being Mrs. Clayton Davenport. And definitely yes to being Mrs. Clayton Davenport without committing bigamy.

Clayton deserved to know the truth about my marriage. However, this was not a conversation to have on a crowded campus, minutes before I had to go to class. We needed privacy. After I prepared a speech. Oh, and finalize the divorce for real this time.

I finally responded, "Well, Andrew and I were friends when we were kids. We sort of drifted apart, sometime after high school."

"Did you know he was going to show up today?" Clayton asked.

"No! Not at all. It was a total surprise." I shook my head vigorously.

"Tia," Clayton said. He turned me around to face him completely, pulling me closer toward him. "It's okay. So you dated before."

"What?" I yelped. "How'd you know?"

He laughed, his hands seeking mine. "You have the most expressive face of anyone I've ever met. Your face is your captions. Anybody would have known how awkward you felt when we were in your office. You two have a weird dynamic, so I just assumed."

Sighing a breath of relief, I sorted through my head what I could admit at this moment. "It ended rather badly between us."

"Of course," Clayton said. "Are there any good breakups? If it had ended happily between you two, you'd still be together. You didn't do something silly like marry him back then, right?"

"Ha ha," I forced out, trying to join in on his joke. "That's funny."

Ai ya ya. Maybe I would tell Clayton about Andrew when we were eighty. Or ninety. He might have a chuckle then. Or, drag my wrinkly butt to divorce court. To be clear, my butt would presumably be wrinkly when I was ninety. My current butt was perfectly non-wrinkly. Ahhh, now I would think about wrinkly and firm butts while teaching my students about the importance of data visualization as a tool to communicate results in data science.

Visualizing butts.

CHAPTER SIX

TIA

December 1, 2009 (never sent)
Andrew,
I cleaned my room today and found a stash of red envelopes that had contained money that my parents and relatives had given me over the years. The envelopes are empty now—all of the money has been safely deposited into savings accounts. I don't think I've ever spent any of those gifts.
I've been thinking a lot lately. I might have panicked too much about the lack of money when we were married. I shouldn't have made you feel guilty and should have trusted you that we would be okay. At the time, it was scary. I was so afraid of getting cut off from my parents and maybe ... too used to having them pay for everything I wanted. Nice purses and pretty necklaces seemed way too important. How silly of me.
Ting

"You're feeling okay? Ready to have dinner with my mom?"

"Yup, yup. Right as rain. Fit as a fiddle. Easy as pie. Pleased as juice."

A small smile tipped Clayton's mouth. "Punch."

"No, no! I don't want to *punch* your mom. I want her to *like* me. Why, did she say something to you?" I frowned, trying to think of my last interaction with his mom. Was interaction even the right word? At the time, it had felt more like a battle, where Judy Davenport was the commander and I the loyal soldier as we strategized through walls of blindingly white wedding dresses. Or rather, she critiqued while I served as the mannequin.

"No, the saying goes 'pleased as punch,' not 'juice.' You don't have to be nervous about my mom. It's just dinner," said Clayton as he helped me step out of his BMW. He handed his keys and a bill to a nearby valet.

It was a reminder of how much I had to learn about Clayton's world. You see, in a regular world, you tip the valet *after* you pick up your car and hope that there were only small nicks on the bumper. In Clayton's world, you *front* a tip to ensure that your brand-new BMW got preferential treatment, as well as a tip *after* when you find that, yes, indeed, your car came back with no suspicious extra mileage.

Unable to stop the rush of words, I asked, "By the way, why is it 'pleased as punch'? How can punch be pleased? The only time I've seen punch is at frat parties, and *that* punch was sketchy."

"Hmm, I'm not sure."

"Right as rain? Is that a judgement that rain is good and sunshine is bad? What about those in-between moments of cloudiness or snow? Unless snow is considered rain since it's water too?"

"Tia, there's no need to—"

My brain told me to shut up. As usual when I was nervous, my mouth didn't listen. "Fit as a fiddle? Is a fiddle supposed to be lean? I thought fiddles were curvy with a thin neck though curvy can absolutely be fit too. Also—"

"Tia."

"Oh, hi, Mrs. Da—Judy!" Drat, we were already inside the country club's lavish dining room.

"Darling Clayton, you look well." Judy Davenport stood and reached over to press an adoring kiss to her son's cheeks. Her blue eyes turned to me, significantly cooler as she remarked, "Tia." Pause. "Do you have pumpkins dangling from your earlobes?"

My hands reached up toward my ears. I tried to shrug Judy's censure off. "It's Halloween next Thursday. I was going for festive."

"Next time, why don't you try for elegant?" she said, smoothing her slacks as she sat down in one of the dark green velvet chairs in the large dining room. I called the things you wore on your legs "pants." She wore "slacks."

Heat blazed across my cheeks, as I stared at my brand-new loafers. From the top of my head, I heard Clayton cut in. "Mother, I think they look cute."

Judy sniffed, as she studied the menu. "Puppies are cute. My future daughter-in-law should be a source of pride for our family."

I shook my head slightly at Clayton, to stop him from protesting. Clearly, I was not Judy's ideal woman for her firstborn son, and all three of us knew it. I was simply going to learn to deal with this. It wasn't worth arguing over.

My nerves were already frayed from Andrew showing up in my office two days ago. He hadn't tried to contact me since, but just knowing that he was still in Boston and coming to the engagement party had resulted in higher, late-night ice cream consumption.

Survive the engagement party! Afterward, I could try to figure out how I could be *more* before the wedding in June.

The waiter came and took our orders. Clayton kept up a steady pace of conversation, while I watched silently except to agree at appropriate moments. Though different in temperament, Clayton resembled his mom physically. Their blond hair shone under the chandeliers, as blue eyes rested under light brown eyebrows. They both had khaki *slacks* and button-down shirts, though Judy had a cashmere sweater draped around her shoulders. They looked like walking, talking Brooks Brothers models.

Under Judy's watchful eyes, I refused the waiter's offer of dessert and opted instead for some hot chai. While we sipped our digestifs (the fancy word for drinking after food), Judy turned her attention fully to me.

I swallowed my tea. *That was a mistake*. I clenched my teeth against the pain of scalding hot tea going down my throat.

"Tia, did you get my message this morning? I made those changes you had asked for." One elegant eyebrow arched up in question.

"Yes, Judy. Thank you for considering my feedback to add some Chinese food to the menu. It does mean a lot to me and to my parents. But, um, could we pick different food options? Not to be difficult."

Her eyebrow rose higher, as if that eyebrow doubted my claim of not being difficult. "It was very fortunate that the hotel was able to accommodate those *late* menu changes."

Frustration brewed. *Clayton's mother, his mother. Remember, she matters more than food.* Yet, my mouth came back with, "That was very fortunate indeed. It's just that, crab rangoon and fortune cookies aren't authentically Chinese. Actually, there are some theories that say that crab rangoon was invented by a Caucasian American and that fortune cookies stem from the Americanization of a Japanese tradition. Some historians even think that fortune cookies became more closely associated with Chinese-Americans around World War II when Chinese manufacturers started producing them when Japanese-Americans were sent to internment camps. So you see, it just feels odd to serve just those two dishes when there are so many other, *more authentic* options. How about Beijing roast duck, or maybe even steamed dumplings? Those are Chinese *and* from where I'm from in China."

I stared at Judy's disapproving face. Hastily, I added, "Both dishes are pretty palatable and common in the US too. You don't even need to have a server cut the whole duck in front of you—you could have it pre-cut beforehand. I mean, taco bars are sort of the rage. You could think of it as a hip, make-your-own-duck-wrap taco thing ... No?"

"Tia, you're marrying my son, whose father is a United States senator. This party is in Boston. For goodness' sake, we're not trying to fly everyone to China for an immersive experience. You insisted on wearing that, whatever that dress is called—"

"Qi pao."

"That thing. I think you've made your point clearly. No one is forgetting that Clayton is marrying a Chinese girl. At least, your name is pronounceable."

Silence.

"Mother, I don't think Tia is trying to—"

"Clayton darling. I mean it. I want our guests to feel comfortable too."

"Mother, the guests can deal with having dumplings or whatever food Tia wants. No one is coming for the food," Clayton pressed, looking more and more uncomfortable with the exchange.

"If no one is coming for the food, then why is it a big deal what we serve?"

Breathe.

Contorting my face into a placating smile, I cut in, "You're right, Judy. I'm sorry to have made a fuss. As you said, it was very nice of the hotel to make changes at the last moment. I really appreciate you changing the menu."

"Good, I'm glad that's settled. One more thing that I wanted to discuss with you, Tia." She folded her hands in front of her as she studied me. "I was hoping you would have signed the prenuptial agreement before the engagement party. Considering it's tomorrow, it doesn't seem likely. Was there an issue with our proposal?"

"Your proposal," muttered Clayton, red tinging his cheekbones. "Mother, I don't think we should talk about this here. I'm not sure we even need one."

"It's fine," I said. Had I been slightly offended when Clayton's parents had their lawyers draft a prenup? Sure. But I understood. The Davenports had a lot of assets to protect. It was my lawyer's review of the contract that had unearthed my non-divorce. In comparison, what was a prenup request when compared to the fact that I wasn't legally allowed to marry Clayton?

"My lawyer is still reviewing it, Judy," I hemmed.

"You're still okay with the background check? It's not that we don't *know* you, but you never know." Judy's voice was gentle, yet her blue eyes looked at me in challenge. In my periphery, I could see Clayton open his mouth to protest.

"Yes," I fibbed, keeping my toes crossed. *As soon as I get a divorce and burn the evidence. Would the almost-kiss show up in a background check?* Maybe Andrew had security cams, and someone hijacked it, and then that person sold it to the Davenports. Had I been watching too many British detective shows? Or was that my guilt talking?

"Good, good, then." She glanced subtly at her probably Swiss-made watch.

"I'll grab the check." Looking relieved that we hadn't caused more of a scene, Clayton waved our server over enthusiastically.

With my mind unsettled and filled with discontent, I let Clayton steer the conversation back to safer ground. He quickly paid for dinner, and the three of us left the cavernous dining room for the valet station. After seeing his mother into her Mercedes, he turned to me, with a boyish smile on his face.

"How about a walk, before I drive you home?"

I smiled in response. Without Judy around, it wasn't hard to remember why I was planning to marry this charismatic, handsome man.

Clayton: the perfect man, the perfect boyfriend, the perfect fiancé. He would probably be the perfect husband, father, son-in-law. And I wanted that perfect life.

So what if I wished that he defended me more in front of his mom? I knew that he stayed silent to keep the peace, not because he actually believed his mom.

I had lucked out when I met him during a visit to my friend Pippa in Manhattan. I had tagged along on a sunset cruise chartered by Pippa and chanced to sit next to Clayton during dinner. He had no one else on his other side, and it had been too loud to converse with other people across the table. Unlike most of my attempted conversations with men under the age of eighty, this conversation was easy.

A few months later, Clayton accepted a job at a law firm in Boston, and we reconnected as friends. We commiserated together while he studied for the Massachusetts bar and I despondently procrastinated over writing my never-ending thesis. Before I could write, there had always been one more puppy video to view or another book waiting to be read.

Writing a thesis was like finding matching socks after doing laundry. You were forever putting more socks into the washing machine than what you would end up with when the cycle was done. Likewise, I was endlessly typing and researching, and after what felt like a million words later, my word count would mysteriously increase by only two hundred. There must be a black hole filled with charts and words from my dissertation floating somewhere in space.

More than two years after we had become friends and thankfully with the bar and thesis successfully checked off, Clayton and I had found ourselves single at the same time. He had broken things off with his long-term girlfriend, and I was taking a break from online dating after a string of disappointing dates with guys who were only looking for hookups.

It had been easy to slide from friendship into a relationship. Relationships were just friendships with kissing, right? With Clayton, there were none of those half-terminologies and questions that my friends were plagued with—dating but not exclusively, hanging out, hooking up, how many other girls was he talking to on dating apps? In a cute, old-fashioned way, Clayton had asked if I wanted to be his girlfriend.

Our interests aligned, our friends liked each other, and most importantly, our parents approved. Or at least, my parents were Tom Cruise jumping on the couch in front of Oprah. Minus the Scientology.

After the roller coaster that I had been on with Andrew and being burned too many times dating afterwards, it was a relief to be in a no-drama relationship where the guy respected me. We supported each other and enjoyed spending time together, but we also gave each other room. Similarly, I suspected that Clayton liked the steadiness of our relationship and that I was independent, a far cry from his previous relationship.

A few weeks ago, my parents' dream came true. My perfect boyfriend had replicated our first meeting by taking me on the most perfect sunset cruise around Boston Harbor and had gotten down on his knee. I barely heard Clayton's question, my eyes mesmerized by the giant diamond glinting in the last of the sunlight. On autopilot, I nodded.

So what if my feelings for Clayton weren't comparable to what I had once felt for Andrew? I had learned the hard way that too much feelings led to broken hearts. At least with Clayton, my heart was safe. Marrying a Davenport was the pot of gold at the end of the immigrant rainbow. I was convinced that my feelings would grow over time.

Besides, what are you supposed to say when someone that you've dated for six months bedazzled you with a giant sparkly ring? I should have been more prepared for his question. Marriage was a logical option for people who had been happily dating for a while. Heck, marriage occurred between people who met each other at the altar—there's a whole reality show about it if you don't believe me. Google it. Or better not. Because then you'll stay up all night getting invested in strangers trying to figure out married life with cameras in their faces, only to find out that some of them had only gotten married to boost their social media following.

Anyways, for someone who spent hours every day creating, writing about, and teaching about data, I had missed the indicators that there could be a second marriage for me.

The first one had been too much.

Yet here I was, preparing for my engagement party. For my second marriage.

"Are you feeling okay?"

Clayton's voice pulled me back to the golf course where he had led me. I nodded.

His blue eyes probed mine. "I know my mother can be difficult to deal with. Sometimes, it's just easier to let her have her way. You'd let me know if you were truly uncomfortable or didn't agree, right?"

"Hmm, sure." I nodded weakly.

Not looking entirely convinced, he dropped the topic. "I actually have something else I wanted to ask."

Uh-oh.

What could it be? My heart raced as my mind flew over possibilities. Did he find out about Andrew? Was this dinner a lure before I was cast away? Had the Davenports found a political bigwig with a marriageable daughter and made an alliance? Like back when women still needed a dowry, except without cows and whatever else they traded. What was the offer—we get rid of the fiancée, and in exchange, your daughter brings to the marriage a well-funded PAC?

By the time Clayton stopped somewhere on the golf course, I was fully prepared for the news that I had been thrown over for a blonde virgin from Texas named Sally Sue. A traitorous thought snaked through my brain. *What if this is meant to be? If there's no fiancé, should I give my husband—*

No! I figuratively slapped my heart back down. My heart was not the brightest of organs, nor was it good at remembering. I thought I had trained it to listen to my brain, but every now and then, it broke through the restraints of reason.

Shaking myself out of the midst of a mental boxing match, I noticed with surprise that Clayton was starting to kneel. "What are you doing?" I said to the top of his golden hair.

He looked up at me, laughing self-consciously. "I know I surprised you a few weeks ago, but I figured you'd know the second time. When a man gets on his knee, with a ring …" He shrugged adorably.

Gah, I didn't deserve his goodness. Feeling guilty that I wasn't more delighted, I plucked at his arm to get him to stand. "Aren't you forgetting something? We're already engaged. Remember the party tomorrow—it's for us."

Clayton held up the same ring that he had proposed with and slipped it over my third finger. "I got it back yesterday from the jeweler. It should fit better now."

The ring felt like chains. I was unbearably itchy. There were no visible mosquitos that I could see, but I felt as attacked as if I stood in deep woods in the summertime with honey slathered over me.

Just like last time, I focused on the ring to calm myself. It blinded me with its size and sparkly-ness. This was a statement piece, as clear as if Clayton had branded me. I should have been happy and proud that he wanted me.

And, just like last time, I reminded myself that Clayton and I loved each other. Our love was based on a solid foundation of common interests and goals. That was more sustainable than passion.

Getting up from the manicured grass, Clayton leaned down to kiss me. On autopilot, my head turned at the last second. Pausing for an indecisive breath, Clayton gently kissed my cheek before pulling back quickly.

Even though I couldn't see his expression, I could tell I had hurt him. However, ever since I had gotten back from that disastrous trip to Chicago, it hadn't felt right to do anything besides hold his hand or allow him to kiss my cheeks, as if we were fifth graders with chaperones watching. I didn't know why I had put up this wall, and I needed to figure this out before I screwed up this engagement.

If I still planned to marry Clayton, I had to get over Andrew completely. Because, even with Clayton's ring on my finger, I couldn't stop thinking about Andrew. When I closed my eyes, I saw Andrew—his dark hair mussed from my fingers, that crooked smile of his, with a hint of a dimple.

And that made me the worst kind of person.

CHAPTER SEVEN

TIA

December 15, 2009 (never sent)
Andrew,
I dreamed of a big white dress and flowers everywhere. Instead, we got married by someone who was ordained online, in some random chapel that smelled like vomit and alcohol. Yet, I was still so happy that day! Because I was getting married to you, and on that day, we were going to ride off on our happily ever after.
That day seems so far away. There are no signs left that we had ever been married. No ring, no photos of the day. Even the physical pain has mostly receded, just like the doctors and nurses promised—the last tangible reminder that we were once together.
I wonder if the mental and emotional pain ever fades away?
Ting

Feeling like an imposter at my own party, I walked around the tables in the Ritz ballroom. There was nothing left for me to do. Judy and the wedding planner she had hired had taken care of everything. So what if I had vaguely mentioned that I'd love something small and casual, maybe in a barn somewhere with twinkly lights? The Ritz ballroom was a close second, with lights twinkling from the hundreds of candles in the centerpieces. Clayton's mom must have added a zero to the number I had given her for my desired guest list. Thirty, three hundred, what was the difference? Judy was out of my hair, and I had much, much bigger problems to worry about.

"Hey, Tia." Clayton entered the ballroom.

"Hey," I called back. We had arrived separately tonight, not having talked since the awkwardness of the re-proposal the night before.

"You look beautiful," he said.

He was the beautiful one, looking out of my league in his tailored, dark blue suit. I looked up at his handsome face. I could never understand why people said they were looking at someone's eyes. Plural. Maybe I was a defective eye-looker, but with our faces only inches away, it was easier to focus on one of Clayton's eyes at a time.

Looking into his left eye, I said, "Your mom called me this morning to make sure that I knew to put on something, as she called it, 'more elegant.'"

Clayton sighed. "She means well."

"Yes, I agree." I tried to smile at him, looking at his right eye. "Don't worry about it. I'm appreciative that she's throwing this engagement party for us."

Speaking of the very nice devil, Judy waved us over to where she stood near the doors with Senator Davenport and my parents. "Tia, Clayton, please come over here to welcome the guests. They should be arriving soon."

Sighing, I plastered a boringly pleasant smile on my face and crossed over. I shook the senator's hand and greeted Judy with air kisses on her professionally made-up cheeks. Her dress probably cost more than my monthly salary, and I didn't even have to look down to know that her nails had been buffed and polished more than even her wineglasses at home. And those were meticulously polished daily with silk cloths and steam from filtered water by housekeepers wearing gloves.

She looked me up and down. Unlike the admiring gaze from her son, her gaze felt calculated. "Not a bad dress choice," Judy said at last. "At least you tried."

"Mother, Tia looks great," Clayton interjected. I felt a rush of gratitude toward him.

Ignoring her son's comment, Mrs. Davenport turned to him. Her smile couldn't have been warmer, as she gave Clayton her cheeks to kiss. "Don't you look so handsome, darling! Like a prince."

My parents smiled at me encouragingly. I was grateful that they hadn't grasped the undertones in Judy's comments. My mom had been beside herself since I told her about the engagement, and now, even my dad looked mildly interested. They had flown in this morning from Colorado, and I felt guilty for immediately dumping them off in their hotel room. It was hard to be around them when they were so proud of my engagement.

With greetings complete, we clustered around the entranceway in awkward silence. I wracked my brain trying to think of something to break the ice. To my utter relief, Clayton nodded towards a distinguished couple heading our way. "There're the Elfas. They're always the first to arrive."

An hour later, my face was starting to hurt from the incessant smiling. The constant smiling was simply put, work. Most of the guests were Clayton's family, friends, or his parents' friends. I kept my small talk to four topics: the weather, what people were wearing, my ring, and how lucky I felt that I was about to be married to Clayton. Each time I restarted my list of topics, I felt a sense of déjà vu.

Of course, Clayton was his regular charming self. Being around people was his jam. I had seen him in action before, but watching him greet every guest by name as if they were his favorite and dole out personal stories was still impressive. The guests, even our few mutual friends, gave me perfunctory greetings before eagerly clustering around Clayton.

"Hi, lady!"

I turned toward the sound, a genuine smile splitting my face. Leaving behind Mr. Someone-or-Other, I rushed over to hug my best friend, Pippa. She was bedazzled head to toe in a sequined hot pink dress, with four-inch heels that had little spikes on the heels. From the corner of my eyes, I could see Judy glare at her in disapproval. Elegant and understated, Pippa was not. She was *new* money, as Judy had pointed out before, in a way that left no doubt that *new* meant *tacky*.

I must have tacky taste because I thought Pippa looked wonderful.

Voice low, she whispered close to my ear, "Is *he* here?"

I didn't have to ask which "he" Pippa meant. As soon as I got to the airport in Chicago, I had called Pippa's cell, leaving a message that was part hysteria, part … well, okay, all hysteria. Andrew's visit to my office had garnered another panicked voicemail.

Though Pippa was also Clayton's friend, she was my friend first. We had met twenty-two years ago at the International School of Beijing, where my parents had enrolled me in preparation for our move to America, and where Pippa's parents had deposited her while they made a fortune investing in Chinese electronic firms. We had reconnected when we found out that we were going to the same college.

"I haven't seen him yet," I whispered back. "He probably won't show up. It's so last minute. Why put yourself in that awkward spot?"

"I hope he comes." Pippa craned her neck around to look at the crowded ballroom. "I didn't fly all the way home from London to miss the drama."

I elbowed her gently. "Hey, what about me? It's your duty as maid of honor to support me."

Laughing loudly enough to attract eyes, Pippa said, "Yes! I'll totally support you as Andrew and Clayton battle it out. Preferably with some ripped shirts and howling at the moon. Can you imagine?"

Grinning, I watched as Pippa pretended to fan herself. "Andrew, yes. He was barely civil when I knew him. Clayton, definitely not! He'd probably fold up his shirt first before fighting."

Our laughter got another disapproving glare from Judy. On the other hand, Senator Davenport smiled broadly at us. Or rather, Pippa. The senator was all politics, all the time, and his spidey senses must have been tripped when Pippa showed up. Whatever his wife thought, Pippa was still the daughter of an obscenely rich family and a valuable connection.

Giving the senator a not-so-subtle wide berth, Pippa pulled me away. My future father-in-law hadn't survived over thirty years in Washington without knowing when to push. For now, he backed off, returning to the receiving line of guests.

Pippa waved a waiter over. She grabbed the waiter's entire plate of hors d'oeuvres and champagne, and plunked down at a table in the corner. I followed suit.

Was it weird for the guest of honor to sit in a corner of the room like a wallflower stuffing her face with little bacon-wrapped scallops? Sure, but you know what? I deserved a few moments of peace. It wasn't as if anyone at the party would miss me. The benefit of having a charming fiancé was that people rarely missed me.

"So tell me, did you jump him in your office?" Pippa asked excitedly.

My hand slammed against her mouth. "Shhh!" Outside of a few curious glances at us, because we were the only lame ones sitting, no one seemed to notice.

Pippa shoved my hand away and continued, "Well? Did you? Was it hawwwt? Did you have some sexy, sexy make-up sex in your office?"

"No!" I yelped. "Hush, Pippa, no one knows about *him*. I'm engaged."

One eyebrow rose. "Are you really engaged?"

Shoving my sparkly finger at her, I responded, "Yes, see the ring. See the party." I waved my hands around the crowded ballroom glowing with lit candles.

"I know that." Pippa imitated my hand gestures. "Are you sure this is what you want? What you *actually* want, not just want you *think* you should want? You haven't been dating Clayton that long, and just because he shoved some giant heirloom at you doesn't mean you have to accept. The least he could have done was buy you a new ring, instead of giving you a hand-me-down from a dead relative with no sentimental value either."

"Yes, I want." I nodded emphatically even as her words sent my nerves into overdrive. "Now, no more about the other *him. Nothing* happened in my office."

Looking disappointed, she said, "Shame. You could have done some kinky role playing in your office. Hot professors exploring each other for the sake of academia. Hot librarian helping a lost soul find the perfect book, only to end up finding each other's hoohoo."

"Hoohoo? Get your mind out of the gutter," I said.

"Maybe you should get your mind *into* the gutter," Pippa retorted. "I would be rolling in the gutter if I was married to Andrew. That man looks like he wouldn't mind getting dirty."

Laughing helplessly, I buried my head in my hands. If only she knew the dirty images teasing my mind ever since the almost-kiss with Andrew. I blushed thinking of how much my body remembered Andrew.

"Seriously, I wish I had known the Andrew from law school and New York was the same Andrew from your past. What a small world," Pippa said, looking thoughtful.

"What would you have done if you knew?" I asked.

She shrugged. "Oh, I don't know. I think the first thing would be *not* throwing myself at him for three years during class."

"You did not. If you did, he would totally have responded."

"I did too. I don't know if he noticed anyone at law school. He was just so focused on his studies. That inaccessibility obviously made him hotter. Second, if I knew he was your Andrew, I would have knocked him over the head for his stupidity for ruining things with you," Pippa said.

I smiled at her loyalty. I didn't have the heart to tell her that I was equally to blame. Hesitant yet too curious not to ask, I probed, "What was he like in law school and at the firm?"

Frowning in thought, Pippa propped her head on one hand. "He's pretty hard to get to know and kept a distance from most people. I'd wager that you still know him better than anyone else. He married you. Oh shit."

"What?" I turned around to look at what Pippa was staring at. There, in the middle of the ballroom stood Andrew. Clayton may be eye candy, but Andrew was some weird whole-person candy for me.

I couldn't take my eyes off Andrew as he approached, his gray eyes zeroing in on mine. There was this odd calmness that I felt around him, as if I had arrived somewhere safe. I was so focused on him that I didn't even notice that he was closely followed by Clayton, my future in-laws, and my parents. All standing in front of me, looking ready to chew me out.

Lucky me.

CHAPTER EIGHT

ANDREW

December 1, 2008
Ting,
I'm sorry for ignoring you these past two weeks. I needed some time alone to deal with the news. I'm sure you've heard from my mom, or maybe she told your parents—my dad is up for parole. I want him to stay in jail, far away, forever. He deserves hell for what he's put my mom and me through. You've never met him, and I thank God that you haven't. Because he was a piece of shit, even before he embezzled at his firm. He manipulated people when he was bored, stole from people when he wanted something that wasn't his. That's the person that I remember, not this well-behaved, reformed person that his lawyer is arguing for. But then, he has always been charming.
Do you ever wonder if we'll turn into our parents? You might think your parents are nosy and overprotective, but they love you. I try so hard to not be like my dad. To keep my head down. But sometimes, I just feel so angry at the world (like this parole hearing) that I wonder if I'm not turning into him.
Do you think I'll end up like him?
Yours,
Andrew

I was irrationally, hopelessly drawn to her. My head told me to fly back to Chicago, that it was over, and to sign whatever thing I needed to in order to move on. Instead, I spent the past couple of days in Boston, working out of a hotel and trying to figure out if I was crazy for attending my wife's engagement party. To a different man.

When I didn't see her at the front of the ballroom, I headed straight inside, barely acknowledging my wife's fiancé. That "f" word was an infection that my body fought against.

Ah, there she was. Instead of being at the center of the crowd at her own party, she was in a corner, in deep conversation with one of my former classmates and colleagues, Pippa. I was reminded again of how small the world was.

My heart pounded faster than the music blaring around me. My feet moved on their own accord. I stupidly whispered, "Hi," even though there was no way she could have heard across the room.

Yet, as if my greeting had been whispered intimately in her ear, Tia glanced up right at me. I couldn't have looked away from her warm brown eyes even if I had wanted to. Some part deep inside of me recognized her, took solace and joy in the sight of her, and could never get enough of her.

I couldn't tell you what she was wearing, because well, she looked beautiful in everything, so what did her wearing this shirt or that dress matter? What I did notice was her smile, her lips parted slightly, the soft and dreamy expression on her lovely face. It was as if she had missed me in the few days since we had last seen each other.

My feet propelled me to her. In the background, I could vaguely hear my name being called out and others heading toward Tia too. Whoever they were, they didn't matter. Nothing mattered except this woman in front of me.

Tia stood up and stepped into my waiting arms. I held her tightly against me, burying my face in her dark brown, almost black hair. She smelled like Lip Smackers, tea, and something so intricately her.

My body fit around her curves. And curves, she did have, I noticed appreciatively. They felt soft and warm around my hard body. Hard because I worked out. But yes, also in *that* way too.

"Ahem. Stop mauling each other right in front of me. You're just rubbing it in my face, when I haven't gotten any action in months. This is a hotel, get a room."

My face reddening, I broke away from Tia, smiling sheepishly at Pippa. Pippa had spent all three years of law school flirting with me like it was her job. From the beginning, I had known that she was doing it more to get a reaction from me than because she was actually serious. She was pretty much never serious—the class clown without a filter. I liked her because of that. You could always tell what she thought of you.

"Are you ready?" Pippa asked, her eyes sparkling with mischief, looking at both myself and Tia.

Confused, I turned around.

Shit.

It was the un-welcoming brigade.

Mr. and Mrs. Wang looked horrified and a little scared, as if I were a zombie coming back from the dead trying to steal their precious daughter from her Prince Charming.

Clayton looked thoughtful and bristling at the same time. No longer the easygoing acquaintance from earlier that week, I could sense his suspicions warring with his desire to trust Tia. As soon as he reached us, he put his hand on the small of Tia's back, tension radiating off of both of them.

Senator and Mrs. Davenport were wearing identical smiles, lips thinned to harsh lines. I didn't know how much Tia's parents or Clayton had told them about me or our relationship. Judging by the fact that I hadn't been accosted by the not-so-hidden bodyguards around the ballroom, my guess was nothing or some partial, glossed-over story.

I was tired of being nothing or some skimmed-over story. Tia and I had a past. A long, intertwined past that had shaped both of us. I wanted to shout to the ballroom and demand that they stop treating me like some dirty secret. Was I so awful to everyone's current lives that I needed to be handled like an explosive? *Yes, compared to Clayton, who do I think I am?*

Even though my first instinct was to throw Tia over my shoulder and escape, instead, I forced myself to stay. "Hello, Mr. and Mrs. Wang. Hey, Clayton." I stretched out my hand to the Davenports. "Hi, I'm Andrew."

As if it was second nature, the Davenports shook my hand automatically. They looked inquiringly at the Wangs, who had drawn Tia over to the side. Huddling together, they alternated shooting questions at their daughter and smiling at the rest of us, as if to say everything's fine.

"Ting Ting, ni zai gan shen me? *Ta* wei shen me zai zhe?"

"Mama, Baba," Tia said, her cheeks flushed with discomfort. "Wo men deng yi xia zai shuo ba."

"Nu er, ni bie gan chun shi, bie gao su Clayton, bie lang fei zhe ge ji hui."

I didn't know exactly what they were arguing about. It had been a long time since I had tried to learn Chinese—ten years to be exact. However, it was not hard to guess that they were furious at seeing me here and probably nervous that Clayton and his parents would find out about us.

Senator Davenport cleared his throat. He was a commanding man and that small sound, despite the noise in the room, drew our attention. "Can someone please tell us what's going on?"

"I went to school with Clayton," I started, tired of having others discuss me like I wasn't standing right there, "and I knew Ting—Tia back in Colorado."

"Knew how?" asked Mrs. Davenport sharply.

"They just friends, kids play—"

"Andrew's mama clean our resort, nothing else. They—"

There it was. With the Wangs' hurried statements, I was reduced to the kid who was only tolerated because my mother was the Wangs' maid. No matter what I had achieved, I was still the poor kid who had to be watched carefully in case I ever turned into my dad.

"Mama," Tia said, "that wasn't very nice."

"Is true, no?" her mom retorted.

"You know he's more than just Ms. Parker's son, and that we—"

"Tia." I put a soothing hand on her arm. She drew back immediately as if burned.

That hurt. Her public rejection, though not a big movement, was worse than her parents writing me off or the Davenports looking at me as if I had purposely come to ruin their son's shining moment. It was a deeper fall from grace that I hadn't thought was possible.

"I invited Andrew," Clayton cut in, his eyes flickering away from the spot on Tia's arm that I had reached for. "I ran into him this week and asked him to come, since he's friends with both Tia and me."

Before anyone else could comment, Clayton said, "Mr. and Mrs. Wang, it must be a surprise to see someone you knew from Colorado. What a small world. Have you had a chance to meet my aunt Jenna Mae and uncle Bob from Texas? They just came back from a trip to Beijing. Mom, Dad—do you want to take Tia's parents around and introduce them?"

I hated that Clayton was Tia's fiancé and that he already had everyone's seal of approval. However, even I could grudgingly admire how easily he diffused the situation and redirected conversations. With his parents and Tia's parents still suspicious but safely distracted by their guests a few feet away, he came back to Tia, Pippa, and me.

"We should talk, away from this," I said, indicating the crowded ballroom with my hand.

"I don't know if there's anything we need to say," protested Tia. "Maybe later? We should probably stay here. I mean, Mrs. Davenport has worked so hard to put this party together."

"She can enjoy it. We"—I pointed to the hellish triangle of Tia, Clayton, and myself—"need to talk."

"I agree," said Clayton. "I don't know what's happening here, but it's more than you two dating in the past. On the other hand, I agree with Tia that we need to stay. It is *our* engagement party, and we don't want any gossip. The party's supposed to end around eleven p.m. Let's talk then."

I watched as Tia and Clayton walked away to mingle with their guests. I was surprised that Tia had told him that we had dated. Did she tell him that we were married?

If I had to be honest, I would admit that they looked good together. Her dark brown hair contrasted with his blond hair. He was social and comfortable with himself. She was quieter in crowds but one-on-one with someone, she was funny, self-deprecating, and charming. Tia was not going to leave Clayton, at least, not for someone like me.

So what the hell was I still doing here, waiting for a conversation that would lead nowhere?

It wasn't as if I had actively pined for her for the last ten years. The first few years, she had been a constant in my brain. More recently, the frequency of thinking of Tia had slowed to occasional curiosity. *I should go and leave them alone.*

"Want to get out of here?"

I had forgotten that Pippa was still there, and knowing her, loving all of the drama playing out in front of her. How much had Tia told her about all of this?

I shrugged. "Sure, know a place nearby? As you've heard, I have a meeting back here at eleven."

"Google says there's a bar with great cocktails down the street," she replied, turning her phone toward me. For all I knew, she could have been flashing photos of cats in kilts, with how fast she was waving her phone in front of my face.

"Andrew!" a voice called out to my left. The heavily accented voice made me want to keep walking, straight to the bar and drown myself in shots. Forget my one-drink-max rule. This was a special occasion.

However, the part of me that had always wanted his approval stopped. I steeled myself against Mr. Wang's lecture. When we were kids, Mr. Wang disciplined Tia not by grounding her or taking away privileges like TV. Instead, he gave lengthy lectures that somehow ended in cautionary tales about Communism and becoming zookeepers. It didn't matter what Tia had done. In Mr. Wang's lectures, she always wound up as a zookeeper if she didn't listen to her parents. Occasionally, Mr. Wang's affinity for lectures extended to me too, like when he heard from my mom that I had skipped school one day. Apparently, I was also destined to clean monkey shit. I was still wary of zoos.

"Hi, Mr. Wang," I greeted for the second time that evening, trying to keep my voice friendly.

Pippa the Nosy One made no move to step out of earshot. Oddly enough, I was glad to have her physically by my side, even if there was no way she was actually on my side of this Tia-Clayton-Andrew triangle.

"Andrew." Mr. Wang paused, as if searching for the right words. The Wangs had moved to the United States when Tia was eight years old and Mr. Wang had decided to personally oversee some of his real estate investments in Breckenridge. Mr. Wang's English was perfectly understandable once you got used to his cadence, but clearly this topic required words outside of his familiar real estate jargon.

He cleared his throat and started again, "You and Ting Ting are no more. You two—too young before. A big mistake. You leave, she get back up. Now, she has good, big chance to do good things—" He waved his hand around the ballroom as if this room could capture all that she had accomplished and her potential.

"She's already doing great things," I insisted.

Looking pained, Mr. Wang said, "Yes, she is a good girl—she go to good college, get PhD, now professor. Her mama and I are proud of her. She have chance to marry a senator's son now."

I waited for him to say more. He didn't. As if marrying a senator's son was self-explanatory, Mr. Wang rocked back on his heels. We stood there silently assessing one another.

I liked Mr. Wang. Truly. Yes, he had a propensity to lecture, was overprotective and doled out too much advice. However, in comparison to the deceitful father I had who hadn't cared a shit about me, I appreciated that Mr. Wang protected his only child.

"Mr. Wang," I said. "I care about your daughter. I want the best for her."

"You care about her?" he asked. "Go away. Let her marry Clayton."

"I didn't know they were getting married until this week. I'm not trying to take her away from Clayton. I'm just trying to figure out—"

"You think I not see? I see you look at Ting Ting—same now, same when you as a boy," he spat out, his voice rising with a hint of desperation. "After you leave, she in big pain. You make her sad. Andrew, I always like you, even as kid. You better than your father. You think my wife and I need so much clean in the house? No! We very clean people. Your mother not want to take money for your college cost, so we give her more work. So, I like you—you good boy."

I was stunned. Like law school, my college tuition had been covered by scholarships. However, there had still been costs for the dorm rooms, food, and books. Waiting tables at the local diner only covered so much, and I had been too grateful to ask when my mom slipped me extra money whenever she visited me in college. To think that it was Tia's parents who had funneled the money to help me was … It shocked me to the core.

I had always thought the Wangs disapproved of me. And maybe they did. But they also saw enough good in me to help me in a way that wouldn't hurt my mother's pride. Or, maybe they helped so that I'd stay at college and away from their daughter. Either way, I was grateful to the man in front of me.

"Mr. Wang," I said, simply. "I didn't know you had helped. Thank you."

He dismissed the thanks, looking slightly embarrassed to have said anything. "You a friend to Ting Ting and need help. We help a little."

"How much did you give to my mother? I can pay you back, with interest," I insisted. I didn't want to be in debt to anyone, much less to Tia's dad. It put me at a disadvantage, and I needed all of the advantages I could get.

Mr. Wang looked at me, assessing. "You want help? Leave Boston. No call Ting Ting. No email. No WeChat. She marry Clayton. He give her good life. He take care of her. He maybe be senator or governor—my daughter have better and easy life with him. Listen, Andrew, okay?"

He made so much sense. I should agree. Yet, words refused to come out.

At my silence, Mr. Wang waved me off, muttering Chinese under his breath as he headed back to intercept his wife who was making a beeline for us. Mrs. Wang was a woman who liked things settled, and by the time she thought of something that needed to be done, she was already impatient to have it complete. I was unsettling her daughter's life, and I could see the stress on her face.

I didn't like the thought of disappointing or stressing Tia's parents. However, I also didn't want to promise to leave Tia alone if I couldn't be a hundred percent sure that I would keep the promise.

I stole another glance around the ballroom, looking for Tia. She was half hidden in a crowd of people our age, a forced smile on her face, as they laughed enthusiastically and talked over each other. I wanted to rescue her, to steal her away from this loud crowd and take her somewhere private where we could just be.

Before I could do something stupid, Clayton leaned in to whisper something in her ear, earning him a genuine smile. *She's not mine to rescue.* I needed to get it through my dumb head—she wasn't mine. She hadn't been mine for a long time. I needed to support her in whatever she wanted to tell Clayton later that night and to pull myself out of this situation as quickly as possible. When I got back to Chicago, I vowed to sign those stupid divorce papers. No more.

"I think you need a drink even more than me," Pippa said, at my side. For such a chatty and loud person, she sure was quiet when drama was unfolding. For the second time that night, I had forgotten about her.

"Let's go, then."

We headed to the bar down the street. It was too trendy for my taste, and the alcohol menu had too many pages of drinks with punny cocktail names. But they had little booths for privacy, and the lighting was dark enough to hide my turmoil.

"So, are you single?" asked Pippa suddenly. She hadn't spoken a word to me since we left the ballroom.

"I date," I said vaguely.

"What does that mean? I swear, this is the problem with dating nowadays. Everyone's so ambiguous and afraid to define a relationship or non-relationship, you end up not knowing what you're dealing with," huffed Pippa, clearly passionate about this. "It's even worse with dating apps where there are so many choices. Don't get me wrong, I've been forced to get on the apps: Bumble, Tinder, OkCupid, CoffeeMeetsBagel, Cowboys Singles."

I barked out a laugh. "Why are you on a cowboys app?"

She shrugged. "Why not? It's not like I'm having success in Boston."

"Not that it's really your business, but I am single," I conceded. Looking back, I hadn't realized how boring my dating life had been recently. With buying a townhouse and getting a new job at Cipher Systems as their in-house lawyer, I had been busy. That and dating had seemed so draining lately. I hadn't been interested enough to even go on a second date in over a year. What's the point if I could tell from the first date that it wasn't going anywhere? I knew what it was like to fall in love, and it felt like a waste of time to string someone along if I knew that I wasn't going to fall in love with them.

"Would others consider you single too? Are you sure there aren't any women in your life who think they're in a relationship with you?" Pippa quizzed.

"No one expects anything from me. What's with all of the questions?" I asked.

"I just want to see what we're dealing with. Love triangles are tough. Can you imagine dealing with a love square or pentagon?" She shuddered.

"Not sure it's even a love triangle. A love line perhaps, with some legal procedures mucking it up," I said, resigned to my role as the soon-to-be ex-husband. Sure, I'd step out of the way, as Tia wanted, but don't expect me to be happy for them. Whoever said that, if you really loved someone, you'd just want them to be happy, was full of bullshit.

Pippa shook her head, a thoughtful frown on her face. "You know the only side I'm on is Tia's, right? Clayton's a fantastic guy. But you know what I keep thinking about? Tia and I knew each other back in Beijing, and we restarted our friendship in undergrad. She took a gap year or something after high school, but she had so many AP credits that she eventually caught up, and we ended up in a ton of classes together. She was not the same as the girl from Beijing, nor was she who she is today. She was devastated, like a ghost. That Tia from college makes sense now. If divorcing you hurt her that much, then it's a logical assumption that there were a lot of intense feelings to start with." Pippa paused before asking, "Do you ever get over feelings that deep?"

No!

It tore at me to hear about how devastated Tia had been. It made me want to get up and throw things, punch a wall, punch myself for hurting her. It made me more resolved to step away from this whole situation and to give Tia what she really wanted—a clean slate with a marriage to the man of her dreams. Yet, a traitorous part of me clung to Pippa's question with pesky hope. Do you ever get over feelings that deep?

Had Tia?

Could I?

CHAPTER NINE

TIA

December 17, 2009 (never sent)
Andrew,
It has been more than ten years since we met. A decade of knowing you.
It was incredibly awkward to be the new girl. I was doomed to be the outsider. Until you came over to sit at my table at lunch. We were two loners sitting together every day at lunch—you eating a sandwich that never seemed enough for you, me eating leftovers from the food that my mom had cooked the night before. I tried asking if I could bring sandwiches or get school lunch, but she insisted that homemade Chinese food was superior.
I really tried to listen to my mom, but sometimes, I just wanted pizza. You were the pizza that I craved. Turns out, maybe my mom was right, and too much pizza was not good for me.
Ting

Ugh. I'd had better days.

I should have been celebrating—my family and friends were around, the food was great. I'd stress eaten at least a bazillion bacon-wrapped scallops in the last hour, and even conceded to eat one crab rangoon. All I had to do was stand there, smile and say thank you whenever people congratulated me, and let Clayton guide the conversation.

However, all I could think about was the impending doom once this party ended. Which was why I was stuffing my face as if it was my last night on earth. What were calories if my life was going to be in ruins tomorrow?

I HATED that I was putting Clayton through this mess. I HATED that I had pulled Andrew back in. I was the person who got secondhand awkwardness from watching *The Office*. Now, I was going through the motions at my own party, feeling preemptively awkward for my future self.

By eleven p.m., the guests had mostly filtered out. The remaining guests were clustered around the bar, too drunk to care what we did. With every person who came to say goodbye, I mentally counted down the minutes of my life. After trying unsuccessfully to keep Clayton's uncle Bob and aunt Jenna Mae from leaving by sprouting every fact I knew about Texas (which was unfortunately not a lot) and ignoring Clayton's hints to leave, I decided to try all of the leftover desserts. Or just plain eat everything until I passed out and had to be taken to the hospital, where I could feign amnesia or something.

While eating my sixth little pastry, I had finally run out of excuses when Clayton tracked me down by the lemon bars. Outside of the small frown between his brows, I couldn't tell what he was thinking. "Hey, Tia, let's go find Andrew. I want this conversation done with."

Gulp. I stuffed my seventh lemon bar into my mouth and proceeded to chew as slowly as I could. Clayton stared at me patiently. After a minute, I slowly nodded and let myself be led along the path to doom. Otherwise known as the hotel hallway.

"I booked a room upstairs and texted Andrew to meet us there. I want privacy for this," Clayton said, letting go of my hand, as we went into the elevators.

As the doors to the elevators closed, Clayton leaned back against the opposite side of the enclosed space, eyes closed. He looked weary. I'd always thought that he found other people energizing. For the first time since I've known him, I wondered if being charming wasn't as easy as he made it seem.

"Are you—are you okay?"

Eyes flying open, Clayton laughed dryly. "Why shouldn't I be? I just watched my fiancée and an old friend … I don't even know what I saw. What did I see?"

Panic silenced me.

He pressed on, "Andrew said he was in Boston for business. Is that 'business' you?"

Miserably, I nodded.

Eyes narrowed, he said thoughtfully, "I spent nearly every day with him for five years at school and at our old firm. He's very good. Calculated and not a risk-taker. Why would he randomly visit you?"

"I might have visited him first," I whispered. I was the worst human. "I'm sorry."

The elevator dinged, and the doors opened. Ignoring my apology, Clayton put out his arm to hold the elevator doors as I walked into the empty hallway. He didn't look at me as he led me to a room at the end of the long hallway.

As he swiped a card against the reader, I grabbed his arm. "Please, aren't you going to say something? Yell at me, curse at me, something."

"What can I say? What's the right thing to say to your fiancée after she tells you that she flew to another city to visit an ex?" Frustrated, Clayton took a deep breath, as I physically felt the weight of his acute disappointment. "You know, one of the things that I used to admire about you was that you didn't invite or cause drama. It's too much. It's not like you."

"I'm sorry, I'm sorry," I whispered. Clayton didn't deserve to have me stuck on another man. He didn't deserve me obsessing over what kissing Andrew would be like, when I could no longer stand the thought of kissing Clayton.

"Let's get this over with, Tia. When Andrew gets here, I want to hear everything," Clayton said, seemingly back in control again.

Inside the hotel room, we waited in silence. Painful silence that stretched. The silence was a sign of my fall from grace—for someone so adept at small talk, Clayton didn't deem me worthy of conversation.

Metaphorically strengthening my spine, I steeled myself for what was to come. *I will get through this. I will get through this.* If I survived, I'd reward myself with a giant piece of fudge brownie. And ice cream. Maybe another lemon bar.

"Am I interrupting something?"

I turned quickly at the oh-so-familiar voice. Hair mussed with day-old stubble shadowing his face, Andrew stepped into the room. He glanced at me, a line of worry between his eyes, as he tilted his head to the left in question.

"Hi, Andrew," I breathed out. Every time I saw him, all of me reacted to him. Without thinking, I took a small step toward him. "Where did you go during the party? I didn't see you stay."

"Pippa and I went to a bar down the street," he said.

He might as well have declared that they had a quickie in the alleyway, the way that my body recoiled. I thought they were just acquaintances. Pippa had told me that there had been nothing between them in law school. Could something have sparked after all these years? *No!* My brain protested, reeling my conjectures in—Pippa was my best friend and loyal. *Relax.*

From somewhere behind me, Clayton said, "Let's get this over with. I can deal with the two of you dating in the past. Everyone has a past. But tonight, I found out that Tia visited you in Chicago. What is going on here?"

I froze at Clayton's directness. I waited with my breath held to hear what Andrew would say. Instead, he lifted an eyebrow slightly, but said nothing.

Ai ya ya. He was giving me an out, letting me take the lead. Even now, he wanted to protect me. Part of me wanted to let him shield me, as he used to do in school when kids teased me for my accent and occasional English flubs.

"I flew to Chicago"—I swallowed hard—"because I needed to ask Andrew for a divorce."

Silence.

"I thought I heard you say divorce. That can't be," Clayton protested.

I could feel an uncomfortable heat flushing through my face, my neck, my upper chest as I nodded.

Clayton's blue eyes darkened, a tic in his jaw working overtime. His hands clenched into fists. Looking at both me and Andrew, he said in measured tones, "Explain, please. I thought maybe there were some leftover feelings. Now, you're telling me that you're also *married* to him? Tia, did you think I was a fool?"

"You're not a fool!" I said, trying to pat his arm as if I were soothing an angry kitten.

Andrew interjected, his tone surprisingly calmer than before, "No one's trying to make anyone look like an idiot, Clayton. Tia and I dated in the past, got married too young, and got a divorce. Except, the divorce never went through."

I added, "I just found out a couple weeks ago when my lawyer was starting to work with your lawyer around the prenup. My lawyer called me, and I flew out to Chicago to ask Andrew to sign the divorce papers."

"Did you sign, Andrew?" asked Clayton.

"No."

To ease Andrew's defiant response, I rushed in, "Don't worry about it. Andrew and I will sign tonight, and I'll give the papers to my lawyer on Monday to file immediately. Then, we can get married next summer like we planned. Right?"

"You said, 'Andrew and I will sign.' You haven't signed either, Tia?" Andrew asked sharply, picking up on the tiny, embarrassing detail.

I shook my head miserably.

From my other side, Andrew turned quickly towards me, his eyes piercing. His expression was hard to read. He seemed untouchable.

On the other hand, I could tell that my non-signing had triggered something for Clayton. He began pacing. Every now and then, he would glance at his watch—a nervous habit, I knew, whenever he was feeling stressed. He wasn't looking at either Andrew or me, but his fierce concentration made me wonder what he was thinking. Was he thinking of the best way to tell his parents that our engagement was over? Was he thinking how quickly he could get out of this mess?

What a shock this must be for him. How chaotic, how dramatic—all things that Clayton was not. He was articulate but not demonstrative. Yet, with our engagement starting to crumble, I expected him to be angrier. Instead, he was too calm. Why wasn't he showing more feelings? If you truly loved someone, wouldn't you care more?

After watching Clayton pace for a while, Andrew cleared his throat to get my attention. He pointed to my shoes. "Tia, you should sit for a bit. Your feet must be killing you."

Looking down at my feet, I was surprised to see that I was still wearing the only pair of heels that I owned. Now that he mentioned it, yes, my feet were frozen in pain, carved by the unforgiving lines of the stilettos. Clayton barely spared a glance at us, as he continued to pace. He didn't look anywhere near done, so I sank onto the king-size bed that dominated the hotel room.

Gingerly, I took off one of my shoes, groaning in relief. I wanted to cry with happiness that my foot was free at last.

Across from me, Andrew sucked in a ragged breath. My eyes were instantly drawn up to his. There was a flicker of heat in them, as his eyes dropped to my mouth. Slowly, careful not to disturb anything, I took off my other shoe. I couldn't help a small groan from escaping. Andrew's eyes shuttered at the sound. When they opened, the edge of heat was blazing with hunger.

I stared right back at him. I couldn't have looked away, even if there were a mountain of lemon bars having a pillow fight next to me.

It was hard to remember to breathe, as we stared at each other. Andrew had the singular gift of making me feel like the most important person. His eyes didn't roam when he looked at me. Instead, they observed and absorbed. They forced me to focus on him, on this moment.

I devoured the gray of his eyes, the darker flecks in his pupils, the high cheekbones that reddened under my gaze. Andrew held his body tight, tension of a different kind radiating from him. With every raspy breath we drew, our bodies leaned infinitesimally closer.

The thud of the shoe falling from my hand onto the ground shook us out of the spell. Clayton looked up from his pacing. If he had noticed our flushed faces, he didn't say anything.

I immediately leaped up and retreated to a side table in the large room, padding over in my bare feet, to grab a bottle of water with shaky hands. I needed distance from Andrew—physically, mentally, emotionally. The five extra feet wasn't enough.

From the reflection in the window in front of me, I saw Andrew sit down. He looked deceivingly casual, his arms spread out on the back of the chair, his legs sprawling.

It wasn't just Andrew's physical appearance that was dangerous to me. No, the greater danger was *him,* the indescribable mix of *him.* He made me want to trail after him, to try to be the lucky one to uncover his secrets. I remembered the joy I had felt when he bequeathed a rare smile at a joke or shared a fear or desire—chasing those emotional highs had been addicting when we were younger. And like an addict, the withdrawal crushed me.

"Tia," Clayton said, interrupting my thoughts. I hadn't noticed that he had stopped pacing in front of me. He gave me a forced smile that didn't fully reach his eyes. "I've been going over the last couple of weeks. I knew something was up when you disappeared two weeks ago. You've been so anxious and jumpy. Every time I tried to kiss you, you'd draw away. I thought you were nervous about the wedding planning. Now, I know why. I've seen the two of you together, and in that short amount of time, even I can see there's still something there."

"Clayton, I can explain."

To Andrew and in a colder voice, he asked, "Why did you come to Boston? You could have called her, emailed her, communicated via lawyers. Why show up in person?"

Andrew said, not bothering to get up, "I wanted to see if Tia would be open to exploring a relationship with me."

As if that statement confirmed some conclusion that Clayton had already reached, he told me, "Maybe we rushed into this engagement. I still think we have a great friendship and could make a marriage work. However, if we get married, I want to know that it's because you are absolutely sure you want to, not because it was the easiest choice. Right now, I don't think you can say you are sure. I don't want to force you to pick me if you aren't certain. If you are sure, I'll believe you. We'll forget about this."

He looked at me, his blue eyes questioning, a spark of hope in them. I opened my mouth to tell him that of course, I was one hundred percent sure that I wanted to be Mrs. Clayton Davenport and eventually laugh about the craziness that happened before our wedding. But one hundred percent was such an absolute number. A black and white number that brokered no doubts or questions. And I couldn't lie to myself. Or to him.

Shaking my head, I admitted, fighting back tears, "I think I need some time apart to figure things out. Please don't hate me." I waited for him to hate me.

"I could never hate you," he said, sighing, looking frustrated and confused. After a long pause, he added, "I—I need to remove myself from this."

"We'll call it a break, a pause."

Clayton laughed bitterly. "A break is too ambiguous. At this moment, do you know if you'll sign the divorce papers?"

I hesitated for a second before saying quickly, "Of course."

Clayton raised an eyebrow at me. "Without regrets?"

There was nothing that I could say. I should push the divorce proceedings through. Yet, he had guessed right—no matter what I said, I hadn't signed the papers myself, and that must mean something. The truth was that, every time I looked at them, I felt sick.

"I thought so. Tia, if the Band-Aid is going to come off, let's rip it off now. Let's make this clean. And in the future, if you decide that you do actually want to be with me, without any doubt, let's talk then." His blue eyes shone with stubbornness.

This was too big of a decision to be made in the middle of the night. Part of me wanted to argue that we needed more information, more time, before making any decisions.

A traitorous part of me felt … relief.

It was that relief that gave me enough foolish bravery at the moment to twist off my ring. "Here." I held it out in my palm.

Both of us stared at the twinkling ring, before he reached to accept it, a finality in his movement. With the symbol of our future casually dropped into his suit jacket pocket, he headed for the door.

Andrew stood up finally, as silently, the two men assessed each other. Andrew's hands were curled into tight fists at his side. His stance was wide and arrogant, as he looked coolly at Clayton. I couldn't tell what he was thinking. Clayton however was easy to read. Waves of resentment and exhaustion rolled off of him. He opened his mouth to speak, then stopped himself.

I moved closer, in case they decided to settle this with fists.

Finally, Andrew spoke, "I am sorry that you're involved. You've always been respectful toward me. But I'm not sorry that you're breaking up." His voice tightening, Andrew smiled without humor. "Unlike you, I'm a selfish asshole."

Jaws tightening, Clayton ignored Andrew's taunt. He looked at me, his eyes both hurt and resolute. "Call me if you change your mind." With that, Clayton opened the door and walked away from me.

Both Andrew and I watched the door close slowly behind Clayton. We kept staring at the door, even after it clicked shut. The click seemed so final.

Different emotions floated through me—confusion, sadness, guilt that I had ever let Clayton's and my relationship progress so far. Above all, there was a dark anxiety when I thought about the future. My perfect world was crumbling. *How am I going to tell my parents that I let Clayton go?*

From the corner of my eyes, I saw Andrew sink back into the chair, his body bent and head down. We were alone.

I shivered. Was it fear or anticipation? I didn't know.

I was considered an expert in training machines to understand the human language—both the words and the context around the words. Using advanced analytics to parse through a doctor's unstructured instructions to create an easy-to-understand visual of how much medication a patient should take and when? Doable.

This situation with Andrew? I didn't understand, and I didn't have words, nor a path to solve it.

Three weeks ago, I had a perfect fiancé and was content in that relationship, looking forward to the future. Two weeks ago, I had learned that I was planning for a wedding that could land me in jail for bigamy. Twelve days ago, I had impulsively bought a ticket to Chicago to confront my not-ex-husband and ended up in his arms. Today, I was sort-of-but-not-really single, with no fiancé, and a definitely-here-husband.

You're free. What the heck was I going to do now? More importantly, could I handle whatever the wreckage came after? Because there was definitely going to be major metaphorical bloodshed and carnage.

I looked from the door to Andrew. Instead of staring at the floor as I had expected, he was staring at me with unmistakable hunger. In a fluid motion that surprised me for a man his size, he strode forward and was in front of me before I could suck in a breath.

"Tia?" he whispered, his voice a low strum across my body.

Too close.

"Tia?" he repeated. I saw the ask in his eyes.

This was my chance to tell him to leave, to remind him that there was only doom for us. Leave before we could do anything stupid, before I could make another mistake. I didn't need more heartbreak in my life. I needed to make smart decisions. Kissing Andrew was not smart. Kissing Andrew was stupid.

For goodness' sake, I had just broken up with my fiancé ten minutes ago. What kind of person was I to even think about kissing another man?

Stop thinking about kissing Andrew. Stop, screamed my brain as I closed my eyes and leaned toward him.

Yes, yes, yes, shouted my body.

"Wait, Andrew."

Immediately, Andrew pulled back as if burned.

What are these words popping out of my mouth? Get back in and kiss the man. That was my first thought as I took a step groggily back from Andrew. I felt like a comet who had hurled too close to his orbit and was at risk of getting sucked into his gravity, forever meant to circle around him, at his will.

Uh-oh, what have I done? I had pushed away Clayton, my safety net, and the regrets were making a revengeful comeback.

Lifting my head, I looked up at him in question. Andrew was staring at the bed behind us, his jaw tense, as if he too was unsure. Taking a deep breath, he looked down at me. I gasped at the hunger and possession in his eyes, defying me to deny the chemistry between us.

Chemistry—physical, emotional—had never been an issue with us. Even when we were younger, our chemistry had been great. But this was something unexpected.

What did he want? He said he wanted to try again, but how serious was he? Was this really about me, about us, or a middle finger to Clayton and what he represented?

"Andrew?" My voice was soft, hesitant and husky.

"Shhhhh. I need a moment to calm down, and your voice reminds me of sex."

Well. I smiled, despite my warring thoughts.

"Fuck," came another curse, as he turned away from me. Bracing his hands on the wall in front of him, he muttered, his voice so low that I could barely make out his words. I thought I heard something about "nondisclosures," "state laws," and "limited liabilities."

"I'm the boss, applesauce!"

"Huh?" Whirling around, Andrew stared at me in confusion. "You want applesauce now?"

"No, silly, I'm pretending to be Judge Judy."

"Why?"

"I don't know. You were muttering about legal stuff. This is a weird situation, and you know, when things get awkward, random words spill out of me."

"You don't have to try to lighten the situation, or be funny all the time. You don't have to pretend. Be you, it's enough."

My cheeks flamed in pleasure and confusion. Sweet Andrew scared me.

There was too much to discuss, and I knew Andrew had to have questions. I had questions that I wanted to air out. But not tonight. I needed to dissect and panic by myself before I could have a real conversation with Andrew. I needed time. I needed space from this complex, intriguing man before he pulled me back in.

Without putting his hands on me, Andrew leaned down to whisper in my ear, his voice a caress against my sensitive skin. "One more thing. I want you, Tia, so badly. When, and not if, we sleep together—and I promise you, there will be no actual sleep involved—it will *not* be as a rebound. You will only be thinking about me. Think about that tonight."

My cheeks were on fire. Sexy Andrew slayed me.

Nodding at his fierce promise—what else could I say—I left the hotel room with my shoes in hand. One of these days, I would part from Andrew with shoes on.

CHAPTER TEN

TIA

December 25, 2009 (never sent)
Andrew,
We went to Christmas Eve service last night. It was the first time I had left my house since I came home from the hospital. The doctors said that I could have "gone about my regular business" a few weeks ago, that I was recovered enough, but I had nothing to do and nowhere to go.
A few people looked at me funny during the service, but my mom must have warned them not to stare. I'm not sure what my parents told Pastor Smith or the other folks—probably that I just had a health scare and to pray for my soul. Those prayers must have done some good, because last night, when I was sitting and listening to the choir sing, was the first time in a long, long time that I thought that I might be okay. Not now, not for a while, but sometime in the future, I think I could be okay.
Ting

Zero.

That was the number of calls or texts or emails or knocks on the door from Clayton or *him*. I could understand Clayton's silence. We had just broken up, and he rightly needed some time. I didn't know if I could ever face him again after how our engagement fell apart.

But *him*? My phone number had been the same since high school, not that Andrew would know for sure. But he worked for a security company out in Chicago. Don't security companies have secret ways of finding people? He had no excuse for not reaching out.

Of course, he could not *want* to talk to me. Was I even ready to talk to him?

What was up with that sexy promise last night?

"Ai ya ya, you're a fool," I muttered to myself, as I kept walking around Boston. Halloween was next week but it seemed as if the parties had started early. Candy wrappers were scattered around the usually clean streets, alongside the occasional lost sweater, feathers, and glitter from costumes.

If last night's memories weren't painfully clear, I would have thought someone had dressed up as me and doled out a trick on my life.

"Ai ya ya." I smacked my hand against my forehead. A lady walking past looked at my messy hair and lemon pajamas peeking out from my bright turquoise overcoat, and crossed to the other side of the street.

I yelled after her, "Hey, I'm not dangerous! I just didn't have any clean yoga pants left." With a nervous look back at me, she half ran away from me into a nearby coffee shop.

I sighed and kept walking.

Nine hours, 55,000 steps, six cups of coffee, and one blister later, I turned the key to my apartment and fell on my couch in relief. My body was exhausted. My mind was numb enough that I could half ignore my inner dialogue. I had walked more of Cambridge and Boston than I ever had, though I couldn't tell you exactly what I had seen.

It had been an utterly unproductive day. I was no closer to "clarity" than I had been when I woke up from a fitful sleep at four o'clock this morning. Sadness over breaking up with Clayton, confusion about what I wanted from Andrew, anxiety that my life was heading down a path where I couldn't control the endpoint—I was battered from too many feelings. Threading through my ping-pong of emotions was the question of, what did I want?

Say, hypothetically, I realized that I wanted to be with Andrew, did he want the same? After his impromptu visit to my office and last night, I was confident that he wouldn't mind a romp in bed. Or against a wall. However, despite our two almost-kisses, I was not a one-night kind of woman. I couldn't have a meaningless fling without expectations.

Or say, hypothetically, I decided I wanted to go back to Clayton, which was so clearly what I should choose. Could we ever get over the specter of Andrew's and my first marriage? If Clayton was the right choice, shouldn't I feel worse about how our engagement ended? Instead, I felt guilty about not feeling guiltier.

Thinking more was not going to solve anything, apparently. Tired of wallowing, I got up to grab a pint of ice cream from my freezer. No point in spooning some into a bowl when, let's face it, I was going to eat all of the ice cream tonight anyways. Sitting cross-legged on the rug, my back leaning against my bed with a blanket over me, I opened up my phone. I shot off a selfie of myself eating ice cream to Pippa to assure her that I was alive, and reluctantly dialed my parents. Fifteen missed calls and twenty messages on WeChat, the Chinese texting service my family used, were leading indicators that my parents were about to show up at my doorstep armed with food, a plane ticket to Colorado, and a never-ending lecture.

"Wei?" I greeted my parents when they picked up.

"Ting Ting, ni zai nai er?!" shouted both my parents into my ear.

"At home," I answered, putting them on speakerphone, so I could free my hands to continue eating my cookie dough ice cream.

"Who with you?"

"Mei you shui." I shook my head at my phone. Even over the phone, I could feel the tension lessening, as they mentally sighed in relief.

"Where you go today? You not there when we come to apartment," my dad repeated their earlier question. "You too busy, not spend time with us today? We go home tomorrow."

"Oh, I'm sorry. I thought you were resting. I just took a walk around Boston. It was a nice day out," I said.

"Dai mao zi ma?" asked my mom, concern in her voice.

Smiling slightly at her question, I fibbed rather than worry her about exposing my head to the cold and getting sick, "Yeah, I had a hat."

"Hao, walking very healthy. Good job," my mom told me. Now that they were assured that I had not been kidnapped either willingly or unwillingly by Andrew, they had moved on to more important things. Like wearing hats, and how I needed to stop sitting so much and exercise. It wasn't as if they wanted me to lose weight—they didn't really believe in diets. But they did believe in the importance of moving around.

When I first started my job, I had told them that I did exercises all the time—my brain was doing all sorts of stretches and mental sports. They had stared stonily at me through WeChat's video chat and muttered something about kids in America these days.

"… zhu yi shen ti, yao bu yi hou shen ti …" My parents took turns lecturing me about staying healthy. In a few minutes, this litany would devolve into their typical lecture about the future. Over the years, their lectures had switched from warning me that I would wind up working at a zoo, cleaning monkey poop if I didn't listen to them, to ending up in the hospital if I didn't take care of my body.

"Uh-huh," I agreed robotically to the value of eating fresh vegetables daily even as I took another giant bite of ice cream.

Half listening, I opened up my work email. I tried not to be one of those people that worked around the clock, but I made concessions to check my email on weekends for any frantic notes from students freaking out over upcoming tests. Last year, when I had first started teaching, one of my students had accused me of "having it out for her since day one" because I "took, like, forever" to respond to her emails. What was the saying? An apple a day kept the doctor away. Well, ten minutes of work emails on the weekend kept the bad teacher reviews at bay. Eh, not as rhyme-y, but whatever.

"Mm-hmm," I responded to my dad's question about something.

Seeing no desperate emails as I quickly scrolled through my inbox, I was about to start browsing my library for a good book when my heart stuttered. Sandwiched between an announcement about a department lunch and an invitation to speak at a local conference, was an email with the simple subject line of, "Hi" from an A. Parker. It wasn't the same email address that he used when we were younger, but how many A. Parkers did I know? Hands trembling a bit, I touched the email to open it.

To: TWang@mit.edu
Subject: Hi
Hi,
What are you doing tonight?
Andrew

My heart thumped as I stared at the screen. I typed quickly, then erased, then typed … Ai ya ya, I tossed my phone away.

"Ting Ting?" came my dad's muffled voice against a furry pink pillow. "You okay?"

Digging into the pile of pillows on my couch, I grabbed my phone and practically yelled into the speakerphone, "Zai jian! Got to go."

"With Andrew?" asked my mom suspiciously. Darn, she could still read me like a book, that astute woman. It's as if she raised me or something.

"Maybe dinner with a friend," I said vaguely. "Zai jian."

"Pippa? Hao, hao, good. She a good friend," my mom said approvingly. Crisis averted.

"Who's Pippa?" asked my dad to my mom. He was the worst at remembering names. "The pharmaceutical girl? You should be friends with her. She CEO of own company."

"No, that's Kat—"

"You has cat? You should have my grandbaby first, then pets."

"Bu shi de, aiya, Kat shi …"

"Okay, I'll let Mama explain. Got to go. Zhai jian!" I clicked the red button on my phone before I ended up having to draw charts of my friends and acquaintances for my dad.

Taking a deep breath, I looked back down at my half-written email. Urgh, I deleted what I had written, typed out a message, and hit send before I could change my mind.

To: Andrew.Parker@gmail.com

Subject: Re: Hi
Hi,
My number is the same as before.
T

Two minutes later, my phone rang. Without glancing down at it, I picked up, "Wei, Mama, Baba, wo ming tian zai geng ni da dian hua, hao ma?"

A voice cleared on the other side before speaking, freezing me with its husky timbre, "Hi, Ting Ting."

As if to lessen its effects on me, I yanked the phone away from my ear. Nope, my heart was still pounding. Taking a deep, fortifying breath, I said slowly, "Hi, Andrew."

"I've always loved listening to you speak Chinese. There's a melody to it."

"Huh," I said stupidly. What a great conversationalist I was. Thinking hard, I managed to squeak out, "I wasn't sure you still had my number in your phone."

"I don't. I erased your number," came the short reply, before he admitted quietly, "I didn't forget it."

A warm glow filled me up, lifting my cheeks into a smile. Never mind that he had tried to erase me from his life. I couldn't fault him for that, as I had tried to do the same. Shyly, I whispered, "I'm glad."

"Do you want to have dinner?" There was a streak of uncertainty in his voice.

My voice was casual, belying my pleasure. "I could eat."

"My colleague Dan said that there's a great Greek place near Seaport. I could swing by in thirty minutes to pick you up."

"Huh." Images of Boston traffic on a Sunday evening floated through my mind. Food wouldn't be in my tummy until eight at least, and I was a grumpy hungry person. Plus, what if someone who knew Clayton and me was at the restaurant? A shudder ran along my spine. I was not ready to explain our relationship status to busybodies, especially when I was still trying to find answers myself. "How about takeout?"

"Takeout?" Andrew repeated, sounding a little disappointed. Recovering quickly, he amended, "Sure, um, do you have a favorite place? I'll give them a call and pick it up on my way to you."

Twenty-nine minutes later, my apartment was somewhat clutter-free, and I had showered and had on my fifth outfit. It also felt as if I had run a marathon, from running like a maniac around my little apartment. My closet was bursting with clothes, yet I had nothing, absolutely nothing to wear. Was it too late to call the restaurant to tell them to lose our order so I could try a few more outfits?

Bzzzzzzz. Bzzzzzzz.

Yelling like my inner Tarzan, I leaped over discarded dresses to press the intercom button. Out of breath, I shouted, "Who's there?"

"Butter chicken, lamb vindaloo, and naan. Lots of naan."

With a groan, I reluctantly pressed the button to let Andrew into the building. Best-case scenario, if the elevator was busy, I had three minutes. With a panicked look around my studio which now resembled a clothing store at the end of Black Friday shopping, I grabbed a deep red sweater dress and shimmied into it. It was a little tighter than what I typically wore, and I spent precious seconds debating whether to swap it for a loose sweatshirt. This was just a casual, friendly hangout, right?

The knocking on my door, two feet away from where I was standing, shook me into action. Red sweater dress it is. I would just suck in my breath and eat tiny bites. My discarded clothes flew into my closet, and I slammed the closet door shut.

Deep breath, just a casual hangout. Hand shaking a bit, I pulled the door open. Beyond the takeout bag and bouquet of flowers, I could see Andrew's eyes light up and his face relax into a smile. Either he was down to his last clean outfit, or he had dressed up for this *casual* hangout. A light blue button-down peeked out from a gray cashmere sweater over dark jeans. There was no denying it. Andrew Parker had turned out very, very well.

"Can I come in?" he asked, still smiling.

"Yes!" I shouted, before clearing my throat and repeating in a more subdued voice, "Yes, please come in."

Even though my studio apartment wasn't huge, I'd always thought it a decent size, with the high ceilings, big windows, especially for Boston's Back Bay district. It was roomy enough to have a few guests over, with enough space to move around.

However, I didn't realize until Andrew stepped inside just how close my bed was to everything. With his long legs, the bed was less than ten steps from where he was currently standing in the living room part of my studio. I glanced nervously at my bed, back to him. Was it too late to suggest going out to eat?

Whatever my worries, Andrew didn't seem to notice. At ease, he took off his shoes and glanced around my apartment before moving into the kitchen to find plates and utensils. The ease with which he navigated my home unsettled me. I liked it too much.

From over his shoulder, he remarked, "I like your place. It feels like you."

"What does that mean?" Was he implying that I was disorganized? Had bad taste in décor?

"Relax. I meant that it's warm and inviting."

"Oh," I said, my anxiety deflating. Reaching into a cabinet, I grabbed a couple of glasses. "Water or tea okay? I have a bottle of wine somewhere."

"Water is good," he replied.

For a few minutes, we focused on eating. Actually, I focused very intently on sucking my stomach in, taking tiny bites, and *not* looking at Andrew. Since I was definitely not peeking at him, I was only ninety-five percent sure that he was staring amusedly at the top of my head.

I was absurdly nervous. How does one act with your ex-turned-still-husband after you and your fiancé broke up? School hadn't taught me how to decode this, and Google was not helpful. Also, don't google "heartsick" and "confused" in the middle of the night, because then you'll end up going down a rabbit hole thinking you need to call either a cardiologist or neurologist. Or maybe a therapist to talk you out of calling both.

"Tia?" he asked, his gaze tender and soft. "You look beautiful tonight. Actually, yesterday and two weeks ago in Chicago too—I forgot to tell you. I can't stop thinking about you."

Whoosh. There went my breath. My eyes locked with his. In that moment, it was just us. No specters of others or the past.

Of course, my big mouth had to ruin that moment with, "I don't know. I could lose some weight, especially on my butt and legs."

Incredulity shone in his gray eyes, as he stated firmly, "From my perspective, I can assure you that there are no complaints whatsoever."

With a little moan of self-consciousness, I plunked my overheated face into my hands. Andrew's laughter surrounded me, carefree and joyful. If anyone needed to laugh more, it was Mr. Too Serious over there.

Peeking out from behind my hands, I asked, "What are we doing here?"

Pretending ignorance, he answered teasingly, "You live here. I'm eating."

"How long will you be in Boston?"

"How long do you want me to be here?" Andrew asked.

"Don't you have a job in Chicago that you need to get back to?" I continued my very serious game of twenty questions.

"It's flexible. My boss, Quinn, doesn't care where I am as long as I keep his company out of legal trouble. I only need Internet, and I have my laptop. Besides, one of my colleagues moved to Boston a few years ago for his wife and just travels as needed," he explained. Red tinted his cheeks, his eyes not quite meeting mine.

"Huh."

It was a lot to take in. Was he offering to stay in Boston while we figured this out? My head was reeling, and I alternated between excitement to see what might happen between us and horror over how far my life had veered off my safe and predictable path.

The risk-averse part of me trumped. "What about getting a divorce?"

"What's the urgency? You don't think there's something between us that warrants exploring, now that we're both single of sorts?"

I opened my mouth to say something sarcastic. Then, sighing, I went for the truth. "I do feel *something*. I'm also terrified. We did a lot of damage to each other before. I'm not sure it's worth the risk to try again."

The gray in his eyes dimmed, as he leaned back into his chair and crossed his arms. Immediately, I wanted the easygoing, laughing Andrew back—the man who flirted with me and called me beautiful.

In a flat voice, he said carefully, "We were eighteen and nineteen when we tried before. I'd like to think we have both matured. We don't have to commit to a lifetime again, but why not use this opportunity to put any second thoughts and questions away? Give me a month where you fully commit to exploring this thing between us, and at the end of the month, I'll sign whatever you want me to sign—no arguments."

"A month?" The idea intrigued me. A defined duration was less scary. Maybe I needed to see how badly Andrew and I would end up again, before I could come to my senses. And do what at the end of the period? Tell Clayton that I'm sane again and beg him to take me back? The thought didn't hold as much appeal as it should have.

"One month—no holding back," Andrew repeated.

"How about a week?"

"Ten days."

I nodded. I could do ten days. Two hundred and forty hours. Surely that would be enough to remember all of the issues we had. And short enough to not get my heart broken.

Elbows on his knees, Andrew leaned forward. I could easily see him at a boardroom, wrestling contracts to favor his clients. "I don't want you to disappear and come back in ten days, saying that you tried. Here're my terms: I'll stay in Boston the whole time, and we'll see each other every day."

"Every day!" I squawked.

His voice dipped. "We don't have to be handcuffed to each other all day. But I want to see you every day."

Before I could linger too much on the thought of handcuffs, I scrambled for reasons to turn this proposition down. My mind immediately found one. "What about Charlie?"

His expression closed as he said through his teeth, "What about Charlie?"

"In Chicago, it sounded like she was still in your life. This is already messy. I don't want to intrude on anything."

"I'm not *dating* her."

His voice was final. If he went back to her once he signed the divorce papers, it wasn't my business. Not. My. Business. At. All.

"What do you expect us to do together?" I asked.

"I don't know. What normal people do—dinners, breakfasts, movies, checking out the city, talking. I'm sure we can come up with some ideas," Andrew said, shrugging his broad shoulders.

"What about, um, you know …?" I gestured wildly between us and the bed that was too, too close.

Andrew's eyes heated even as his voice remained steady. "You mean sex? Do I want to fuck you? Yes."

At his crude words, my insides liquefied and warmth pooled low in my belly. His deep voice was even lower, his words vibrating in the air around us, creating a cocoon around us.

Voice dropping to a hoarse whisper, Andrew continued, "I'd want you in your bed, on that couch, on the floor, against the walls, in the shower. I want evidence of us all over your home. However, am I expecting it? No. You set the pace for us. I'm just asking that you don't hold back for the next ten days."

I nodded, relieved that he was giving me control. *And what control have I ever exhibited around Andrew?* My mouth parted a little. "When do we start?"

With a triumphant gleam in his eyes, Andrew moved closer to me so that our faces were just inches apart. "Now."

My breath coming in faster, I waited in anticipation for the inevitable sparks. It was too soon. *You'll never be ready, so why not jump in anyways?* I needed more time to prepare, to fortify my heart, to … My eyes fluttered shut, as I gave into my needs.

Thump! Thump!

We stared at each other in confusion, frozen in our chairs. The jolting sound came again, spurring me into action. As I jumped off my chair, I called out, "Hello?" My voice sounded unfamiliar, huskier than usual, as if I had just woken from sleep.

"Ting Ting? Shi Baba he Mama."

"Oh crap!" I looked frantically at Andrew.

His gray eyes narrowed as he stared at me. Standing up, he asked, "What do you want to tell them?"

Thump! Thump! The knocking came again from outside my door. My parents must have followed another tenant into the building, to bypass the intercom downstairs. There was no way to pretend that I wasn't at home. Knowing my parents, now that they knew that I was at home, there was no way they were going to leave.

My eyes settled on my closet. Grabbing Andrew's shoes and throwing them at him, I took his hands and dragged him over. When we got to the front of the closet, he cursed. "Hell no. I'm not hiding in a damn closet from your parents!"

"Shh! Please? Please?" I pleaded. I didn't know what I was going to do if he remained stubborn. "I know we have our deal, but my parents—they're not going to understand. I don't want them to worry. Please?"

"Two weeks," he bargained.

I nodded, happy to agree to anything to avoid further conflict. With a stony face, Andrew squeezed himself against my hastily tossed clothes and closed the door.

Taking a deep breath, I patted my hair and straightened my dress. Forcing a smile on my face, I opened my front door. "Mama, Baba."

With arms full of bags and what looked suspiciously like rolls of toilet paper, paper towels, and Saran Wrap, my parents barged in. With a gruff hello, my dad dropped his bags in the middle of my apartment before sitting on the couch with his phone. Probably to check WeChat. He worked with Chinese investors who tended to impatiently pepper him with questions about their real estate investments regardless of the time difference.

Whack.

My mom gave a firm pat to my back, a reflex after years of trying to get me to improve my posture. Requisite back slap out of the way, she started taking groceries out of bags. "We bring you some food. You eat more vegetables and fruits."

Thrusting a roll of paper towels at me, she continued, "We buy for you. You too busy."

"Thanks," I said accepting their gifts, while simultaneously glancing surreptitiously at the closet to make sure that Andrew was staying put. "I have things delivered. Next-day shipping is pretty handy."

She looked skeptically at me and my millennial ways that didn't require me to actually verify that toilet paper was toilet paper before purchasing it. Seriously, who had time to go to actual stores these days and lug back detergent and Kleenex boxes, when you could just subscribe and have everything automatically delivered every few months?

Suddenly, my mom stopped doling out presents like a practical Chinese Santa Claus and glanced at me suspiciously. "Why you have nice dress?"

"You're always telling me that I need to stop wearing sweats."

"Pippa eat meat now?"

"Huh? No, she's actually vegan," I replied, confused at the non sequitur.

Finger pointed at the half-eaten butter chicken and lamb vindaloo on my small dining table, she cocked her head. "You say you go to dinner with Pippa today, no? Who this eat?" Face brightening all of a sudden, she asked hopefully, "Clayton here?"

I shook my head. *Ai ya ya.* I hadn't even thought about what I was going to tell my parents. It felt too *real* to tell them that Clayton and I had broken up, and that I planned to embark on a two-week *something* with Andrew. I already knew what my parents' reactions were going to be, because they would say exactly the same thing that my diminishingly rational brain was screaming at me. *Tia, you're crazier than a bag of salted cashews!* Then, my parents would finally do what they had threatened to do throughout my childhood when I misbehaved—send me to a Chinese boot camp in the rice paddies. Or worse, look at me in disappointment.

Both threats scared me, never mind that I was supposed to be an adult and didn't need their approval. Which is why I kept my mouth firmly shut.

Still in the afterglow of the engagement party, my mom ignored my muteness. "Oh, Ting Ting, party so good. We so happy. You do good job, catching Clayton. If no Clayton here, who eat meat?"

By now, my dad had apparently deemed our conversation interesting enough to tear his gaze from his work messages. Darn my mom's memory for everything I've ever told her about my friends. My gaze shifted between their overly curious eyes, before I elaborated, with my fingers crossed behind my back to counter my lie, "Well, yes, *Pippa* did come over here, and she accidentally ordered chicken. She thought it was, um, tofu! After she tried some, she realized that it wasn't tofu, and um, left to find um, vegetables."

A chirp sounded on my dad's phone, pulling his eyes back toward the screen. Shaking his head as his index finger drew characters on the phone screen, he said, "In China, when I a little boy, poor people eat vegetables. She family has so much money. She has money to eat meat."

"It's a choice nowadays, and she doesn't—"

Not distracted and definitely not convinced, my mom contended, "Where your ring?"

"It didn't quite fit," I hemmed.

"Clayton no take it and fix it before?" she countered. Ai ya ya, too astute and too good of a memory.

"It still needs some adjusting," I insisted, shoving my hands into pockets that didn't exist. Why didn't dresses automatically come with pockets, like guys' pants?

As if just noticing that my apartment looked too neat for me, she looked around my place as if it was a crime scene and she was the TV detective charged with solving the episode's mystery. I half expected her to start looking under my bed or behind my curtains. "Where Andrew is? He fly to Chicago?"

Sheer willpower kept me from looking over my shoulders at my closet, as my heart thudded in my chest. Faking calm, I shrugged lightly. "I think he has some business in Boston." It wasn't a lie technically.

A huge sigh came from my mom. There was a reason why I didn't play poker. I could calculate odds for poker hands easily, but my face would bankrupt me. Try as hard as I could, I was pretty sure I had not fooled my mom.

A second sigh from her. "Ting Ting, ni yao xiang dao ni de jiang lai."

"I am thinking of my future, trust me," I assured her, even though I could not predict with any confidence that this whole "experiment" was going to take me to a place that my parents approved.

More nervous than I had ever seen her, my mom started moving around my studio, picking up books, rearranging my shoes, wiping invisible dust off of my kitchen counters, constantly in motion. In the middle of her frenzied activities was my dad, well-intentioned but oblivious, and me, so obviously aware of the cause of her anxiety. I braced myself for whatever uncomfortable topic she was preparing herself mentally for.

"When I in university, I have a boyfriend. Before your daddy," she started as she got close to me, and I groaned internally. There was nothing more awkward than to hear about your parents' prior relationships, especially when the other was within listening distance. "All so exciting. I worry so much—ta bu shi hen wen ding. Then I meet your daddy—"

"And let me guess, he was the opposite and so steady."

"Yes. I choose your daddy, and look now—good life. Sometimes, you need lot time to love. You know Andrew many, many years. You know Clayton only little. You choose Clayton," she stressed.

"I could be happy with Clayton," I agreed.

"What is problem, then?" She looked very confused.

Welcome to my world of mental turmoil. Thinking through my words carefully, I said, "What if Clayton and I are better as friends? What if our love doesn't grow? I don't want to have regrets or question whether I made the right decision later. I want to have as much information as I can."

Looking over at my dad to make sure that he was still occupied, my mom stated matter-of-factly, "Andrew is good-looking boy, hen shuai. He tall and strong."

"Mama." My face burned, as if I had swallowed a shot of Sichuan peppers.

"I'm not young, but I see, I understand," said my mom, with another huge sigh. "You smart girl. Use your nao dai"—she tapped the side of my head—"and choose happy with Clayton. Forget Andrew and past. He too messy. Okay?"

CHAPTER ELEVEN

ANDREW

December 16, 2008
Ting Ting,
I took three showers yesterday, and I still feel gross. I went to Denver for my dad's parole hearing and saw him face-to-face for the first time in eleven years. Maybe his lawyer's letters got to me—I'm ashamed to admit that I almost believed my dad. Then I saw his eyes in the courtroom. They were dead eyes. He smiled at me as if he was including me on the secret that he was just fooling everyone. I'm glad the judge denied parole. I wouldn't want his type of evil anywhere near us. I'm glad you listened and didn't join me in Denver. I wouldn't want him to know you existed—not because I want to hide you—I just don't want him to somehow hurt you.
Three more days until I'm done with exams and come home to you.
Yours,
Andrew

Secrets destroyed lives. Living for the first seven years of my life with scum like Brandon Parker taught me that lesson early on. He hurt everyone around him whom he was supposed to care for. My dad was always cheating and lying about cheating, gambling and lying to my mom that he hadn't just gambled our grocery money away, conning people and trying to pretend he was an upstanding citizen—it was a never-ending cycle of lies. Eventually those lies caught up to him and landed him in jail for a blessed eighteen years. It was nowhere near long enough.

It had been a few years since he finished his sentence, and the state declared him "reformed." I knew better than to believe that to be the case. People like him didn't reform. They got smarter about hiding their evilness.

My mom said that she had no idea Brandon was scum at first. When they met, he had a legit job. It terrified me to think that one day, something could snap within me, and that I would turn out to be just like Brandon. It was unsettling to be uncomfortable with myself.

As for most things in my life, I tried to do the opposite of what my dad did. He drank until he was punching mad, so I didn't touch alcohol for the first twenty-one years of my life. Now, I forced myself to drink a beer every now and then just to prove that I could imbibe without losing control. My dad gambled his and my mom's paychecks. I had never gambled, never even filled out a March Madness bracket. His smile hid lies. I tried to be brutally honest rather than charming.

Except for that one time, when I had wanted, truly wanted with everything in me, to tell the truth. Except that it hadn't been my secret to tell. And ultimately, even if I did tell Tia, what did it matter? I was a broke college student with no connections and tainted blood. I was too big of a risk to take on.

Now, squished in Tia's closet, with hangers poking at the back of my head and clothes falling around me, I stood in the darkness like her dirty secret. I hated that she couldn't admit to her parents that she had broken up with Clayton, as if there was even a chance she might go back to him. I hated that she had asked me to hide from her parents, as if she couldn't face potential criticism about us. I hated that she couldn't, or wouldn't, defend me to her parents.

So what if I got an extra four days in our arrangement by being treated worse than dirty laundry? Because if she was still ashamed of us and wouldn't even acknowledge what was between us to herself or to her parents, then we were doomed regardless of how many days we spent together.

The closet door was pretty thin, and I had no trouble hearing her mom ask her to forget about me and focus on Clayton. Tia hadn't responded, and that non-response was enough to make me feel like gum stuck to the bottom of a shoe. It didn't matter that Tia hadn't explicitly agreed. What stuck out to me was that she hadn't vehemently tried to shoot down the suggestion, or better yet, yanked open the closet door and shouted "ta-da!"

My hands balled into fists so tight that I could barely feel them, itching to open the door and show Tia and her parents—what? *Mr. and Mrs. Wang, I'm bribing your daughter into a pretend relationship by withholding my signature from our divorce papers*. Because bribery always made you look great in front of people you'd like to impress.

I hated to admit it, but it was time to face facts. I wasn't anything more to Tia than a rebellion. So, what did it say about me that I was willing to accept that role, if it meant having extra time with her? What did it say about my greed for her? *Maybe this is how Brandon started turning, maybe he had wanted something that wasn't his.*

Pacing internally and growing more and more irritated—whether at the situation, myself, or both—I waited for Tia's parents to leave. They stayed for a few more minutes, chattering in a mix of broken English and Chinese.

A long time ago, I had tried learning Chinese in an effort to be seen as a more acceptable husband to Tia's parents, to the point that I could converse about as well as a moderately articulate three-year-old. Years of disuse had atrophied my Chinese to the level of a one-year-old. I could understand very, very simple phrases but couldn't produce more than basic sounds myself. In this situation, I didn't need to understand everything to know that Tia's parents were fussing over her, while she bristled at being treated like a child.

Their dynamic had always fascinated me. Maybe because theirs was the only other family dynamic that I had the chance to observe at close range. It was night and day compared to my own family's. One, none of the Wangs had a criminal record. Beyond that, while my mom was an amazing woman who had survived a horror of a husband, she had been too busy working multiple jobs and making sure we had a roof over our heads.

On the other hand, Tia's parents' world revolved around her. It wasn't just the material things, but also the time and care they took with her. In middle school, when Tia asked if she could go to summer camp, her parents had spent days researching the best programs around the country and polling their friends. When Tia had expressed an interest in math, her parents learned how to use YouTube so they could watch videos of college math lectures.

Once upon a time, I had hoped that love and care would expand to include me. Clearly, they hadn't and still didn't feel the same.

When the Wangs finally left, I opened the closet door, holding my shoes that Tia had tossed into the closet, to find Tia staring contemplatively at her floor-to-ceiling windows. Try as I could, regardless of what my mind was telling me, self-preservation was simply not in the cards for me when it came to this woman. Just seeing her was enough for me to throw out my resolve. Forget about resetting expectations.

Knowing with every cell within me that our arrangement was going to end up with me being left behind, I still pursued blindly on. "It's a little touristy, but I've heard good things about the Esplanade. I was thinking we could start day one with a picnic by the Charles River."

Eyes widening slightly, Tia stuttered, "I thought … um, I wasn't sure … after, um …" Trailing off, she gestured in the general direction of my closet jail.

Forcing a light laugh that I didn't quite feel, I affected a teasing, casual tone. "It's a first for me. Next time, let's find a more spacious hiding spot?"

"How much did you hear?" Her hands twisted strands of her long, dark brown hair, twirling around and around her elegant and ring-less fingers. Thank God she gave back the ring yesterday. I didn't want to see another man's mark on her.

I read the worry in her. Whatever my trepidations were, hers were tenfold. Now was not the time to push her. "Hey, listen. You didn't want your parents to worry. I get it." I hated that I did. Brandon Parker's son did not have the same ring as Senator Davenport's golden son. "Let's just call it a night. Do you teach tomorrow?"

"No, only Tuesday through Friday. I usually make Mondays a quiet work day."

"Do you want to play hooky from work and go on a friendly picnic tomorrow? I'll pick you up here."

"Friendly picnic?"

"The friendliest of picnics." My lips quirked up in a smile. "I'll find an unassuming basket with no expectations, maybe some peanut butter and jelly. I'll bring some tea too. How serious can you get while debating the merits of crunchy or smooth peanut butter and drinking tea?"

Her chuckle felt like a bigger win than having a tricky defamation suit against my company tossed out last month. And that had been cigar-worthy.

Smiling slightly, Tia countered with, "What if I told you that I like neither? Almond butter, sunflower butter, Nutella are all the rage now."

"Okay, okay, my difficult lady, you can have your flower butter and pea milk, and I'll stick to my old-school PB and J, full of allergens and sugar."

"Ew, pee milk! Who drinks that?" Tia's scrunched-up face made me want to kiss her puckered lips.

"P-E-A, not P-E-E." I smiled at her, trying not to think about kissing her. "Get your mind out of the toilet."

In mock seriousness, she explained, "Well, another new craze is drinking cat poop coffee, made from coffee berries that civets eat and then poop out. I thought it was a natural extension that someone figured out a way to make artisanal P-E-E milk."

Damn. It was hard to have her real smile turned on me and not want to grab her closer. Her turned-up lips made me want to kiss the corner of that smile and absorb the laughter bubbling underneath the surface. Let her warmth and light chase away the darkness lurking inside of me.

I could have kissed her then.

I wanted to kiss her then.

If I leaned in closer, she might even kiss me back.

Instead, I stepped around her to the little dining table and started dumping the half-eaten food back into their containers to save for later. From the side, I saw Tia reach out as if to stop me.

Damn, I was used to saving every last scrap of food, even if I didn't have to anymore. "Sorry, did you want to throw this away instead? You didn't eat much, so I thought—"

Shaking her head as if she knew exactly what I was thinking, which she probably did after years of seeing me clean my plate better than any high-efficiency dishwasher, she said, "No, let's save it. I might need a backup lunch, depending on what's in that unassuming picnic basket of yours tomorrow."

My shoulders relaxed. I stepped out into the hallway outside her apartment. "Good night."

"Good night," she whispered.

I knew that I could have easily stayed longer, now that the crisis of her parents' impromptu slap of reality had been averted. However, if I wanted any chance of proving that we were more than sex buddies, I needed our two weeks to *not* start with sex. And while I didn't know exactly where I wanted this thing with Tia and me to end up, I also wasn't ready to give up something real and substantive with her.

I forced myself to keep walking away and my eyes in front of me. Because if I looked back, I might have given in.

I wanted to give in.

And by giving in, we'd doom our relationship.

CHAPTER TWELVE

ANDREW

December 17, 2008
Ting Ting,
I couldn't sleep last night, thinking about my dad. What if I become him? None of my college buddies or even my roommate knows about my dad. I am too ashamed. My whole life I've been so ashamed to be Brandon Parker's kid. It's much better that no one on campus know about him. He's my dirty secret to carry.
Two more days until I see you.
Yours,
Andrew

Monday was sunny. My hotel room overlooked the city and its crooked streets that made no sense. I could see pedestrians crisscrossing Copley Square near my hotel, minding their own business, ignoring cars and bikes.

Boston was the epitome of a city that was built before the introduction of city planning. I had been here a couple times before for work and, honestly, hadn't given the city much thought before. Now, it seemed charming and accessible in a way that New York City or Chicago wasn't.

Or maybe *someone* had casted a rose-colored glow to the city.

Usually, I was great at compartmentalizing. It was what made me a top lawyer, able to work on multiple cases with different clients, and what had enabled me to leave behind the baggage of my past. But all my usual tricks didn't work when it came to Tia. Thoughts of her popped up when I went for a run this morning and when I cleared my calendar for today. When I grabbed coffee, I wondered if she drank hers black. I turned on the morning news and thought of how she had preferred reality dating shows in the past. Did she still? It was as if ten years of trying to compartmentalize our marriage had suddenly blown up in my face.

Did I believe in fate? Not really.

However, I believed in being ready and seizing opportunities. Except I wasn't sure if I was ready or wanted to seize this opportunity. Or what the opportunity even was.

I had moved on.

Really, I had.

I had examined our marriage, identified what went wrong, internalized my mistakes, and accepted the situation. Case closed.

Except now, it felt as if the case had closed with incomplete evidence. The fact that we were still married was a wrench in my case—a game-changing Hail Mary, a half-court-shot wrench.

Like any good lawyer worth their retainer, I couldn't disregard new evidence without at least considering it. Which is what I planned to do. I reminded myself of my decision last night to not lead with sex. We could just talk for the next couple of weeks.

Liar. I couldn't even fool myself.

Promptly at noon, I rang the intercom outside of Tia's building. This time, she buzzed me in almost immediately, without even checking who I was. Maybe I was too suspicious, or maybe my work in the security industry had made me jaded, but I reminded myself to tell her about some of the reasons why our clients hired us in the first place.

All thoughts of security soon fled my mind when she opened her door, wearing jeans that hugged her just right and a fleecy sweater that both covered her up and made me think of snuggling under blankets. Naked snuggling, that is.

Hell, this woman was going to send me to the hospital.

Diagnosis? Perpetual hard-on.

"Hi," she said, waving slightly before bundling herself up.

"Hi," I parroted, trying to decide on a proper greeting. Not naturally a hugger or toucher in general, I had an urge to do just that. Luckily, Tia, who was a hugger, stepped into my space to wrap her arms around me briefly before bouncing back.

Suspiciously, she looked around me. "Where're the unassuming picnic basket and the PB and J you promised me?"

A grin broke out on my face at her disgruntlement. "Patience, I have them stashed in a safe spot."

Mollified, she turned to head to the staircase. With mock sternness, she called out over her shoulder, "Well, let's go, then, Andrew. I'm hungry."

"Yes, ma'am."

We headed toward the river. It wasn't exactly a comfortable silence, as I was too aware of her next to me, but I wouldn't call it strained either. It seemed that a night's sleep had calmed her nerves. I was hopeful that she was opening herself to whatever this was between us.

Or I was being delusional, and she was just sucking it up in order to get rid of me in two weeks' time.

When we reached an intersection, Tia moved to cross the street. My left arm shot out to stop her. "No, this way."

"No, this is the quickest way to the Esplanade. That's where we're still going, right?" Tia asked.

"I know a different spot. Trust me, you'll like it." Taking a chance, I grabbed her mittened hand in my bare hand and tugged her to the right.

A thrill shot through me when she didn't pull away. A couple weeks ago, I had gotten into a heated discussion with some of my coworkers on whether sex or hand-holding was more intimate. I was firmly on the side that sex was—how could it not be, when you were literally sticking a part of your body into someone else's body? Yet, I had to admit that there was an intimacy in holding Tia's hand in public, like a little visible acknowledgement of our togetherness.

I glanced down at Tia. A giant red hat with a pomelo-size pouf at the top hid most of her face. As if she could feel my gaze, she looked up, smiling tentatively, before averting her eyes. I squeezed her hand through the thick mitten to reassure her.

A long-withheld breath later, I felt the flutter of a squeeze back. Whatever happened in two weeks, I would relish this single moment of complete contentment of holding hands and walking the streets of Boston together.

Soon, we approached the address that I had memorized. Ignoring her confused look, I pulled her into the lobby of an upscale residential building, decked out in marbled columns and plush rugs. I stopped by the concierge to greet him.

"Welcome back, Mr. Parker, please go right ahead and let me know if there is anything else you need." The portly man in uniform pressed a button to open an elevator door.

"Thank you, Bobby. Please make sure we're not disturbed." I nodded my head as Tia and I walked into the elevator.

Once the door closed, Tia turned to me, her face scrunched up in a question. "Where are we? What are we doing here? How does that guy know you?"

"It's a surprise," I said, anticipation blooming for once with Tia in a non-sexual way.

"You hate surprises," she said as the elevator dinged to signal that we had reached the top.

"I hate to *be* surprised," I clarified, covering her eyes with my hands. I guided her out of the elevator and through a door. "I enjoy surprising you."

"As long as the surprise isn't some couples CrossFit class," Tia joked.

All I heard was "couples." Batting down hope, I chalked the word up to a slip of her tongue. I dropped my hands from her eyes. "What do you think?"

"Wow." She spun around the rooftop garden that overlooked the Charles River. On the side closest to the river, I had set up a cluster of pillows and blankets on top of a red and white checkered picnic cloth that covered an air mattress, alongside a plain basket filled with food. Dozens of flower pots and string lights transformed the roof into a secret garden.

So what if I had to call in several favors to get this space, pay exorbitant prices to get a florist to decorate the rooftop, and run around like a maniac this morning to find everything? The delighted look in her eyes was worth it. I could never tire of pampering her, just to see her smile at me, wide and inviting, with no hesitation.

"Wow, all it needs is a random hot tub and some red roses," she said, bending to smell some flowers whose name I didn't know.

A laugh burst out of me. That's one question answered—she still watched awful reality TV shows. And I had watched enough with her in the past to recognize her reference. "Are we on *The Bachelor* or *The Bachelorette*?"

Feigning seriousness, she tapped a finger to her chin. "Hmm, *The Bachelorette*. I like the idea of women having the upper hand. Or maybe *Bachelor in Paradise* where anything goes and tacos are aplenty."

"Definitely that, then." I nodded solemnly.

"How did you find this place? All these blankets, pillows, and this basket?" she said, pointing to everything before plopping down on the mattress.

"The blankets and pillows I borrowed from my hotel room. The basket, that was tricky. I had to steal it from a family in the park."

Her eyes opened wide. "What?"

The warmth that was ballooning within me ever since she had let me hold her hand deflated. "It was a joke. I convinced a bakery to sell me this from their window display."

"Oh, I didn't mean to imply that you—that you … I'm sorry," apologized Tia, her cheeks flushing.

Shrugging slightly, I tried to hide my hurt. I was used to people judging me and had learned to easily brush it off, but damn it, I cared about what she thought. "It's not an illogical assumption. I mean, my dad did go to jail for identify theft and stealing. Don't worry about it."

Silence cast a pallor over the rooftop, even as the sun continued to cover us with brightness. Tia started haltingly, "I wasn't comparing you to your dad. From everything I've heard about him and from everything I know about you, you are not your dad's son except via biology. You've always been … you. And being you is pretty great."

The passion in her voice caught me off guard, as my heartbeat slowed in an effort to freeze this snapshot. When we were younger, her belief in me had scared me as much as it had pulled me to her. Whatever mess was our past, I was grateful for and touched by her confidence in me.

Now looking extra awkward, she wrinkled her nose. "I was just surprised that you joked about stealing. You wouldn't have poked fun at yourself before. It threw me for a loop. Not for a minute did I think you stole this basket."

And… I was an idiot. "I guess I'm still a little sensitive about being compared to Brandon. I'm sorry for jumping to conclusions."

"You're forgiven as long as you feed me," she said, a genuine smile peeking out.

I was relieved that this hadn't turned into a blow-out fight, as so many of our minor miscommunications had in the past. For fuck's sake, she had once asked if I wanted to sneak snacks into the movie theater to avoid paying for twenty-dollar popcorn, and I had accused her of associating me with criminal activities. Instead of enjoying date night, we had argued about finances, and I had ended up sleeping on the couch. Yeah, not my best moment. There were unfortunately a lot of not-my-best-moments in our marriage.

Out of the basket, I pulled out jars of crunchy peanut butter, smooth peanut butter, the gross organic kind that was basically peanut butter liquid, almond butter, sunflower butter, cashew butter, Nutella, hemp seed butter, and even a jar of Vegemite. "I wasn't sure what you preferred, so I have some options."

Laughing in surprise, Tia opened up the jar of Vegemite. Her sniff turned into a gag, as she waved a hand in front of her nose and held the jar far away from her. "Ew! Next, please."

"It's not that bad actually," I said, taking the jar from her and opening up the hemp seed butter for her to smell. "I tried it in Australia last year."

"You left the country? I didn't think I would ever see the day. You never seemed interested in traveling. Not bad," she exclaimed, taking a whiff.

"I'm full of surprises. Here." I spooned some of the hemp seed butter for her to try. Big mistake. Her pink tongue swirled around the spoon, licking it clean. Her eyes briefly closed, as she focused on the taste. Immediately my brain was filled with lurid images of what else her tongue and mouth could taste. My hand squeezed the jar so hard that the top popped off, the sound startling both of us.

I stared straight at her, willing myself not to hide my thoughts, needing her to see the raw hunger she stirred in me.

Clearing her throat, she brushed the invitation aside and said huskily, “I might go for a little bit of each.”

With meticulous attention to detail, she spread strawberry jam on a piece of bread, cut another piece into four squares and spread crunchy peanut butter, Nutella, hemp seed butter, and Vegemite onto each of the squares.

I watched in hunger. Not for food, for I had years of ignoring hunger pains under my belt, but for her. For her laughter and wide smiles, for her scrunched-up face when she was thinking, even for her innocent moves that were tortuously sensual.

“Aren’t you hungry?” She held out one of her perfectly made sandwich squares.

“Starving,” I whispered, taking a bite from her hand.

She gulped, realizing too late where my mind was living. “The Vegemite isn’t too bad,” she remarked, trying to move the conversation to safer ground.

I humored her, banking the hunger for her within me temporarily. “It’s definitely an acquired taste. It kind of tastes like kombucha or beer.”

“Look at you—traveling the globe, eating all sorts of things. Though, it seems some things don’t change.” She smiled as she watched me pile a mountain of chips inside my peanut butter and jam sandwich.

“It’s the best way.” I crunched down, enjoying the crackle as I chewed, making me deaf to all sounds except the crush of chips against my teeth. This had been my dinner for years when I was a kid—easy enough for a kid to make, and loud enough to drown out my dad slinging insults.

Going back to her earlier comment, I asked, “What’s so different about me?”

“Besides the obvious.” She gestured, her hand waving circles in front of me.

“What’s the obvious?” I looked down at me. Was it my clothes? Yeah, they were nicer and cleaner than before. That was to be expected. We weren’t nine-year-old kids running around the woods behind her house with dirt on our knees anymore.

“You know.”

"No, I actually don't." I looked at my hands and touched my hair. My hair was still the same black, my eyes still this lame gray color, and as far as I knew, I was still six-two, same as ten years ago.

Sighing dramatically but still not articulating an answer, Tia waved off the question. Under her breath, I thought I heard her mutter something to the effects of, "Clearly, you don't own a mirror." That couldn't have been correct, as she had been inside my house and most likely saw the mirror in my bathroom.

"What's the nonobvious?" I asked, hoping it would be clearer.

Eyes narrowed and face scrunched in concentration, she looked at me with her head tilted to the side. After a moment, she responded, "You seem more comfortable with yourself,

yet more willing to be uncomfortable."

Okay, that made no sense. I sniffed the Vegemite jar. Had I bought an expired jar, causing Tia's loopiness?

Nope, smelled fine. Or rather, smelled like Vegemite. "I give up. What's the answer to your riddle?"

Her smile widened, showing off her very straight teeth. "I don't know. You don't slouch anymore, your voice is louder. You feel less angsty. Actually, I don't know if that's true. You still feel a little angsty, but there's a sort of … gravity? Gravitas? Presence? Something around you, as if you're more in control. You're going to places like Australia and trying foods that you would have scoffed at years ago. You seem more worldly, which I would have never guessed, especially with how stubbornly stuck in your ways you were."

"A far cry from the kid who claimed that he would never leave Colorado. Actually, traveling to exotic places never seemed attainable as a kid, so I never thought much about it back then." I didn't add that a lot of the changes that she had just described were a direct result of her leaving me. It gave me a push to be different. No, not different, because I was still me. No, just … more. And better.

We ate in companionable silence for a few minutes, enjoying the sunshine and view of the river. When Tia shivered in the chilly air, I wrapped a big blanket around her legs. She kept stealing glances at me, as if not quite believing that we were here, ten years later, and not throwing things at each other. To tell the truth, I couldn't believe it either and certainly had never expected to see her again.

I could tell there was something on her mind. Instinct told me that she would be unable to keep the thought to herself. Unlike me, she had never been the type to bottle her feelings.

After rearranging her blanket around her legs, then around her shoulders, back to her legs, tucking them around her this way and that, smoothing out some imaginary wrinkle, she asked in a too offhanded way, "Why didn't you sign the papers this time? You couldn't have been pining for me all these years, so why not sign them and move on with your life?"

Despite her casual tone, the weight of her question made me pause. I didn't have answers for myself, never mind for her. Deliberating my words, I admitted, "I don't know. Even though it sucked that our marriage didn't work the first time, I've moved on."

"Wouldn't signing the papers help you stay 'moved on'?" she asked, leaning forward a little.

"What if I don't want to? Seeing you again, I felt a spark. It felt like a second chance."

"When you found out about Clayton, why did you stay?" probed Tia, leaning even farther forward until our heads were nearly touching. I became distracted by the black and brown flecks in her eyes, lightened by the glow of the sun around us.

Pushing away the distraction of her eyes and tamping down the sense of discomfort at her questions, I focused on her words. Ever since I knew her, she had asked a lot of questions: What do you like? What don't you like? What would you do in this situation? And way too often, why did you do that and how do you feel now?

Feeling defensive yet trying not to raise up walls unnecessarily, I forced myself to continue, "I couldn't tell how serious you were about each other."

"What does that mean? We were engaged. How much more serious could you be?" she retorted.

"Married," I said, not fully able to keep the sarcasm out of my tone.

Her burst of laughter was a surprise to both of us, loud peals that faded in the open air and turned into giggles, as she eventually collapsed against the blankets in front of her. Mirth still evident in her crinkly eyes, she looked up at me from her pile of blankets. "Oh, Andrew, what a mess we're in. How do we get out of it?"

Unable to resist any longer, I reached out to play with the strands of hair peeking out from her hat. Teasingly, I replied, trying not to scare her, "We go on lots of dates for the next couple of weeks, find out that we hate each other and go along our merry ways."

"Or leave as friends," she whispered dubiously, clearly not convinced by the idea.

I nodded, even though I couldn't imagine the prospect of having her in my life only as a friend. Even if I wasn't worthy of Tia, my heart squeezed at the thought of watching her go back to Clayton or start to date someone else. No, I'd much rather be called a sore loser than pretend to be okay.

Before I could overthink it, I threw in, "Besides, if there was no chance for me, you and Clayton wouldn't have broken up so easily. Neither of you fought very hard for each other."

Outside of the slight widening of her eyes and the sudden stillness of her constantly-in-motion hands, there were no outbursts, no throwing plates, or leaving. Instead, she sat silently, staring off into the scenic view behind me. I could sense her mind treading water, turning over information and filtering what words to say aloud. Making no sudden movements, I waited, matching my breaths to her slow and controlled ones, as if that adjustment could tie us together.

Great going, dumbass. You couldn't just stick to stupid jokes for the first day. My first reaction was to soothe her, even as another part of me needed to know the depth of her relationship with Clayton. It had been a question that was tickling at the back of my mind ever since I saw them in her office.

Shut up, I told that part of me. *This is not the time. Don't disturb the peace.*

"You don't have to say anything, Tia," I said.

"No, no, no." Her eyes cleared and sharpened. "Don't brush it off. You asked for both of us to be fully in this 'arrangement' or whatever this thing is. That means talking and asking questions, and actually answering them, which we were pretty bad at before."

As if taking a big mental breath, she continued, "Your comment struck a nerve with me. Maybe I read too many Scottish Highlands and Regency novels and have unrealistic ideas of what love is… When Clayton and I started dating, we had our careers squared away, and our lives in order. It felt like the right next step to be in a serious relationship. Now, I can't help wondering if Clayton and I rushed into a relationship because we were convenient."

Right! I wanted to shout. Well aware of the emotional spikes below me, I stepped carefully onto the metaphorical thin tightrope. "I'd be lying if I said that I wasn't happy that you two broke up. Looking back on our relationship, I wish I would have fought harder for us. It's the biggest regret that I have."

"Do you regret Charlie?" Tia asked suddenly.

"I don't want to talk about her. She's not going to be an issue for us."

"She was an issue ten years ago," Tia insisted, her voice rising with hurt frustration. "She wasn't the only issue and not even the biggest, but …" Her voice trailed off, as her shoulders drooped.

"But what?"

"It's hard for me to even consider whatever this is between us, when I keep wondering what your relationship is with Charlie or if you're on Tinder sending dick pics, or sliding into someone's DMs or whatever people do on TikTok."

"I promise you, there are no nudes of me out there. I am fully focused on you." I didn't know how else I could make that clear to her. "Do you want to check my phone?"

"No, I don't want to be that kind of partner. I want to trust you. I know I'm being hypocritical, since we almost kissed while I was still engaged to Clayton. I already feel rotten about it. I can tell myself that it was because I was overwhelmed, surprised—"

"Or maybe you almost kissed me because you knew that Clayton wasn't the right person," I said.

"So if you thought I was the right person when we got married, why did you still bring Charlie back to our apartment?"

"I never cheated."

"Let's call it a difference of opinions about the definition of cheating, then," she said in a pacifying voice, even as her eyebrows rose sardonically.

"No, not a difference of opinions. I'm pretty sure our definitions are the exact same. The answer is still no. No cheating, no bases, no home runs, nothing," I insisted, frustration bubbling up inside of me. I didn't want her to think the worst of me, to distrust me, not then and certainly not now.

Looking unconvinced, she took a deep breath. "Fine, at least an omission of the whole truth, then."

That silenced me, for she was right. For months after we broke up, I had thought about picking up the phone to tell her the full story. Each time, I stopped myself, because what was the point? This had been the proverbial straw that broke the camel's back but the load had been too heavy to start with.

My palms out in a gesture of peace, I tried to shove my frustrations aside. "I don't want to fight with you, not today. All I know is that I think there might be something between us still. Maybe we just need closure, maybe there's something here. We can't *not* try. Remember our agreement?"

I hated that I was using the divorce papers to get Tia to spend time with me, but I was desperate. It was risky, since she could still have her lawyer file without my signature. It would make the proceedings harder, but if she wanted to, she could still force our divorce through the courts. And I would lose whatever time I had with her.

"Andrew, if you want a real chance, then you can't hide. I'm taking a risk now. Take this risk with me," she pleaded urgently.

I remembered the tears and hurt on Tia's face when she stormed out years ago. As I looked into her face now, I could see the tears that she was trying valiantly to fight back. There was no hope for us if she couldn't get over her distrust of me. And I desperately, more desperately than I was expecting, wanted that hope for us.

My mind made up, I watched Tia's face closely. "Charlie is my sister."

A beat passed before Tia's face scrunched up in surprised. "What? She looks nothing like you."

"She's technically my younger, half sister—we have the same sperm donor. I look like Brandon unfortunately, whereas Charlie looks like her mother."

Now that the confession was out, I realized how stupid it had been for me to withhold this. Now that I had started telling the story, the rest was easy. "After we got married, I got this call out of the blue from someone. She was rambling about our dad, and that she was my sister. I thought it was a prank call. A day later, she showed up at our apartment."

Horror and guilt shone on Tia's face as she dropped her face in her hands.

Reaching out hesitantly, I took her face in my hands, even as my heart constricted with regret. "I'm so sorry, Tia. I should have told you when you asked."

Shaking her head, she whispered, her words spoken in bursts, "I think I should be the one apologizing for running away and filing for divorce before you could explain."

"It looked bad, I admit. That evening, Charlie showed up after our fight, and I was shocked as hell when she told me the story. She was a mess, crying, soaked from a rainstorm. I think she had driven all the way from Chicago. It was no secret that my dad cheated on my mom regularly before he went to jail. It was very plausible that he could have fathered more kids. Charlie had a DNA test, documents that her private detective had found. It sounded crazy, but I believed her. So I let her shower and gave her some old sweats to warm up. That's the situation you walked in on."

"Why didn't you tell me the truth later? Or called me? Or argued about the divorce?"

"Charlie begged me not to tell anyone. Her dad—not Brandon—he was in the middle of an election campaign. She wasn't sure what her mom had told him. More importantly, I didn't think it mattered for us. Even in jail, Brandon was still everywhere. It was another sign that my life was screwed up, and that you deserved someone better. It seemed easier to let this be the thing that broke us up."

Blinking rapidly, Tia whispered harshly, "First, how presumptuous you were to make that decision for me. Let me decide who I want to be with. Maybe we would have broken up anyways, but at least, I wouldn't have thought you were a cheater all these years. I thought you regretted getting married to me, and this was your way of destroying the relationship."

I shook my head vehemently. How could she think that? How could she think that I would cheat on her? Yet, her observation about me being self-destructive was spot on.

Her voice softening, she said, "Part of me is still mad at you for giving up on us so quickly. Part of me is mad at myself. I *knew* you, and I still let my insecurities get in the way."

"It's not your fault. I held you at arm's length our entire marriage, in some misguided attempt to not get hurt. To be honest, I didn't know how to function in a relationship. I'm sorry that I didn't tell you earlier," I said.

"I wish I had known back then. I hated you for a long time afterward."

"Do you still?" Blood pounded through my body, as if it didn't know where to go. My hands were icy cold, my ears were ringing with my shouting heartbeat, and my heart was bleeding. Waiting for her answer.

"I don't think I ever did."

And I could breathe again.

"I was mad at you for not fighting for us, and it took me a long time to realize that I was equally mad and disappointed at myself for leaving. I wish you had told me," she repeated. Her voice was self-deprecating and that tugged at my heart. I didn't like the thought of Tia being disappointed in herself and beating herself up. She deserved to live in laughter and light, not self-doubts and regret, especially not when caused by me.

"Thank you for telling me today," she whispered, her gaze soft. "If you're still interested, I'd like to continue our two weeks."

Ignoring cautions and my earlier promise to myself to slow down, I pulled Tia towards me … an inch … another inch … until our lips touched. A whispered hello. It was deceptively gentle, belying the tumultuous need that threatened to take over. Desire thrummed and rocked through my body, focusing on this singular person in my arms.

With a groan, I leaned back slightly. Her eyes were hazy, her mouth puckered slightly as if in mid kiss, my touch still imprinted on her.

I couldn't have moved. I was caught in a web in that moment, waiting for ... *something* from her. Impossibly, as if she was as drawn to me as I was to her, Tia closed her eyes and swayed towards me.

Without waiting for my body to draw another breath, my mouth was on hers, probing, seeking her response. When her lips parted, I yanked her between my legs, devouring her lips. I couldn't get close enough, as I trailed kisses against her soft cheeks, down against her neck, sucking lightly.

Had her skin always been this soft? Her scent always this intoxicating?

Shyly, her hands came up to stroke my shoulders, my arms, my chest. Even through the layers of clothes, her hands left a trail of want. I was shivering with need. I was burning with desire. This fire that Tia stirred inside of me, this turmoil wracking my body, was enough for me to forget my mind.

When I slid my hands into her coat to palm her full breasts, she gasped against my mouth. Even through her sweater and bra, I could feel her nipples harden against my marauding fingers. Whimpers spilled out of her, each sound a direct shot to my cock.

For an insane moment, I imagined tossing her down against the blankets and burying myself in her. That image of me losing control when I couldn't afford to make mistakes with Tia was enough to sober me. With a groan, I pushed her gently off my lap, holding her shoulders to keep her at arm's length.

For a suspended time, we sat on that rooftop, staring hungrily at each other as we tried to control our ragged breaths. I thought seriously of pulling her back.

I already missed her.

Tia was the first to recover. Her gaze still a little dazed, she whispered, "I guess, we're going to give us a go. As long as you tell me the next time you discover a sibling?"

Relief mixed with happiness rang out in my laughter, as the pressure building within me dissipated. A broad smile took over my face. Going for a lighter note, I teased, "You'll be the first to know. And, I promise, you'll be the only person I send dick pics to.

"Hey!" I dodged a strawberry that Tia chucked at me.

"You're the worst," she said. The lift of one side of her mouth belied that comment. "No dick pics, please. I've done enough online dating to know that no dick pic is as impressive as the guy thinks. If you're going to send nudes, at least send some shoulders or your back."

"Really, my back?"

She shrugged, blushing as she refused to meet my eyes.

"Also, online dating? What kind of pickup lines got you to respond?"

Two eyebrows rose as she looked up at me. "The non-pickup lines that don't come with requests to send photos of my feet."

Grinning at her, I realized how much I missed this type of interaction. I loved talking with her, teasing her, arguing about ridiculous things with her, and hearing what she had to say. She was interesting and made me think and relook at my perceptions.

One question haunted the back of my mind even as we basked in each other. How in the world would I pick up the pieces again when she realized that she wanted someone better than me? Someone who didn't have my baggage.

The chances that I was going to be okay with only a brief affair were looking slim.

CHAPTER THIRTEEN

TIA

December 31, 2009 (never sent)
Andrew,
It's 11:17 p.m. I gave in and went to my parents' friends' New Year's party for a little bit. Now, I'm sitting in my room alone waiting for the New Year to start. Will I feel differently in 2010? Will I be back to myself again when the ball drops? It's weird seeing the crowd of people in New York on TV. They look so excited. I can barely remember what that feels like.
I wonder where you are, who you're with, what you're doing. I still hate you ... but if I'm honest with myself, only a little. If I don't hate you, then what am I left with?
Ting

I was in trouble. Deep, deep, where's-the-light-at-the-end-of-the-tunnel trouble. It was eighty percent my fault. Maybe seventy-five percent, with a margin of error so big that my PhD dissertation advisor would have failed me for allowing.

I made assumptions that this two-week arrangement with Andrew would be a way for me to figure out what I wanted, which was obviously to beg Clayton to take me back. My assumptions sucked.

I could not have foreseen the truth about Charlie. Now that I knew, even though I agreed with Andrew that we wouldn't have survived anyways, I still regretted how our marriage ended, especially when I still had my own secrets. But most of all, I had a hard time tamping down the euphoria of being with Andrew again. Whatever hesitation I had about exploring this *something* with him was draining like water out of a leaky pool, leaving me with the space to hope.

To dream.

To start afresh.

Since our rooftop picnic on Monday, we had seen each other every day. On Tuesday evening after work, he took me on a bike ride around Castle Island that ended in a secluded dinner lit by candles. On Wednesday, I had an evening meeting with my department that lasted far too long, so he came over with lemon squares and hot chai. On Thursday, he cooked for me in my apartment. It was an extremely gourmet meal of pasta with tomato sauce from a can and what looked suspiciously like salad from a bag. We laughed about the fanciness of it.

There were no helicopter rides to Newport, or sunset private cruises, or giant, bedazzling jewelry, like there were with Clayton. Yet, now that I knew that Andrew had not cheated on me, I was enjoying myself more than I should. I liked the normalness and unfussiness of the time that Andrew and I spent together. It was easy to fall back into the happy part of our past relationship—the teasing, the discussions about everything from the best pizza topping to systemic racism in the workplace, the non-judgement and ease in which we spun around each other. In the most telling sign, in just a week, I had relaxed to the point of forgetting to suck in my stomach around Andrew.

The more time that I spent away from Clayton, and critically, the more time that I spent with Andrew, the less I wanted to go back to my safe life. I *liked* being around Andrew. Both of us had changed, and yet, we had changed in ways that were, as I was discovering, still compatible.

Or maybe even more compatible.

Little things didn't trigger big fights, like before. I didn't have to tiptoe around subjects like his father or money. When I offered to split the cost of the bike rentals on Castle Island, Andrew had insisted firmly that he was going to pay. However, he didn't shut down and accuse me of thinking he wasn't good enough. Similarly, I wasn't as overwhelmed. Yes, I still fretted about what my parents would think and whether this experiment would blow up in my face. But, for the most part, the two-week time limit kept me from self-destructive behaviors, like deliberating picking fights with Andrew.

The realization that Andrew and I could become *something* was scary. I couldn't imagine leaving him after two weeks, and yet, I still hadn't told anyone besides Pippa that Clayton and I had broken up. Whatever my colleagues thought of me not wearing my ring, I ignored their looks, and I let my mom still talk about wedding plans on our calls. Even though Clayton didn't feel like an option anymore, telling everyone that Clayton and I were completely done felt huge and irreversible.

To top off my confusion, Andrew's behavior was weirdly gentlemanly. After that schmexy kiss on the rooftop, the man made no moves. Whatsoever. Just easy, friendly conversation. He was so respectful that I wanted to shake him and demand what the heck did he want from me? What was with the pissing match between him and Clayton, if it resulted in one of them walking away so easily from an engagement and the other only wanting me as a friend now that he had "won" me for a couple weeks? *What if Andrew changed his mind?*

So yes, I was in a conundrum—a headache-inducing, exhausting conundrum. Muddled, fuddled, a proper tweetle beetle noodle poodle bottled paddled muddled duddled fuddled wuddled fox in socks. And the blame was one hundred percent, with a ninety-nine point five percent confidence level, Andrew's fault.

Tonight, I faced a different conundrum, still with Andrew to blame. That morning, while in the middle of a lecture, I had glanced down at my phone to see a message from him pop up: *"Let's do something different tonight. I'll come by at 6 to pick you up."*

Thirty very long minutes later when the class finally ended, I texted back: "*What does that mean?*"

Waiting for his explanation, I spent the next fifteen minutes answering questions from overachievers. It was my universally acknowledged truth that only high achievers asked questions or came to office hours. Either they had paid enough attention to my lectures or read ahead to know what questions to ask, or because they thought asking questions boosted the participation part of their grades. Never mind that I and my syllabus said that there was no participation score from the lecture portion of my class.

Andrew's text while I was getting lunch made me immediately stress-order an extra side of fries. "*My coworker Dan, who lives in Boston, invited us to his house for dinner. Want to go?*"

Stuffing fries into my mouth to calm the sudden jump of nerves, my fingers typed a message.

Me: Who's going to be there?

Andrew: Dan, his wife, us—casual.

Me: What do they know?

Andrew: Nothing. Dan invited me over since I'm in Boston. I said I'll bring a friend.

Me: Is that friend me?

Andrew: No, my other wife.

I made a face at Andrew's sarcasm. Curiosity got me. Without thinking too much about it, I typed with my eyes closed.

Me: Okay.

The excited part of me was jumping. *What's he like as a coworker? Was Andrew good at his job?* The risk-averse part of me was lobbing concerns left and right. *Oh no, oh no, we're meeting friends, and that doesn't feel like a two-week affair. What if they know Clayton?*

Promptly at 6:30 p.m., our cab stopped in front of an unassuming house on a quiet street in Jamaica Plain. Andrew nudged me toward the door, one hand pressed firmly against the small of my back, as if worried that I was going to run away. I wouldn't blame him for thinking that, because I was definitely pondering how far I could run in my heels without tripping over myself.

His voice was a hot whisper against my cheek, as he leaned down. "Tia, what can I do to help you relax?"

"Um …" *Don't go there, don't go there. Oh fudge, here come the mental images.*

"I wouldn't put you in an uncomfortable situation. I think you'll have a fun time. And we can leave whenever you want." Hesitating a moment before adding, "They'll like you. Just as you are. Just as I do."

Leaving me beflustered at his admission, he rang the doorbell. The heavy, wooden door swung open almost immediately, revealing a burly man in his late-thirties with stripper eyes. His broad smile widened even further as he saw me. “Fuck.”

“Excuse me?” My head tilted to the side as I considered his word. Andrew laughed, so I assumed this guy wasn’t mean-cursing at me. I think.

“Fuck a duck. So you’re the one that’s got this fucker all wound up trying to woo you.” His laugh was booming, as he turned to yell over his shoulder. “They’re here!”

A blush tinted Andrew’s cheekbones, as he denied half-heartedly, “I don’t know what he’s talking about.”

“No wooing here,” I agreed solemnly, my lips curving up slightly.

“Say I was trying to woo—”

“Hi, you must be Andrew,” came a soft-spoken, gentle voice. “Tia?!”

I glanced up at the newcomer, wearing khakis and a light blue Oxford shirt. My eyebrows shot halfway to my forehead. “Kat?”

In a daze, I looked between Kat and her husband. They looked like opposite ends of magnets—Kat was polished and reserved, and her husband had greeted me with curse words. I had heard that Kat had married some random security guy, but I had figured that he was more like a Secret Service guy. The kind who wore suits and whose job was to blend into the background. Gosh, I didn’t even know this guy’s name except he was a security man, as Clayton’s parents had—

Ai ya ya. Fudge. Fudge. Fudgey fudgester. I had completely forgotten. Even though Kat wasn’t close to Clayton, they had known each other growing up. In her current position as head of a large pharmaceutical, we had crossed paths a few times at various charity and social events. I had heard plenty—trust me—*plenty* of gossip about some long-ago drama of Kat running away, only to return to kick her cousin out of the family business. Was it too late to bolt?

“Tia, I didn’t realize that Andrew was bringing you. Last time we met, I thought you were with um … hmm … I didn’t realize that you two …” Looking very uncomfortable, Kat turned to her husband for help.

Kat’s security man put a reassuring arm around her shoulder and pressed a kiss to the top of her head. “I’m Dan, by the way. Let’s get some fucking drinks and food, yeah?”

“Sounds good, man. Great to meet you, Kat. Thanks for having us over.” Andrew grabbed my hand and gave me a reassuring squeeze, prompting me to remember my manners and mutter greetings.

As we followed our hosts down a hallway, Andrew looked at me in question, one eyebrow raised. Trying not to be too obvious that we were talking about our hosts literally behind their backs, I mouthed, “Through Clayton. They grew up together.”

The confusion in Andrew’s eyes gave way to something I couldn’t quite read, as he nodded absentmindedly. Stopping me before we entered the dining room, he pushed me against the wall and bent to kiss me. This was no gentle kiss. This was possession and devastation, as he trapped me against his hard body.

Still reeling from the collision of my two worlds, I was so caught off guard that I could only respond with a needy whimper at the brutal kiss. By the time I had gathered enough control over my body, Andrew had pulled away, his eyes a little hazy and all territorial as they locked on to mine. We stood there, in the dark corridor, not saying a word, trying to calm our breaths. Through our clothes, I could feel Andrew’s hardness, triggering a low ache in my body. I arched into him, biting my lips against the pleasure. *More, more...*

From inside the dining room, Dan’s voice cut through our daze. “Stop pawing at each other in my fucking hallway like fucking rabbits. Get a fucking room *not* in my house, or come in for a drink.”

Andrew had been right—I did have a fun time. Dan was hilarious and had no filter, and unlike me, seemed completely comfortable with whatever came out of his mouth. Once she had gotten over the shock of seeing me in her house with someone other than Clayton, Kat was as sweet as I remembered her.

Maybe it was the combination of Dan’s crazy stories and Kat’s calmness, or just being around his true friends, but Andrew was a revelation. Once upon a time, I had taken pride that he could be himself around me, in a way that I didn’t observe him with others. So it was an utter surprise and joy to see Andrew relax so completely. I couldn’t take my eyes away from him as he and Dan went back and forth, ribbing each other, telling stories of the weird requests from their clients.

“My favorite has to be the guy who asked that his contract state that his bodyguards only wear tie-dye, bell-bottoms, grow out their hair and beards, and carry disinfectants to spray the air around him when he walked outside,” said Andrew, a broad smile lighting up his face, his arm draped casually over the back of my chair.

“Fucking idiotic move agreeing to those terms, Parker,” bemoaned Dan. “I had to sub in when one of the guys got ‘sick.’”

“Must have missed that clause when I signed.”

“No you didn’t, you fucker. I’ve never seen anyone so fucking detailed in my life.”

Kat reached over to touch Dan’s short hair, suppressing a smile. “I actually liked the long hair and beard.”

Putty in her arms, the big, potty-mouthed Bostonian turned to his wife and asked in a much gentler voice, “Really? Want me to grow it?”

“I wouldn’t mind a beard,” she replied, before turning to the rest of us self-consciously. “Um, Tia, do you want to help grab some dessert from the kitchen with me? I found some great cheese at the local farmer’s market this week.”

“I have suddenly discovered space in my stomach for dessert,” I said, following Kat. “We can gossip about the guys behind their backs too.”

“As long as all of the gossip starts with how amazing we are,” called out Andrew, winking at me. *Be still my heart, was he cute when he was happy.*

“Of course. We’ll discuss how amazingly arrogant you two are.” I winked back, except my wink was more of a face scrunch. He laughed anyways at my attempt.

In the spacious kitchen, Kat busied herself plating cannoli and cheese, waving off my offer to help. “How long have you and Andrew been dating?”

What rumors had she already heard? One thing that I had learned while dating Clayton—you didn’t need to be best friends with someone to share gossip. Drama was the most infectious of diseases, and no amount of social distancing could eradicate it, only slow the rate of spread. And breaking up with the golden boy after his own engagement party was juicy gossip indeed.

“Umm, we’re not really dating, just hanging out,” I managed to get out.

Kat’s eyes widened. “Really? You two seem really good together.”

Dropping the topic when I didn't respond, she steered the conversation away from the bee's nest that was my dating life. "So, I heard Andrew call you 'Ting' once during dinner. Should I call you that too?"

I shook my head. "No, no, you can call me Tia. Andrew and I grew up together, and back then, I went by Ting."

"Why did you change it?"

"It seemed easier when I started college. Easier to blend in, I guess." Even though this wasn't a topic that I really wanted to delve too deeply into even with myself, Kat's warm brown eyes made me want to spill. Or maybe it was my second glass of wine for someone who was the definition of "lightweight." "I didn't grow up in exactly the most diverse town. No one was mean per se. However, kids in middle and high school were either too curious or judgmental. 'Tia' seemed like someone who would fit in more, and it's not that different from 'Ting.'"

"Names carry weight," came Kat's quiet voice.

We looked at each other, and I knew that she understood my need to don a certain image. While unconfirmed, according to the rumor mill, aka Clayton's mom's friends, Kat had assumed a fake identity to run from her family legacy.

She continued carefully, "I understand the need to blend in, though I've found that sometimes it's okay to stand out too. Different and weird can be liberating, especially if you're with someone who lets you be you."

My mind flashed to Andrew and the comfort that I felt around him. Shaking the image away, I confessed, "I've thought about changing my name back actually. Ten years ago, 'Tia' felt like an escape and a projection of what I wanted to be. Nowadays, it doesn't feel like a rejection of myself. I think I've grown into that person, and going back to 'Ting' doesn't feel right anymore. Weird, right?"

"Not weird," Kat said firmly, smiling broadly at me, before her eyes lit up. "Oh, hi, Dan!"

I looked over my shoulder to see the guys amble in. My eyes went straight to Andrew's. We made no move toward each other, but I felt his tender gaze on me, as if checking to make sure I was doing okay. For someone who proudly considered herself independent, I was oddly touched by Andrew's care.

"Are you feeling okay?" Dan asked as he crossed over to Kat. She pushed away the cheese plate and wrinkled her nose.

"Yeah, my mind really wants cheese. But the baby is grossed out."

Silence.

With a sheepish smile, as if just realizing her words, Kat looked at us shyly. "I'm four and a half months pregnant." She pulled her loose shirt tight, revealing an undeniable bump.

"Congrats!" Andrew shook Dan's hand and patted Kat's back, smiling broadly, as if there was nothing better in the world than babies.

As for me? My ears were ringing, and all of a sudden, I couldn't breathe. My body was physically still in the kitchen, rooted to the tiles underneath my shoes, even as my arms automatically wrapped around Kat in a swift hug. But I wasn't really there. My mind had separated from my body and had floated back in time and space, awash in memories so painful that I physically recoiled.

As if he could read the pain behind my smile, Andrew narrowed his eyes, studying me. I shook my head. This was not the time for *that* particular conversation. There would never be a time for *that* conversation. I was never going to be ready to tell Andrew. Yet, after seeing his delight, I couldn't not tell him.

I wasn't sure how I got through the rest of the evening. Even though Andrew spoke way more than I have ever seen him in public to cover my complete inability to get words out, there was still this new tension. My awkwardness made others uncomfortable, and I had no energy or the wherewithal to try to fix it.

What felt like both a blink and hours of torture, Andrew and I said goodbye to Dan and Kat. Well, he said goodbye, while I forced my face into a smile-grimace. We didn't talk the entire cab home to my apartment—me stewing in my thoughts, and Andrew probably wondering what in the world was happening. I knew that I had embarrassed him in front of his friends. I only had to be normal for one evening, and I had ruined it by freezing up at the end.

It had been a long while since I had felt embarrassed about my actions. I had basked in the residual glow that Clayton's charm casted when we were together. My propensity to talk too much and act like a nerd was considered cute with his friends since Clayton had already deemed me worthy of his attention.

At school, nerdhood was celebrated. Arguing about Machine Learning Platform features and open source code were my drugs, and elegant lines of PySpark were more interesting than heels. I spent most of my days with whiz kids who reprogramed their parents' Roomba to chase after their dogs and treated coding as a major league sport. Seriously, I had students who hosted coding parties to solve difficult problems, like how to use Natural Language Processing to highlight key sentences in their readings. Since I taught computer science, I could only be happy for them that it took half a semester and all of spring break to create a shortcut that saved them two whole hours of reading.

Tonight, I didn't want Andrew to think me weird, or be embarrassed about me somehow. It was different from when we were kids—he had no other friends, he'd been stuck with me. Now, he was a major catch.

Ugh, not the time to freeze up over the past. Idiot me.

As the cab pulled up to my apartment building, I leaped out before it had fully stopped. Not something I'd recommend trying, as I lurched forward on the sidewalk, barely keeping my balance.

"Wait!" Andrew's voice grabbed me with its urgency. Before I could free myself from the hold of his command, he was in front of me, crowding into my personal space. His hands reached up as if to grab my shoulders, then lowered as he growled in frustration. It was a pure sound of irritation. At me.

"What the hell is happening?"

"Don't be mad at me," the people-pleaser in me automatically implored.

Sighing—his second sound of irritation within the last minute—he ran a hand through his thick hair in exasperation. "I'm not mad at you. I'm mad at whatever circumstance is making you act this way. Tell me what the fuck I did wrong."

"You?"

"Yes, me. Andrew Parker, the boy who will never amount to anything. Andrew Parker, the boy who will screw up just like his dad." He repeated the taunts I had heard too many times when we were growing up. "What was it? Did I push you too hard? Should I have listened to you about not going to Dan's house?"

"No, that's not it."

"Did they say something?"

"No, they're great."

"Then, I don't get it. I thought this past week was great, amazing. I thought you were enjoying *us*."

"I did. I do. I think?"

"What's not enough? Why do you keep running away?" His voice was bleak. Sadness and anger directed inward. At that moment, instead of the muscly, smoking hot, confident Andrew Parker, I saw my friend from years ago, who carried a chip on his thin shoulders and the unconscious, internalization of self-doubt.

I instinctively understood that his "*what's* not enough" was in reality a cover for "*why am I* not enough," and that made my heart hurt for him.

As he leaned his forehead against mine, Andrew's voice lowered to a harsh whisper, the words ripping out of him. "I want you. My whole life, I've only needed you. Tell me what I did wrong and let me fix it. Please, Tia. Please. Let me make it right."

I couldn't take it anymore. It was too much. Ever since my trip to Chicago, I had been inundated with Andrew. Smart Andrew, sweet and thoughtful Andrew, charming Andrew, and now vulnerable Andrew. My defenses and reasons for keeping him out were falling apart with his words. They were crumbling before his gray eyes, illuminated by the moonlight. I could see how terrified he was at putting himself out there, yet he seemed determined to fight for us. This was it. The drawbridge crashed down for him to cross over.

Taking a deep breath and knowing that this was a decision that I couldn't take back once made, I asked, "Do you want to come inside? I think I made a mistake."

CHAPTER FOURTEEN

TIA

January 1, 2010 (never sent)
Andrew,
Made it to another year. For a while, I wasn't sure if I was going to be able. Then, for a while, I didn't really care if I did.
I took a walk outside today. That's my New Year's resolution—to go outside and walk a little bit each day. I saw your mom while I was out. She asked how I was doing. I didn't want to see her pity, so I walked away.
I should have told her that I still hurt physically and emotionally every day, that I cry for no reason, that I have never made it back to our park. The fact that I haven't been there just breaks me. I should have told her that, despite all of that, I'm getting stronger. I'm not one hundred percent myself yet and maybe will never be the pre-Ting, but I think there's a post-Ting that I could be okay with, sans speaking in the third person. Ha! My first kind of, awful, not-funny joke since ... Even if it's on a letter that will never be mailed.
Ting

It was a full twenty or thirty minutes before we spoke. I took my sweet time rummaging around my freezer to find an unopened box of mochi and boiling water for tea. It became imperative that I not say anything until my tea was steeped to perfection and the mochi defrosted enough for the ice cream inside to be soft. They were my flimsy umbrella against the upcoming thunderstorm of unpleasantness. Andrew sat on my couch, silently observing my movements as if I were some fascinatingly odd creature under the microscope.

When my mochi balls were threatening to become pools of melted ice cream, I heaved a great big sigh and threw my figurative hands in the air. So many sighing, breathless moments and thundering hearts since Andrew re-entered my life. It was as if I lived inside a Fabio-covered romance novel instead of real life.

Except this was my real life. And I had no expectations of a flowing-haired, shirtless hero to save me from the painful parts.

Andrew's gray eyes tracked me as I sat on the other end of the couch. He no longer seemed vulnerable. The depths of feelings that he had allowed himself to show momentarily were now carefully locked behind impenetrable doors.

"So," I started.

"So."

"Um, hmm … oh no!" Vanilla ice cream dripped onto my pants from my mochi, my outside now reflecting my internal mess. Novice move—I had waited too long to eat them. There was nothing to do but stuff the rest of the ball into my mouth, as I dabbed frantically at my pants with my sweater.

"Here, let me." Suddenly, Andrew's hands were everywhere, trying to dry my jeans and sweater with napkins.

I froze.

He froze.

As if he just realized where his hands were, one hand stilled on my upper thigh, before he resumed slowly, purposefully. My breath hitched as one napkin-covered hand brushed close but not close enough to where my senses were pooling. The other hand rubbed my side up and down, a tantalizing tease. It was too much, and yet not nearly enough.

I was aroused by his ministrations. Scared of what I needed to confess. Distracted by the sweep of his dark, dark eyelashes as he leaned over me. Tempted to let him make me feel better, so tempted to just live in this moment. So, so tempted to give in to what we clearly wanted and needed.

Andrew lifted his head, his gray eyes pinning me with hunger and possession, and moved slowly toward me, his hands shifting to cradle my face. They were gentle, a direct contrast to the ferocity in his eyes. My eyes drifted shut as I felt his intake of breath against my skin, seconds before—

"Hold on."

The words surprised both of us, as we blinked at each other. His eyes were still a little hazy, as mine must have been.

"I have to tell you something first."

This time, my voice was stronger, even if it sounded as if someone else had spoken. My mind was apparently stronger than I had given it credit for. It recognized the foolishness of trying to defer conversation post-physical relief, especially when said conversation would probably lead to Andrew never wanting to talk to me again. Never mind touch me.

With my body wrangled in by my mind, I pushed at Andrew's chest. *Urgh*, his stupidly solid, very warm chest. He backed away immediately, tensing as he stood up. From where I sat, he loomed impossibly large yet still withdrawn, his shoulders hunched as if he had weathered a downpour. His hands were stuffed inside his pants pockets, and one leg crossed the other at the ankle, as he leaned against my door for support. It was as if he had already made up his mind to leave and was impatiently waiting for my words to confirm his decision.

"Okay, start. What's this thing that you have to tell me about?"

I flinched at his voice. It was harsh and impersonal. It was the voice he used when talking to other people. Not with *me*. I didn't want it directed at me, and I also knew that I better get used to it. "So … hmm …"

"Wait, I want to get one thing clear before you start." Determination shone on his face, daring me to argue. "We still have nine days left. I want those days."

"Nine? I thought it was eight more days." I was momentarily distracted by his math. "It's fourteen days, and since we started on Sunday, then next Saturday should be the last day."

"No, we made the deal on Sunday night, so day one was Monday." Andrew's mouth was a stubborn, defiant line.

“Sure, whatever.” I shrugged. It wasn’t as if an extra day would even matter. No, he’d skedaddle way before then. So what if my heart twisted as if pinched by a thousand knives at that thought? When he had told the truth about Charlie, I should have spilled. I had only one word for myself for withholding this information—coward.

His stony eyes scanned my face to ascertain whether I was telling the truth about keeping our bargain, before relaxing noticeably. He asked, “Okay, so what’s the big deal, Tia?”

I narrowed my eyes at him. Before I could lose my final reserve of courage, I blurted out, “Remember when we had sex?”

Okay, not the best start. Andrew smirked. Definitely not the best way to start this.

“Pfff, okay, okay. Remember that night we had run out of condoms and decided to wing it? Apparently, neither of us were paying attention in sex ed or had watched *Teen Mom*. Sooo, the pull-out method isn’t the most reliable birth control.”

Andrew’s smirk fell. He didn’t say a word, yet I could physically feel his body and mind buzzing with questions.

“I don’t, we don’t anymore. There’s no secret nine-year-old.”

That was painfully true. *She* would never turn nine or nineteen or even one.

I waited for Andrew to respond. He stared at me blankly.

I waited for him to understand. Shock colored his face, as my words and what I left unsaid started to sink in.

When he finally spoke, his words were guttural, ripped out of him against his will. “I don’t understand. Not anymore. There was a baby?”

Past tense. Shuttering my eyes against the emotions shining from his eyes, from the walls torn down around his armor, I whispered, “I had a miscarriage.”

I hated that last word. What a clinical, unfeeling term for something so life-altering and life-shattering. I hated that word used to describe the dearth of the tiny flutters and movements that I had just started feeling. In no way did it fully describe the terror when I realized something was wrong or the utter agony in believing that my body had failed me or the months besieged by numbness afterwards.

“Did you know when we were together?” His halting voice pulled me from the past.

As much as losing her had torn me apart, I had had years to—not *get over* it, as I would never be one hundred percent over it—but to learn to live with the reality and finality of it. Andrew was just starting the process, and I felt sympathy for him.

I opened my eyes. "No. I mean, not officially. You know my periods have never been regular. I thought something was weird, but I never experienced any of the typical symptoms. No nausea or morning sickness."

"Why didn't you tell me your suspicions then?"

I breathed out through my mouth. "I was eighteen. We were arguing all the time and stressed out. I wasn't sure how you would have felt about adding a baby to the mix. I was too scared to tell you."

Something clicked for him, as he nodded. "I remember you being really nervous those last few days, and the focus around money." He laughed bitterly. "I thought you were regretting going against your parents and were missing your creature comforts. Makes sense now, if you thought you were pregnant. So, you found out after?"

"I had an appointment with my ob-gyn the day that Charlie showed up. I was ten weeks at the time. I had planned to tell you, and I wanted you to tell me it was going to be okay. When I saw Charlie, I freaked out and thought the worst. I was overwhelmed and didn't know how to handle a baby, a crumbling marriage. In the moment, it seemed easier to run away than deal."

"What shitty timing for everything to blow up. Fuck! If I had known—"

I grabbed his hand. This wasn't his fault. I had made a choice to leave. "How could you have known about her?"

"*Her*." Stunned, Andrew slid down the wall, his arms holding his knees in an almost protective stance. "Girl," he repeated hoarsely. "She was a girl."

For a brief moment, an image of Andrew reading goodnight stories to a sleepy, dark-haired, dark-eyed little girl stained my mind. I swallowed hard.

"When did you um, when did—" Andrew dropped his head against the wall behind him, focusing intently on some point on my white ceiling. "How many months?"

"Four months. Seventeen weeks and two days. I started bleeding." I hadn't thought much of the stain on my underwear at first, but the cramping, the intensity of it, was not normal. My parents had found me doubled over in the driver's seat of my car, shaking and in pain, and they drove me to the hospital.

"I couldn't stop—I couldn't—" The sob burst from me, and he jumped up. For half a second, I thought he was going to leave.

Then, I felt his arms around me as he picked me up to place me gently on his lap. His strong arms wrapped around me, as he whispered platitudes against my hair.

"It's not going to be okay!" I whisper-yelled at him, my voice breaking in the middle.

Andrew's arms tightened around me while he stayed silent. Now that I had started, I had to continue. He had to know what had happened to our baby girl. "The doctors had to do a—cleanup—after my body couldn't …"

My tears flooded onto Andrew's shoulders as I curled into him.

For months afterwards, I had done nothing but cry until there had been no more tears. I had found out the gender right before … And I had finally started to feel excitement about what was happening, hopeful about what the little girl could be. Until everything crashed.

I hadn't cried in years.

Now, in Andrew's arms, there was nothing that I could do to hold back the storm. The wound was raw and open and fresh, except this time, I was in Andrew's arms, where I had wanted to be ten years ago. Where I had needed to be.

CHAPTER FIFTEEN

TIA

February 1, 2010 (never sent)
Andrew,
I opened up a package today from Harvard. Since I deferred last year, they have been sending me information periodically. I finally opened up one of their envelopes. They sent a letter asking me to confirm whether I am planning to attend in the fall. I have to let them know by May. I don't know if I'll be ready to make a decision by then.
I looked at the brochure they sent—the students all look so happy and excited. I'm not sure I fit in, yet I want to. I want to be that happy and excited one day. I'm just worried that I'll need to forget her to achieve true happiness, and by wanting to be happy, am I betraying our daughter?
I still despise you ... but I wish you were here with me.
Ting

Andrew held me in his arms, as I sobbed through his sweater. At some point, he took off his ruined sweater, and I continued to sob through his shirt. My tears weren't dainty, ladylike tears that I could blot with a handkerchief. They were giant drops of pain that streaked the stupid mascara that I had put on earlier across my face, stung my irises from the soot of mascara falling into my eyes, and triggered a leaky nose. I was a nose-blowing, clown-looking, eyes-squinting puddle of muddle.

Poor, startled Andrew patted my back as I wailed into his neck, while continuously supplying me with tissues from a box he must have found during my daze.

This crying business was exhausting, as one moment, I was crying me a river, and the next moment, I woke up in bed.

In my pajamas, which I did not remember putting on. Nor did I remember getting into bed. Or cuddling with a warm male body. SPOONING ALERT!

In my revisionist mind, I made a quick dart out of bed, hair flowing sexily around my shoulders. In reality, I fell off the bed in a shower of blankets and pillows.

Thumpf.

The floor was hard. I definitely did not consider the impact of landing on the floor when I had the carpeting pulled out in favor of wood a few months earlier. Weakly, I made a lame attempt at getting up, but I was so discombobulated from last night's events that I decided to stay sprawled on the floor while I regained my memory.

"Hey."

Andrew's head peeked over from the side of the bed, his hair wonderfully tousled, his eyes still groggy. A small smile lingered on his face as if it was the most natural thing to find me lying on the floor.

And ... I regained my memory. Eyes wide, I whispered, "Hey."

His hooded eyes skimmed over my body, which I tried to subtly rearrange into a more artful pose, except I didn't know how, before landing on my face. "Oh shit." And ... he regained his memory too. He swung his legs over the bed to sit up, scrubbing his face with his hands.

I tensed, waiting for Andrew to say more. Last night had been selfishly all about me, and this morning, well, I was about to find out.

"Andrew, I'm sorry for what happened last night."

"For which part?"

Wasn't it obvious? "For crying everywhere."

"Huh." His eyes were quietly assessing, any remnants of sleep gone. I expected anger, hurt, frustration, something, anything. Instead, his voice was devoid of emotion.

I continued miserably, "I'm sorry about not telling you before. I thought about calling you while I was pregnant, but I was scared. After, what was the point of telling you something that wasn't going to happen?"

In a furor of movement, Andrew moved off the bed to kneel next to me on the floor. His gray eyes blazed with anger, and his voice was disbelieving. "What was the point? We created a child together, and what would be the fucking point of telling me about her? You should have let me carry the pain with you. Fucking unbelievable, Tia."

Unable to look at the scorn in his eyes, I flopped over onto my stomach, talking to the dark shadows underneath my bed. "I'm sorry, I'm sorry, I'm sorry, Andrew. I didn't know what to do, and I was so scared of everything. It felt as if my life was breaking apart with you not being in it anymore, being in this weird limbo of not going to school, and then finding out about the baby … I didn't know anyone going through this … especially after. Statistics say this is common, but at the time, I just felt so lonely. It felt like my burden to carry. I'm sorry."

I didn't know who I was apologizing to or for what. I knew that the miscarriage wasn't my fault, but sometimes, it was easy to forget.

Silent tears leaked out of the corners of my eyes. I thought I had cried everything out, but apparently, pain could always squeeze more emotions out. Today's grief was quiet and weary, though no less gashing than the night before or the hundreds of nights and days before. It was an open wound that would never heal completely.

As I lay on my floor, with my eyes squeezed shut to hold the insistent guilt and agony in, Andrew said nothing. I could still sense him kneeling beside me, and I could physically feel his eyes on me. But I had no idea what he was thinking.

Over me, I heard Andrew sigh as he laid a hand on my back, before immediately pulling away. *Great, now he can't even bear to touch me anymore.*

Another stretched moment of silence.

To my back, I heard Andrew ask, "Can you please turn around? I want you to look at me when I say this."

I thought about ignoring his request. Eventually, he would give up and defer this to another day, right? Or leave forever, while I wasted away on my hard, wooden floors?

And that was exactly the kind of scared, non-confrontational attitude that got me into this in the first place. Reluctantly, I rolled over, propping myself up on my arms to sit so I could be eye level with Andrew.

His handsome face was marred by a frown, as his eyebrows pulled together to create unhappy lines. He kept his hands studiously to himself, clenched into tight fists at his side. I could see the white of his knuckles and wished that I could soothe him.

"Okay, let me have it," I whispered in defeat.

"I'm fucking pissed, Tia."

I hung my head. It was too hard to look at him.

Cradling my face with both hands, he turned me back to look at him. "It's not what I expected, and I'll need time to process this, so I don't know what I'll end up feeling. What I do know right now is, I'm fucking mad."

He paused, as if processing his thoughts as he spoke. "I'm mad that you didn't tell me when you found out, or when you lost the baby—our baby. What a crazy, mind-blowing thing to think about… I'm mad that I might have never known if not for this crazy mess that we're in."

His thumb caressed my cheeks in direct contrast to his words. I wasn't sure if he even realized what he was doing. But his words, oh his words were acute jabs of guilt.

More tears streamed down my face, blurring my vision. "I'm sorry, I am so sorry," I repeated brokenly.

"What I'm most mad about is that I—" His voice wavered, and when he continued, it was filled with torment. "I'm mad that I wasn't there. I'm so fucking pissed at myself."

Startled, I blinked rapidly. "What? How could you have known if I didn't tell you?"

"I don't know. I regret not telling you about Charlie earlier. It seems so stupid not to have told you. At least I could have helped you while you were in the hospital. I should have called. I should have asked. I was too proud to ask for another chance when I had nothing to give you and selfishly worried about … I don't know, being rejected. It was a shitty excuse for not keeping in touch."

"Oh, Andrew," I said softly, broken in a different way for him and his misplaced anger. I ached to touch him, to offer him comfort and to receive comfort from him. While a weight was lifted that he wasn't hurling anger at me, the foundation that we had tentatively rebuilt shifted like sand.

This wasn't light, casual talk between friends. This wasn't lust-filled encounters. This was serious, heart-opening, and achingly intimate. We had crossed a fork in our relationship, and I couldn't see the endpoint.

Andrew's eyes stormy, he said fiercely, "It *destroys* me to think of you going through all of that. A baby doesn't seem real, and losing a baby doesn't seem real, but you *bleeding*—I can't get that image out of my mind."

He asked, "Does that make me an unfeeling bastard?"

"No!" I searched for the right words. "After it happened, I couldn't process it for a long time. Eventually, I found a therapist. One thing that I learned through therapy is that there's no one way or right one to grieve, and we need to give ourselves grace for how we handle it. It took me a long time to realize that the miscarriage wasn't my fault, that I shouldn't blame myself. Just like you shouldn't blame yourself for not being there. Those circumstances were out of our control."

As if he needed to touch me to reassure himself, Andrew yanked me into his lap. We stayed in each other's arms in shared contemplative sorrow, the embrace far different from yesterday's dam-breaking tear-fest. Both were so, so needed and ten years too late.

Lulled into a half-daze by the warmth of his arms and the buzz outside my windows of a city awakening on a Saturday morning, it took me a half-second before understanding that Andrew was speaking again.

"Can I ask what happened afterward?"

I knew instinctively the underlying question that he couldn't voice yet. "I named her Joy. Joy Wang Parker."

I felt him tense around me at that name, before nodding. "I like it."

"It was kind of an ironic name, as I was really struggling at the time and for a long time afterward. However, I wanted so badly to believe that I would meet her again, that she wasn't lost." I took a shaky breath to calm my suddenly beating heart. Andrew squeezed me even tighter as if he could absorb this fresh wave of memories.

"Because Joy was technically a 'miscarriage,' many hospitals don't give out birth certificates," I continued, trying to focus on just the facts. "I couldn't bear the thought of our daughter ... My parents, for all of their flaws, understood that it mattered to me that she was considered real. They had someone make a birth certificate. Even though it's not official, it's meaningful to me. I'm thankful that they had the wherewithal to think to do so."

"Me too," Andrew said.

"Yeah, they were great. We planted a tree for her, so I would have a physical place to visit." Bone-weary and no longer in control of my body, I sagged into Andrew.

He pulled back to look at me, defeated yet determined, looking as if he had aged a decade in the past few hours. "I'm sorry I wasn't there for you or for her."

My hand ran over the stubble shadowing his cheeks and chin, as my facial muscles tried to contort themselves into a small smile. "Thank you for not judging and for letting me ruin your shirt with my tears."

"And my sweater, don't forget," he returned, with a small smile, though his eyes dulled with sadness. With a kiss against my cheek, he promised solemnly, "I'll make it up to you about Joy, I swear. Whatever happens between us, I promise, you'll never be alone again."

CHAPTER SIXTEEN

ANDREW

January 1, 2009 (never sent)
Ting Ting,
I'm not mailing this letter to you, which makes me feel brave enough to say: something has fundamentally changed for me this morning. As we counted down to midnight, in the crowd at your parents' party, I had this inexplicable urge to kiss you. I didn't of course. I was scared my stupid move would jeopardize our friendship, and that, I couldn't bear.
You don't see me in that way. I know *that I shouldn't be thinking about kissing you. However, now that I have this image of me kissing you, it's all that I think about. Would you kiss me back? I ask for scientific purposes.*
Yours,
Andrew

It was the oddest, longest, shortest, most awkward, most comfortable, stress-inducing, thrilling week of my life. If I had to write down a hundred reasons for why Tia had become so upset at Dan and Kat's house, miscarriage still wouldn't have made the list.

A week later, the shock that we—Tia and I—had created and lost a baby hadn't worn off. I was still floored by the news, and struggled with where to begin to processing everything.

In the midst of my struggles, I acknowledged that, if I was this emotional after hearing about this loss ten years after it happened, I couldn't imagine the depths that Tia must have sunk into. Even though she had only known she was pregnant for seven weeks before finding out that she had miscarried, she still had had seven weeks to build expectations, to bond and care for the child that she was nourishing. To have those expectations shatter, along with the physical trauma, coupled with the breakup of our marriage—I didn't know how she had survived.

Clearly, Tia was remarkable.

And I was a bastard for not being there.

"Want another slice?" She dangled pizza in front of me. "I am stuffed. Luckily I changed into pajamas. I'm not sure I would have fit into my jeans."

Grabbing the slice from her fingers, I told her, "You look beautiful."

Red tinged her cheeks, as she smiled at me shyly.

Lucky indeed. She might have tossed them on for comfort, but I was enjoying my view of her bare legs uncovered by her pajama shorts. Let's face it—I would have been checking her out in whatever she was wearing. Or not wearing.

We were once again in Tia's apartment. It was much smaller than my place in Chicago and too cluttered. Despite that, in a short time, it now felt more like home to me than my own. Tia's apartment had Tia…whereas mine looked like a staging for a house opening.

While we carefully ignored the subject of Joy, her specter hung around like a whisper. She was both a door and a bridge for us. Physically, I didn't want to push until Tia indicated she was ready for more, even as the tension between us escalated. However, I had never felt this emotionally connected to Tia, and though I couldn't be one hundred percent sure, I suspected she felt the same. Her previous stiffness around me had relaxed, as if she was allowing herself to enjoy our time together.

Speaking of time together. "Today is Saturday, and tomorrow is Sunday."

"Yes, Mr. Brilliant, and yesterday was Friday. Should we make a song so you can remember?" Tia teased, as she raised her feet to use my thighs as a footrest. I felt like cheering from the rooftop at this small external sign of her comfort with me.

"Ha ha, you think you're so funny."

"Why yes, I do. Funny, smart, nice, obviously a brilliant cook." She gestured toward the soot-covered chicken in the kitchen.

I gave the air an exaggerated sniff. "If your day job falls through, you could open up a restaurant called Tia's Smoky BBQ, where the music is great and the food is burnt. Hey!" My right hand reached over to grab the attacking mochi she lobbed over.

"I want that back, you know." She made grabby fingers at me. "No, don't throw it at me! You know I can't catch—Mmph, than yoo."

My fingers hovered after stuffing the mochi into her mouth, before giving in to the urge to touch her face. Tia had the most amazingly soft skin. Not like silk because that was too cold, or like cotton because that was too common. More like, warm velvet that heated under my touch.

Her eyes widened as I leaned in, her cheeks still bulging a little from the forgotten mochi. It would have been so easy to press my lips against hers.

So *necessary*.

To think that I was once determined to put off sex so we could develop a real foundation. Every time I touched her, my resolve got weaker. I had vastly underestimated her and vastly overestimated my own control when I was with her.

I was tired of acting as if we were just friends, as if there wasn't this crazy chemistry between us. Instead, I should have pushed earlier and gotten us busy horizontally. Screw foundation. We could develop a foundation after we screwed.

"What were you saying earlier about Saturdays?"

"Hmm?" I blinked.

With a big gulp, Tia swallowed her mochi and placed a firm hand against my chest. My whole brain was focusing on the puzzle of whether her hand meant stop or a need-to-touch-me. *Please, be the latter*.

"You were talking about the days of the week. It sounded as if you were going somewhere with that." Her fingers pressed my chest firmly. Away from her. Damn.

My hand dropped from the back of her neck, as I sat back in my chair. I stared at the window behind Tia and tried to remember the argument that I had prepared. "I was thinking, since we started this arrangement on a Sunday evening—actually, if you consider the renegotiations when your parents came over, it was really nine before we finalized the verbal contract—tonight isn't our last night. Hear me out. After we finalized the terms of our contract, we didn't do anything more that night, right? So really, Monday was the start. Which means that we have until tomorrow."

She didn't say a word.

Swallowing a lump in my throat, I forced myself to look at her squarely and said in my most reasonable voice, "I still have one more day, and I'm holding you to that. One more day, and I'll—you can decide what you want me to do after that."

I couldn't speak out loud what I had promised to do in exchange for these two weeks. I didn't want to sign any fucking papers that severed our relationship and took away my flimsy excuse to see her.

Her head cocked in deep thought, Tia looked at me, her eyes assessing and in what felt like judgment. Clearly, I was not going to pass if she wouldn't even grant me one extra day. One measly day to come up with something, anything that would convince her to try again with me.

A low ache spread through my bones, as my lungs slowed to a crawl in reluctant acceptance of what was to come. Which was no more Tia. This was it. These two weeks were a farce, and she'd go back to her perfect life while I was still the son of a criminal. After all of this, I still wasn't good enough.

And this time, I knew it was truly the end. Which made it hurt so fucking much.

"Please." The word slipped out of me before I could stop myself from begging. I was both ashamed and desperate. If the past two weeks were any indication of what we could be, no matter how much the thought made my skin crawl, I would throw myself at her feet and beg. Hell, I'd beg in the streets in front of a crowd for a second chance and screw looking like a damn fool.

A frown of confusion appeared on her face, as if she were examining me like I was an odd species in science class. Abruptly her face cleared as if she had just found the answer to some great mystery.

In a voice oddly tender for a breakup, she started, "Oh, Andrew, about that. I've been thinking …"

Here it comes. Scrambling to shore up my heart, I braced myself. *Accept her decision, accept her decision and walk away.*

"What do you think about, um …"

Accept. And. Walk. The. Fuck. Away.

"Maybe we hang out the Saturday after Thanksgiving?"

"Huh?" What sort of weird, prolonged torture was this?

Red stained Tia's cheeks, as she fidgeted in her chair and tickled her neck with the ends of her ponytail. She looked so uncomfortable that I was worried for her. "Saturday after Thanksgiving. I'll be in Colorado to see my family. Maybe we can meet up after the holidays … in Breckenridge."

Sadness rose within me. *What else could be in Breckenridge?* I said, "Yes."

She must have sensed that I understood what she was offering and with the absolute gratefulness and gravity that I underscored my "Yes," for her whole body seemed to relax visibly in front of me. A warm smile teased the corners of her mouth.

Unable to help myself, yet fully aware that I might be pushing too hard, I asked, "What happens between now and Breckenridge? I want to keep seeing you."

Smiling, she shook her head. "You're growing on me too, Andrew. However, I have some things that I need to do by myself in the next couple of weeks before I head back home for the holidays."

"FaceTime? Calls?"

"I'll be busy."

"I'll be quick. 'Hi, it's Andrew. Bye.'"

"Nah-uh. I need to focus to get everything done before Breckenridge."

"Sexting?"

"Ha! No." Her smile was broad, the best kind that there was. I could bask in the shadow of her happiness.

"Nudes?"

"Gosh no! Remember, no dick pics, please."

"How do you know that I'm going to send dick pics? I listened to you before. Maybe I was going to send an artistic representation of my shoulder. A study of shoulders in black and white." I raised my eyebrows up and down in an exaggerated, come-hither look.

Tia's shoulders were shaking as she tried to look stern, that lovely broad smile still lighting up her beautiful face. "Guess I'll have to miss that masterpiece. What will I do?"

"In all seriousness"—I kept my tone deliberately light, to not scare her—"what am I going to do without you for the next couple of weeks, Tia? I've gotten used to having you around. What am I going to do if I don't have to keep you from walking into walls or burning your food?"

Not fooled by my flippant tone, Tia's smile dipped a little. She countered, "Eat properly cooked food that is not charred?"

Laughter burst from me, catching me and Tia by surprise. Laughter always caught me by surprise. I never expected to laugh. Most of the time, that expectation was correct. But this woman just did something to me—she commanded my respect even as I wanted to protect her. She tickled my funny bone even as I wanted her to stroke something else whenever she was near.

How could I resist the teasing, intelligent, thoughtful woman who was sitting across from me? Throwing caution to the wind, I leaned forward, pausing a rapid heartbeat to give her time to react.

Her eyelids fluttered closed as she swayed toward me. I was already doing the victory dance in my pants, when she put the palm of her right hand against my chest. Damn hand-to-chest blocker again.

I dropped my forehead to hers and struggled to even out my breathing. "Not tonight?"

Shaking her head reluctantly, Tia confirmed, "I'm not ready yet."

I seized on that. "Not yet. Then when?"

Mutely, Tia stared at me, refusing to answer. I wanted to wait until she was ready, but that didn't mean that I understood why she hesitated.

Part of me was pleased to see that her breaths were uneven, as if the close contact had affected her just as much as it did to me. The other part of me was flat-out fucking horny and therefore extremely frustrated.

When I couldn't take the unrequitedness of our proximity anymore, I stood up and walked toward the door. "I should go," I said, even though I definitely did not want to go anywhere.

"Um, okay." Tia followed me to the door and grabbed my jacket from her coat hanger to hand to me. I was careful not to touch her fingers, in case that contact turned me into a caveman and I started demanding what she clearly wasn't ready for. *Or ever would be*, the killjoy part of my brain chimed in.

"Send me the details for Breckenridge, and I'll see you there."

"Okay, will do." Hesitation shone in her face as her hands rose and dropped.

Trying to respect her and wary of the caveman inside of me, I muttered goodbye and turned to walk toward the elevators.

Except, three steps away from Tia, I immediately regretted my decision.

Turning around, my stupid heart leaped to see her staring at me, her body half in the hallway. In a couple ground-eating steps, I was in front of her, my arms wrapped tightly around her, pulling her into me. Pulling her into my heart. Willing her to feel even an ounce of what my heart pounded out.

My body relaxed when I felt her lean up on her tippy-toes, arms wrapping around my neck. A content sigh escaped from Tia, her warm breath tickling my neck, as she snuggled against my chest. This hug wasn't nearly enough, but it soothed my soul momentarily.

With more self-control than I thought possible, I unwrapped her arms from my neck and untangled myself before I could do something foolish. "I'll see you soon, Tia."

"See you soon, Andrew," she whispered, her arms clasping around her waist.

This time, I didn't turn around again as I left. My mind was whirling with ideas. I had two weeks until I saw Tia again, and I needed a plan to extend our "arrangement" into something more permanent.

CHAPTER SEVENTEEN

ANDREW

February 8, 2009
Ting Ting,
We kissed yesterday. This is my testimonial, in case I need it for evidence in the future.
Date: February 7, 2009.
Where: Ross' frat house party.
What: I kissed you. You kissed me back.
How: With tongue.
When can I see you again?
Yours,
Andrew

To: TWang@mit.edu
Subject: Hi

Hi,

You didn't say no to emails, so hi.

What do you call someone with no body and no nose? Nobody knows!

What do you call a pig that does karate? A pork chop!

What did the area say to the perimeter while arguing? I'm trying to talk to you, but I feel like you're just going around my problem.

Should I keep going? I've got lots more.

Andrew

To: A.Parker@gmail.com

Subject: Re: Hi

Hi,

Okay, okay, I'll allow emails. Your jokes are terrible. What else do you have?

Tia

To: TWang@mit.edu

Subject: Re: Hi

Hi,

If a joke is so bad it makes you laugh, is it a good joke, then? Never mind, I got some pickup lines I've been meaning to try on you:

What's at least six inches long, goes in your mouth, and is more fun if it vibrates? A toothbrush. Get your mind out of the gutter, Tia.

I'm a muggle on the streets, but a wizard in the sheets. Want to get magical?

Are you full of beryllium, gold, and titanium? Because you are BE-AU-TI-full.

So, what's the verdict? Are you charmed?

Andrew

To: A.Parker@gmail.com

Subject: Re: Hi

Hi,

Your lame attempts at humor are not *the worst part of my day. Actually, I had a pretty disheartening day today.*

Tia

To: TWang@mit.edu

Subject: Re: Hi

Hi,

Had a bad day? Just pug-et about it.

In all seriousness, want to talk about it? I don't like the thought of you being sad.

Andrew

To: A.Parker@gmail.com

Subject: Re: Hi

Hi, Andrew,

Nope, I'll tell you sometime later. See you in a few days.

Tia

Frowning, I stared at the phone in my hand, rereading Tia's last email. If this problem was bothering her enough for her to mention it, whatever she was dealing with must be bad. I wished I could do something about it.

Was it an angry student? Even though teaching wasn't her main priority, Tia took it seriously and pored over her reviews, trying to get better each semester. Or maybe her research? She was working with some professor out in Chicago on healthcare virtual buddies powered by AI and had been feeling out of her element.

I was in the middle of writing an email back to her to tell her how brilliant she was, when a thought stopped my fingers.

Damn. Of course, she was stressed.

A knot settled into my stomach, a big, uncomfortable knot with thorny tentacles ripping my insides. She was at home with her parents and most likely pretending to them that she and Clayton were okay. Would she eventually tell her parents about us? If she did, how long would it take before she chose her parents' approval over me?

Despite having a nice job and my own house, my blood was still tainted. My dad had kept a low profile since leaving prison, but that just meant he had more time to think up his next scheme. It was only a matter of time before his evilness was caught again.

After our last evening together, I had flown back to Chicago to keep me from running after her. Now, on the Tuesday evening before Thanksgiving, I waited outside a terminal at Chicago O'Hare to pick up my mom who was going to spend the holidays with me.

The first thing that I had done when I started seeing my bank account grow was petition my mom to retire. The second thing was buying her a little condo in Florida that looked just like the magazine cutouts that she hid in her nightstand when I was growing up. Though she never said it, I knew I owed her for keeping us afloat after my dad went to jail. She hadn't been the most hands-on mom, but she could have easily thrown me into the foster system, instead of working multiple jobs to feed my never-ending appetite.

"Hi, Mom." I waved slightly, when I saw her emerge from the terminal. We were not hugging type of people. "How was your flight from Fort Lauderdale?"

"It was so quick. I barely had time to get into my book before we started descending. Are you sure I'm not imposing on you by staying with you?" A worried look appeared on her thin face, as she tapped her nails against her carry-on bag.

I hated how easily the nervous look appeared on her tired face. It was another strike against Brandon Parker. "Don't worry about it. I want you to see my new place. I even made my bed." I gave her my most winsome smile.

Her little laugh warmed me as we exited the airport and headed for my car. It took months after my dad went to prison before I heard her laugh. A true laugh, not the laugh she put on for my father to appease his ego. Another strike against Brandon Parker.

"What have you been doing lately? You sounded so busy on the phone the last few weeks," she asked, once we were settled in my car. "If you don't mind me asking."

"I'm your son. You're supposed to pry." Were all mothers supposed to pry? Actually, I wasn't sure. "I was in Boston for a couple weeks."

"To see Tia?"

Astonished, I glanced at her quickly before turning back to the road. If you ever wanted to see hand-wringing, my mother could teach a master class on it. Like a little bird, her hands fidgeted nonstop.

"I still keep in touch with some people back in Breckenridge. They mentioned that you were at Tia's engagement party. Gossip travels fast."

I waited for her to say that she had heard that Tia's engagement was off. Nothing. I was still the secret on the side.

Worthless piece of shit who'll never amount to anything. I hated that one of my clearest childhood memories was my dad's favorite phrase for me, and I hated that I could hear his voice and recall his sneer as he said it.

"Must have been odd to see her after so many years. Did you know she goes by Tia now? I don't blame her, you know? Sometimes a name change is as good of a new start as any. I thought about going back to being Mary Walden," she confessed, surprising me again.

"Why didn't you?"

"I wanted the two of us to have the same family name."

"We would still have been family with different last names."

There was a long pause before my mom continued, her voice wavering, "I couldn't be sure. You've achieved so much for yourself. With your refusal to come back to Colorado even for a visit after you graduated college, I didn't know if you had room for me."

With an abrupt swerve, I pulled into the breakdown lane on the side of the highway and took my mom's fluttering hands into mine. "I've told you before, you're my mom, and I've promised that I would take care of you."

She scoffed. "I should have taken better care of you. I should have taken you and left long before your father went to prison."

"You and I both know that wouldn't have worked. Brandon didn't take kindly to having his possessions taken away from him," I said matter-of-factly.

Cars rumbled by as we sat in silence. Some things were better left in the past. There was no point in dredging up should haves and could haves. Forcing a lighthearted tone that I didn't feel, I squeezed my mom's hands to emphasize my words. "Let's forget about him. He's not worth our thoughts."

With a tenuous smile, she nodded.

Pulling back onto the highway, I felt lighter. It wasn't as if I had a bad relationship with my mom. It also wasn't as if five minutes on the side of the road would solve the distance between us. But I meant my words—the two of us had survived the deceit and misery caused by my dad, and sometimes, survival was sufficient.

A few minutes later, I pulled into my garage. We busied ourselves getting my mom's luggage into the townhouse and making small talk about my new place. It wasn't huge—two bedrooms, a small yard—but it was mine (plus a mortgage). It was a far cry from the shelter we had lived in right after my dad had been arrested.

When I started with my current company, Cipher Systems, I had lived in a company-owned condo by Millennium Park. It had been the fanciest place that I had ever lived in, but it hadn't been mine. Being a homeowner meant far more.

Inside my not-so-fancy home, my mom pointed out how nice she thought my kitchen cabinets were, how lovely the gray couch was, how much she liked the nice plaid of my oven mitts. When she started commenting on the neatness of the apples and bananas in a bowl on my kitchen island, I cut her off. There was only so much one could talk about interior design, or rather my lack thereof.

"Mom, I know you're not actually impressed with this chair or that pot—"

"Oh, Andrew, I am. You picked such a lovely color scheme. All of these variations of gray—so modern." A master hand-wringing class was being taught right in front of me.

Part of me was amused. Part of me was impatient to hear more about Tia. "Hey, Mom, you mentioned in the car that you still keep in touch with folks in Colorado. Did the Wangs ever say anything about our breakup or what happened afterward?"

Her eyebrows rose as she studied me. "There were rumors that something had happened, though no one was sure what. Her parents tried to hide it, but when the Wangs' star daughter defers Harvard for a year, disappears for a couple months, and reappears looking deflated, people talk."

Those knife-wielding tentacles were stabbing at me again, as an image of a haggard-looking Tia took up residence in my brain. *Fuck*, I should have been there. I should have listened for news of her, instead of burying my head in the sand like a fucking idiot.

"I don't think people knew you two got married, so no one blamed you. You don't have to worry about that," my mom reassured me.

Ouch. Though my mom had meant to calm me, her words served to remind me that Tia and her parents had been too embarrassed to tell their friends about our marriage. *Dumb piece of shit who'll never amount to anything.*

In a small voice, my mom asked, "So are you two friends again?"

Restless and frustrated, I stood up and walked over to the bay windows overlooking the little patio and lawn in the back. It had been one of the features that sold me on this townhouse. I'd wanted to have a little piece of greenery in the city, but now the fence surrounding the little ten-by-eight yard felt constricting. Away from Tia, my brain worked against me.

Because I knew the real answer. I didn't even have to look that deeply within me to know that I didn't want to be friends with Tia. Not *just* friends. I could never be *just* friends with her again. I would always crave more, so much more. So much more than she could ever give.

"Andrew"—a note of warning sounded in mom's voice—"a friendship can be enough. Sometimes, it has to be enough."

Turning, I looked at my mom. For once, her hands were still, and she looked back at me with her patient eyes. A strong breeze could have blown her sideways, yet her message was strong.

Just because I understood didn't mean I had to like it.

"Andrew," she warned again, her voice louder this time. "If she's getting married, then let her be. It's for the best."

"What if she's not getting married?" I asked harshly.

"Oh, Andrew, let the past stay in the past and move on. Let both of you move on."

I hated the pity in her eyes, so I turned away from her. A month ago, I would have been happy to let the past lie.

Now? Two weeks with Tia showed me just how much I needed her in my life. It was a raw-boned, seeping-into-my-every-cell kind of need. A craving for her smile, her laughter, her warmth. The mix of modern, intelligent, professional woman with her clumsy, weird, goofball side.

Could I find someone else who checked off smart and quirky? Sure. I'd bet that there were thousands of women who might describe themselves that way. But there was also this indescribable factor about Tia, or maybe it was when we were together. Some elemental pull that tied my heart to hers. And that, I knew without a doubt couldn't be replicated.

For that indescribable emotional connection, I couldn't give up.

Yet, my mom's words reverberated within me, because they were echoes of my own doubts. Tia might be the best thing ever for me, but was I the right choice for her? Was I being a shitty person for breaking up Tia and Clayton?

Yes, most definitely. I was a fucking asshole for causing this upheaval in her life.

CHAPTER EIGHTEEN

ANDREW

April 7, 2009
Ting Ting,
I have a question for you. Do you want to be my girlfriend officially?
Don't tell me now. Tell me when you're here this weekend. Actually, tell me if the answer is yes. Pretend you never received this if the answer is no.
Yours (if you want me to be),
Andrew

Promptly at three p.m. on Saturday, I stood outside the entrance to Pennypack Park, in Breckenridge, Colorado. I hadn't been back to Colorado since I transferred out of CU Boulder my sophomore year. There was a surreal feeling in returning, as if I expected to find my younger self slouching around. Instead of feeling trapped and judged by this town, I saw it now as tourists must: an upscale ski and vacation town, nestled in the beautiful Rocky Mountains. A place where folks living in bigger cities could take a breather and slow down.

A BMW honked at me from the road, slowing down as it nearer. Tia opened the passenger side window and leaned over. Her smile shone like sunlight on this cloud-heavy day, catching me by surprise and making my breath hitch. "Hey, stranger."

"Hey, you."

We smiled at each other like we had been feeling unsettled until this moment when we saw each other. Like we knew any amount of time together was better than time spent apart. At least, that's how I smiled at her. Tia was probably just being her normal friendly self.

"How'd you get here? Did you take a taxi?"

"No, I rented a car from the airport." I pointed toward the state park's parking lot down the road.

"Oh, okay. Do you want to get in? It'll be easier if I drive than explain the location."

Tia waited for me to buckle up before pulling back to the main road. Reaching into her coat pocket, she waved a bag at me. "Gummies? I've got some granola in the glove compartment too and water in the back if you're hungry or thirsty."

Smiling, I shook my head. Tia's hospitality was one of my favorite traits about her. If she offered food, you knew that you were on her good side. "No, thanks, I grabbed something at Luke's Diner before I headed over here."

"Hey, by the way, thanks for sending me snacks. I don't think I've ever been so excited to see chips and sugar! I was getting so restless with eating healthy food all the time. There's only so much broccoli I can eat without wanting chocolate, you know?" Eyes scanning the side of the road, she wrinkled her nose to show her disdain.

"No problem. I figured your parents would still be health-conscious." I chuckled at the image of Tia sneaking chocolate in her room in the dark, as she used to do when she was younger.

Tia rolled her eyes and said, "They're worse than before. Every day, they're after me about how important it is to eat healthy and exercise when you're young."

"How dare they want you to be healthy," I mocked.

Her laughter reverberated. "How dare they, indeed. But oh, the snacks, you even included lemon squares. It was very sweet of you, Andrew. You definitely earned brownie points in my book."

I wanted all of the brownie points in her book to have my name on them.

As we approached a half-hidden dirt road across from the state park, Tia's laughter stopped abruptly. Her hands gripped the steering wheel tightly. I knew instinctively that this place was tied to Joy somehow.

The road curved around until we got to a small clearing. At the top of the hill, Tia parked the car, grabbed a bag from the back seat, and hopped out. She walked quickly, practically running, toward some trees in the distance.

Trees rose high around us, giving a sense that we were in a cocoon. It didn't look as if anyone had lived here for years. The place had an untamed beauty, made stark by the almost-bare trees against the gray skies. I strode after Tia, catching up with her before she reached the forest. She was out of breath, and that confused me because the clearing wasn't that big. She stopped abruptly and bent over, heaving with exertion.

"Are you okay, Tia? Do you want me to get you some water?" Just in case, I pulled out my phone to look up the nearest urgent care center. No signal. I had taken for granted the omnipresence of Wi-Fi in large cities.

Dropping my phone back into my pocket, I awkwardly patted Tia's back. Startled as if she had forgotten that I was there, she jumped up.

Tia's face was ashen, as her eyes stared at me wildly. In the worst way, I lost my breath as my lungs stopped working. Gingerly, almost reverently, she placed her palm on a tree to her right.

Sensing my confusion, Tia took my hand and placed it on the same spot on the tree. Her voice breaking in the middle of the word, she whispered, "Here."

Underneath my gloveless hand, I felt cool metal. With dread, I lifted my hand. A silver plaque showed a simple inscription, "Joy Wang Parker, 2009."

For the second time that day, I lost my breath. I sank down to the ground on my knees. My vision narrowed on the plaque, as if I could will my daughter to be alive.

This tree was symbolic, I knew that. Yet, I couldn't help feeling a connection to her here. I was aware of the hardness and dampness of the ground underneath my knees, of the wind chilling my ears, of my fingers gripping my thigh to brace myself. I hoped, with every part of me, that my daughter was feeling the wind, watching the seasons, experiencing life somewhere, somehow.

As if from far away, I heard Tia rustling around her bag. She placed a small bouquet of sweet-smelling pink flowers by the tree.

The picture that I carry of Tia is an image of someone who is optimistic, vivacious, and strong. Yet in front of me was someone frail, her face mirroring the anguish that I felt in my heart. Probably more so, since she had carried this baby within herself.

Sitting cross-legged on the cold ground, with her knees touching me and one arm on my back offering me what little remained of her strength, Tia said softly, "One day, I walked over here—"

"All the way from your parents' house? It's got to be at least five miles." A picture of Tia wandering by herself, vulnerable and hurting only served to underline how *not* there I was for her. *I didn't take care of my family, just like my dad.* It was a sobering realization.

Wincing self-consciously, she said, "I was not in a good head space at the time. My parents were ready to call the police by the time I went home. They had been driving all over town trying to look for me. It had started snowing—just a little bit—and well, they were worried about what I was going to do. For a supposedly obedient daughter, I put them through hell."

"It wasn't your fault."

"Sure, some things weren't my fault, but I definitely made mistakes."

The words hung in the air between us, separating us, poking me with their spears. She didn't say it directly, but I knew that I was the mistake. *I* was the decision that caused a rift between her and her parents.

Scooching closer, Tia continued, "One good thing came out of that walk. I happened to pass by this place, and there was a for sale sign by the street. I don't think I ever noticed this place when we used to hang out around here, so I was curious and went to take a look. If we stand up, you can see the state park, and if you squint a bit, you can see the playground. When I went home and my parents stopped fussing, I asked my dad if I could use some of my college funds to buy this land. He didn't even negotiate with the buyer. You know him—negotiations are his jam. I think he was happy to see me care about something."

Looking back at the silver plaque, she said self-consciously, "I planted a little tree here to commemorate her and so I could have a place to visit. In a weird way, I had this idea that as the tree grew, she could, somehow, see the park and playground."

“I don’t think that’s weird. I like the thought of her being symbolically close to where we used to hang out.” Needing to feel her even closer, I pulled Tia onto my lap and wrapped my arms around her. As if I weren’t her biggest mistake, she nestled in closer to my heart.

Softly, she whispered against my neck, so close that I could almost feel the shape of her lips against my skin. “Outside of my parents, I’ve never brought anyone here. Or even told anyone about this place. Pippa guessed, but we’ve never really talked about it. So thank you. For listening to me, for letting me cry, and for visiting her with me.”

I pulled back a little so I could see Tia. Her eyes were focused, and while she still looked sad, I could feel her vitality returning. I wanted to kiss her so badly—and not in *that* way—just to be closer and to offer comfort. Instead, I settled for holding her even tighter. Which didn’t feel like settling, when her arms came around to squeeze me back.

I searched for the right words. “Ting Ting—Tia … I—” There was something in my throat, preventing words from getting out. Something foreign and unwieldy.

Strong and vulnerable brown eyes peered at me, patiently waiting. Her hands came up to rub my shoulders.

What could I say in this moment? How could I articulate what I was feeling when I didn’t understand them myself. I started again. “Um. Tia. Thank you for bringing me here.” Pause. There was that foreign thing in my throat.

Her face fell at my formal tone.

Ah, fuck it, eloquent I was not going to be. Taking a deep breath, I started again, “I don’t know what to say or feel. I’m stumped and overwhelmed and sad. I think you’re amazing for surviving this. And don’t shake your head at me, I know you’re not the only one who has had a miscarriage, but nonetheless, I think you’re amazing. I’m glad you told me, because you didn’t have to, and I would have never found out. I’m not sure what to do. Do I offer you condolences, or make jokes? Should I suggest that we have therapy together and talk more about this? I don’t have a manual for this. Tell me what I can do.”

“Hold me, Andrew.”

I waited for more.

She looked at me hopefully.

My arms hugged her tighter to me. We sat there in silence, holding each other, supporting each other. It felt like a giant step forward for us to be able to sit here and share grief as parents to a little soul who never had a chance.

Something had fundamentally shifted to both strengthen our relationship and put us on an unknown footing. For the first time since Tia entered my life again, I was a hundred percent sure that she was going to stay in my life. As what, I didn't know.

After a while, the peaceful silence was broken by the chattering of Tia's teeth. Her only reaction was to burrow further into me, as I rubbed her back, her arms, her legs to try to warm her up. I hated having to break this moment, but frostbite was not on my list of goals for us.

Reluctantly, I said, "Hey, Tia, it's too cold to be out here. Let's get inside the car."

As if in slow motion, she nodded and stood up, groaning as her body stretched. Immediately, I missed the warmth and weight of her on me.

Tia said, "Why don't you go ahead to the car? I'd like another couple of minutes here by myself."

I nodded. Once back in the car, I turned around to look back at Tia. She was sitting again, and it looked as if she was talking, her hands gesturing. I could picture Tia sitting on a grassy lawn with a little ten-year-old girl with black hair and eyes as warm as hers, as they chatted about their day, their hands extensions of their words.

Because that image made me sad, I pushed it firmly to the back of my mind. Alone for the first time since "meeting" my daughter, I let out a big breath and let my head drop between my legs.

It was too much.

I couldn't turn off my brain. The thought of being a father was scary. I wasn't sure that I wanted to ever have kids. What sort of dad would I be when I had the worst model of what a dad could be?

But the thought of being a deadbeat dad terrified me more. My mind was inundated with images, real and imaginary. Images of Tia in a hospital, of going through this without me, of what our daughter could have looked like. They magnified my sadness and underscored my regret that I wasn't there for her. For them. *I wasn't there for them.*

It was too fucking much.

The door on the driver side opened, and Tia slid in. Sounding concerned, she asked, "Are you okay? I know it was a lot today."

Straightening to look at her, I chased back the intensity of what I was feeling, not wanting her to worry about me. "I'm glad you brought me here. Really."

I took a deep breath. "So, where should we go now?"

"I'm supposed to fly back to Boston tonight at eight."

"Oh."

Damn. I thought I had more time. I didn't know what I was expecting, since we had never discussed what would happen after our two-week arrangement. Outside of the divorce papers. My heart hand planned on spending more time with Tia. Clearly, my heart was stupid.

And also dense apparently. "So I guess we're done with the two weeks, huh?"

"Yes, I'd like to be done with this arrangement."

Fuck. Did she have to sound so normal? Couldn't she sound a little sad? Especially when I was panicking.

I had been stupid to resist sex in the beginning, and stupid not to push for it later. I would have completely respected her if she said no, but I was beating myself up for not even trying. Screw building an emotional relationship first. I should have done something. Something else, something *more*, anything to hold her to me. Because clearly, having friendly hangouts did not cut it.

Was it too late to strip and hope she would be wowed? *And what? Fall on my dick? Stupid idea.*

Way too soon, Tia pulled up to my rental car. After carefully parking, she looked at me, eyes wide. Expectantly.

I wasn't ready to say goodbye. *Say goodbye and be gracious about it.*

Sitting in the car, faced with the prospect of no more Tia, I leaned toward her. Her eyes fluttered shut, as she leaned in to close the distance between us. Closing my eyes, I opened my other senses to absorb Tia in. The soft, fullness of her lips as they met mine. The mix of her fruity Lip Smackers and the lavender scent from her hair circling around me. Her cold hands caressed my face, a dichotomy to the fire she stirred within me. Her low sigh turned into a moan, when I deepened the kiss, unbuckled her, and pulled her into my lap to straddle me.

I didn't need sight to feel how right she was in my lap or know that I could spend the rest of my life relearning her lips and the shape of her.

Trying to show her with my body and hands and lips, I poured all of my want and need into this stolen moment and willed her to understand just how necessary she was to me. At the moment, I would have traded a lifetime of air and water for her next kiss. For her to whisper that I was necessary to her.

I was frantic for her touches. Desperate for the way she moaned my name, as if it was a secret pulled out of her. Blood roaring to the delicious spot where our bodies fit, I rocked against her, drawing out a moan. *Too fucking good.*

All of a sudden, Tia tore her mouth away from me, my lifeboat tossed away in this storm. Her lips were puffy from our ardor. Her eyes heavy with lust. Her broken breaths matching my poor attempt at catching my breath. She was the woman of my dreams and the woman to wreak havoc in them. I had never been so turned on.

I made a move to pull her closer. I would always want her closer.

She pulled her head back to stare at me.

At her pull-back, deflated, I deposited Tia back in her seat and slumped back against mine, trying unsuccessfully to forget how her body had felt on mine. My frenzied and uncoordinated attempts to woo her must have scared her.

I thought about baring my feelings to her, however complicated they were, and hoped that she felt even a fraction of the same. A tiny bit in return would be enough, because what I felt for her was so immense and strong that it could carry both of us.

If I thought that this had the remotest chance of working, I would have gotten on my knees to plead for our future. Except, she had pulled back. And with that motion, I knew without a doubt that she was not ready to reciprocate.

So I tucked the words that I hadn't fully articulated even to myself back inside the center of my heart and allowed numbness to enclose them. They would stay trapped inside as my burden.

The silence stretched, as I acknowledged the end of us. Sure, we might check in on each other every now and then, but that would never be enough. Casual acquaintances were nowhere near what I wanted us to be.

"So." Tia's eyes widened impossibly more as they searched mine. There was a question in her eyes. It was the same look as before I had kissed her. Nervousness hung around her.

Those pesky tentacles with spears gripped my insides. "Oh, I see."

"What, um, what do you see?" she asked nervously.

Of course. Tia would try to be gracious about this and wouldn't want to ask outright, not when I was defeated. She was kind-hearted, and I loved that about her. "I'll hold up my side of the deal. You gave us a try, and it's not going to work—"

"Not going to work?"

"Right." I nodded past the bitterness. "I get it, it was fun hanging out, but fun doesn't mean forever. When I get back to Chicago, I'll sign those divorce papers. You're free."

"Free?"

"You know what I mean, you're free to do whatever. I won't bother you anymore." The thought of being apart from Tia would never cease to destroy me.

"Oh." Her lovely full lips were a grim line of unhappiness.

I didn't like that she looked unhappy, especially when I was the cause. I hurried to add, "I'm still glad you told me about Joy and showed me this place. It means so much to me that you trusted me."

Nodding, she said in a carefully even tone, "Well, you were the father, even if I told you way after the fact. I guess we still have the past."

"Yes, I guess so."

"But no future."

Did her voice rise in a question? Did she not trust me to accept that I lost? Hell, part of me didn't accept and would cling to the memory of her forever. But I said I was going to sign those damn papers, and I would.

"I'll make sure to get those papers to your lawyer as soon as I get home," I stressed.

"Oh, okay. So this is it, huh?"

What was this fucking torture that Tia was putting me through? This awkward, weird, confusing conversation was just prolonging the flood of pain. Exhausted and jittery from the roller coaster of the past month, I opened my car door to escape the pain. "Okay, I have to go, Tia. I—"

"Oh, Andrew—"

My head whipped back to face her. "Yes?"

Red colored her cheeks and nose, as her eyes darted away from mine. "Um … actually, I was thinking, you know, I sort of thought … Never mind."

Big sigh. "I guess I'll see you sometime."

Tia lifted her head finally, her eyes miserable as she stared up at me. Okay, she looked officially sad now. *Good job, Parker, always a great idea to spread some misery on your way out.*

With everything to say and nothing that could be said, I stepped out of the car. Bracing myself, I memorized Tia's face and her sad little smile, as my arm rose to give a wordless goodbye before closing the door shut.

What a fucking metaphor.

Weary, I trudged back to my rental car, feeling the vastness of my empty heart. Tia was gone. That word echoed, like a violent wave pulling me under. It was rare to get second chances, and I hadn't been able to convert my chance into something more permanent. There would be no third chance.

For a loner, I had never really felt alone in my life until this moment. Not only was I literally alone by the side of the road on this blustery almost-winter day, there was an almost-physical hole in my heart created by the loss of Tia. Knowing what it was like to be happy and hopeful, however brief the moment, made this time so much more painful.

And there was nothing that I could do.

CHAPTER NINETEEN

ANDREW

April 13, 2009
Ting Ting,
It's Monday. It's been only a day since I saw you. I might miss you already.
Your official boyfriend,
Andrew

Yesterday, I couldn't wait to fly to Breckenridge.

Yesterday was a different world.

Today, I couldn't wait to get out of Breckenridge. Today ended with a world with no Tia.

Yet, no matter the gaping pain that was dulling my mind and numbing my body, I had to move on. I packed my hotel room in a hurry, throwing the little stuff that I had brought into a small duffel. My flight back to Chicago wasn't scheduled until tomorrow, and there were no more flights tonight that I could switch to. But I simply could not stay in the hotel anymore. I could not do nothing.

It was a fifteen-hour drive back to Chicago. I figured that I could drive partway tonight, find some random hotel, and finish driving by midday tomorrow. I would arrive in Chicago after my scheduled flight but it was crucial that I get out of Colorado tonight.

Once I got home, I planned to throw myself into work. If I didn't have enough work to fill twenty-four hours a day, seven days a week, I was sure there were enough contracts at Cipher Systems and its more than a dozen subsidiaries that I could review. Just to make sure that there weren't any loopholes. Plus, laws changed all the time. Now that I thought about it, I hadn't been keeping up with recent court cases. Sometimes, those judicial rulings and associated statements contained nuggets that I could use in contract negotiations or disputes.

And, I had heard some rumblings of potential work in Tennessee. I could study for the Tennessee bar or apply for reciprocity. Really, I was just being proactive about work. Not avoiding all thoughts of Tia.

In fact, I could even look up instructions for reciprocity right now. Get a head start. I put down the shirt that I was trying unsuccessfully to fold and pulled up my phone.

A text notification stared back at me. It was from fifteen minutes ago.

Tia: Hey, Andrew, where are you staying at? I have something to drop off.

Quickly, I tapped out the name of the hotel and my room number.

This was strange. Part of me was excited to see her—the part of me that was stupid and didn't learn. So I tried not to listen to that part. The other part of me—the rational, self-protective part—was pissed. What the hell was so important that Tia had to come over in person? I preferred ripping off the Band-Aid, not this slow, bloody torture. Clearly, she had only platonic feelings for me, because if she wanted me, she would already be here with me.

I hoped she wasn't bringing me food. I didn't want her to pity me so much that she felt as if she needed to feed me. *No dumplings*– that was the ultimate platonic comfort food.

A tap at the door startled me. I looked at the clock on my phone. Only two minutes since I had texted Tia. Too fast for her to have driven all the way from her parents' house. It was probably someone from the hotel.

Except it wasn't.

My heart tripped over itself at the sight of Tia in the doorway. One of her hands gripped a suitcase, the other was in her hair as if I had caught her finger-combing the long strands.

Her breath hitched, as if she were equally surprised to see me. As if she hadn't just knocked on my door.

A smile spread across my face. I didn't know why I was so happy. "Hi."

An answering smile spread across Ting's face, as she relaxed a fraction. "Hi."

"How did you get here so fast?"

"You used to like this hotel when we were kids. I assumed you were staying here, so I taxied over and was already in the lobby when you texted back." She looked embarrassed at her admission.

Nodding without any idea what I was agreeing to, I let my eyes greedily absorb Tia. She looked oddly dressed up for going to the airport. I didn't know much about fashion, but her dress and tights visible under her unzipped coat caught me by surprise. "So, um, what—"

"Can I come in? I feel weird having a conversation out in the hallway," she interrupted me.

"Um, sure, come in." Opening the door wider, I stepped aside to let her and her suitcase into my room.

"You said you had to drop something off?" I asked, trying to steer my mind back to a safe subject.

A flaming blush colored Tia's cheeks as she looked anxiously at my nose, avoiding my eyes. I was starting to feel discomfort due to her unease. Trying to help her, I prompted, "Where is it? Is it food?" *Please, don't let it be pity food.*

I didn't think it was possible, but Tia blushed even more. Scrunching up her nose, she looked at me briefly before averting her eyes. In a voice so quiet that I wasn't sure I heard her correctly, she whispered, "Not food. Me."

"What?" I nearly shouted.

The booming surprise in my voice caused her to take a step backward, her eyes wide as if she had been caught with her hands down her underwear.

That tiny, two-lettered word, "me," kindled the imagination I didn't even realize I had. My blood and thoughts were torpedoing toward that certain, very insistent area of my body. I saw her hands down her underwear, doing naughty things to herself. I saw her spread out in front of me letting me feast on her like a starving man. I saw her on top using me to achieve her pleasure.

I had to shift uncomfortably and clasp my hands in front of me, to hide my reaction. Unsuccessfully.

Her eyes tracked my movement, as a gasp spilled out of her lovely, full mouth. To the growing tent in my pants, she said, only slightly louder than before. "I'm dropping myself off … With you. If you want?"

Yes, I do want! What came out was, "To do what?" In case she was thinking we sign the divorce papers together, or something platonic, like do a puzzle together. I needed to be a hundred percent sure. I needed her to be hundred percent sure.

"Whatever you want?" Her cheeks blazed impossibly redder.

I didn't think it was possible for my pants to get even tighter. I took deep breaths to control myself. As much as I wanted—no—needed to kiss her right this minute, I didn't understand what the fuck was happening.

Tia glanced up at me, her brown eyes steadier now. "Before I flew out to Colorado, Clayton called me to see where I was at. We chatted."

Fuck.

Anguish stabbed me. I was an idiot. Yet again, I allowed myself to hope. Clayton was Tia's future. Whereas … I didn't know what I was. Best-case scenario, I was a one-night stand.

"He asked if I was interested in getting back together…I told him no. Whatever happens with you, Clayton no longer makes sense for me. Clayton and I aren't a great fit. I shouldn't have let that relationship get that far; I realize that now. Our two weeks together showed me that I still feel something for you. But I didn't want to jump into a new relationship with you until the situation with Clayton was completely resolved. Anyway, I called the wedding planner a few days ago and told her to officially cancel everything."

I was too stunned to say anything.

Tia swallowed hard, blushing once again before continuing. "I was hoping we could forget about the divorce for now and give our marriage another try? A real try?"

"You pulled back in the car," I stated. My head spun from her pushing me away earlier to her asking me now to try again.

She laughed nervously. "I don't know why. Maybe because I'm so used to trying to resist you. I think I got scared for a moment. It's one thing to know what I want. It's a completely different thing to give voice to it and take action. I don't want to be rejected."

Bravely, she took a step toward me, her eyes on me.

Before her next step, my feet were already moving toward her. Toward this courageous, strong woman. My arms pulled her toward me, framing her face, lifting her lips to mine. Euphoria soared in me, as I sank into the kiss. Tia was everything to me, and she had chosen me.

Us.

There was an us.

She wanted there to be an us.

"I'm yours as long as you want me," I promised her. My kiss was a reflection of the desperation in me. I craved the feel of her, the smell of her, the sounds of her. I deepened the kiss, sweeping my tongue into her open mouth, pulling her into mine. My hands moved frantically over her, throwing off her jacket, unzipping her dress.

I knew I should slow down. I couldn't. I wanted to feel her skin against mine. In the most primitive way, I wanted to mark her as mine and be branded as hers.

My lips marked a path toward her neck, where she was especially sensitive. She moaned softly and let her head fall, granting me access to her soft skin. Her hands were just as greedy, fisting in my hair, as she held me tightly to her. Her nails scorched me lightly over my shirt, and I welcomed the pain. I welcomed any sign that I wasn't in this storm alone.

Tia moved one of her hands down to my chest, palm over my heart. For a moment, I froze. "Do you want to stop?" My voice was ragged, deep.

"Does it look like I want to stop?" That hand on my chest fisted my shirt and pulled me thankfully closer to her.

I breathed a sigh of relief before diving back into her luscious mouth. My tongue imitated what my dick was craving to do, drawing out groans from both of us.

My hands unclasped her bra, letting her breasts spill out. Stepping back reluctantly from her lips, I looked at her. Tia shivered as her breasts were bared, though she held herself still for my perusal.

She took my breath away. Her breasts were round and firm, her nipples hardening under my stare. Her heated eyes followed me as I devoured her with my eyes, storing this image into my permanent files. This moment in my forever gallery.

"How could I have forgotten this?" I breathed in awe, my hands reaching to cup her.

There was a light pressure as she arched into my hands. Self-consciously, she responded, "I've changed. My body has changed. I've gained some weight."

Shaking my head, I squeezed her tenderly, loving the weight of her. "You are beautiful. Then. Now." To show how much I loved her body and because I really wanted to, my thumbs brushed over her pebbled peaks. Her low moan soothed my nerves.

Touching her was turning me on. I loved the sounds that she made. Her breathy moans when I flicked her nipples, her intake of breath when I leaned down to taste them, her panting when I sucked her into my mouth. I couldn't get enough.

Tia's hands moved over me, plucking at my clothes ineffectively. She was too distracted to make headway. In a frustrated tone, she demanded, "Andrew, please … please … I need to feel you."

"Anything for you, Tia." I stepped back from her, immediately missing her. As I pulled off clothes, Tia sank down onto the bed, her appreciative look making me overeager and clumsy. I was glad she liked what she saw. Her opinions and expectations mattered to me.

When I finally yanked off my boxer briefs and sprung free, Tia's mouth formed an O. An O that made me think about how her mouth could wrap around me. An O that made me think about just how tight she would be around me.

"I think you've gotten bigger." She chuckled nervously.

"I'm hungry for you," I said, stepping closer to her. Her mouth moved toward that part that jutted fiercely at her.

Yes! I wanted almost nothing more than to lean into her warm, wet mouth. Except I needed Tia to want to do this with me again. And again. And again. Because I was never going to tire of her.

Instead, I kneeled before her. I took off her tights and growled at the sight of her tiny red thong. Tia came dressed to play. If this wasn't the first time in a decade, I might have done something more creative, like taken her thong off with my teeth. But it was the first time in way too long, and I was impatient to taste her. I ripped off the thong and threw it somewhere behind me.

"Lie back," I ordered, as I spread her legs.

"Wh-what? What are you—ahhh, oh, Andrew. More, more … please … more …"

Her encouragements pushed me, as I pushed her toward the edge of the cliff. My whole attention was centered on her center of pleasure. I had one goal, and that was to hear her scream my name.

I brought her legs around my shoulders, angling her so I could reach her deeper. Her hands grabbed on to my hair. I could feel her unraveling, her hips undulating wildly. She was almost there, almost at the edge, and judging by the volume of her moans now, about to fly off.

Reluctantly, I pulled away from the sweet depth of her and trailed kisses along her inner thigh. I wanted her begging. I wanted her incoherent.

Propping herself up on her elbows, Tia glared at me. She looked rumpled and sexy and frustrated.

"Andrew! That's not fair … I was so close." I chuckled at her disgruntlement, as I came up to kiss her.

And then I wasn't laughing anymore. Tia's hands grabbed me where I most needed her. "Fuck, that feels good."

Her hand was firm, stroking me up and down, as the other hand played with my balls. Tia had very talented hands. I would never look at her hands the same way again.

Both of us watched in fascination as her hands stroked me. I loved the hunger reflected in her eyes, and I almost came right there when her tongue peeked out to wet her lips. I was not strong enough for this torture. I wasn't going to last if she kept going.

Pulling her hands off of me, I leaned over her body and attacked her hungrily. There was no playing around this time. In the past, I had been too impatient and too focused on my own pleasure. What a fool I had been.

My tongue found her little nub again and flicked lightly on it. Blowing on it, before sucking it in my mouth. That was enough to tip her over. Screaming my name, her hips arched off the bed as she rocked against my mouth, as I tried to prolong her pleasure. I moved up, kissing her while I held her tightly. Tia was beautiful as she lost control. She tried kissing me back, but her kisses were frantic, uncoordinated, interrupted by lingering waves of pleasure.

"Andrew," she gasped, her hands moving to grasp me. "I need you *now.*"

"I didn't bring a condom. Next time—"

"Don't worry. I've learned my lesson. I'm on the pill. Hurry!"

"Impatient, aren't you?" I teased, relieved that I didn't have to wait until next time, as I lined myself up at her entrance. She was so damn wet.

"More, more, more ..."

Heart soaring, I kissed her gently, slowly, as I slid inside of her. We both gasped. She was so fucking tight. And warm.

Sex before had been good. This—I didn't remember it being this amazing ever. I tried to go slowly, to savor this. Until Tia lifted her hips and wrapped her legs around my waist, pulling me deeper into her. "Let go, Andrew," she whispered against my cheek, squeezing my cock with her warm pussy.

I lost control.

There was a beast inside of me that only she could soothe. I drove into her again and again and again. I was mindless to everything except how her body gripped me, welcomed me. "Tia, I can't—I'm going to—" I growled. The tension was building. I was chasing after release even as I wanted to prolong the pleasure for her.

"Let go, Andrew. I'm right here."

I pummeled into her again, spilling my seed inside of her. It was pleasure so intense that I wasn't sure I would survive. I held onto Tia. Her hands stroked my back gently, as if she understood. Collapsing against Tia, our bodies wrapped around each other, for once in my life, I felt peace.

She had chosen me, and I was hers.

CHAPTER TWENTY

TIA

April 10, 2010 (never sent)
Andrew,
Sometimes at night, I dream of you. I wake up wanting and lonely for you.
Ting

I hadn't realized until now how exhausting it was to argue with yourself. You knew all about your own weaknesses and, unlike arguing with others, you couldn't slam the door and leave.

For the first time in over a month, I was finally at peace. The emotional, heart-led part of me had taken over my scared self and made the decision to run toward Andrew. And I couldn't have been happier.

After that tremendous, out-of-this-world, fantastic orgasm, I drifted off to sleep in Andrew's arms. This time when I woke up in bed with my *husband*, I stayed in his arms.

With sleep still hanging over me, I traced the lines of the muscles on his arms, over his chest. Andrew should parade around naked all the time. With me wrapped around him, holding a sign that said, "Hands off. He's mine."

Mine.

I sighed dreamily.

The first sign that he wasn't asleep was the rising, insistent hardness pressing against me. Surprised, I looked at his face.

A smug grin met mine. Oh, how I loved his crooked smiles. Looking relaxed and younger, he kissed me.

Unlike the earlier tempest, this was gentle, slow, as if we had all the time in the world. He was sampling me, exploring the parts that he had missed during his rampage earlier. The tenderness did nothing to slow down the hunger that grew for him.

I wrapped my arms around his neck, my legs around his waist, and rocked against him. Growling, his hands moved to cup my ass, squeezing as he ground against me.

"I need you again, Andrew," I demanded, no longer caring how needy I sounded. I just needed him. Inside of me. Filling me. "Now, Andrew."

Chuckling, he dipped his fingers inside me, drawing out a moan. He growled against my ear, "Tia, you are so wet."

I blushed, but what could I do? Andrew was a sexy, sexy man who knew how to use his tongue and his cock and, now, his fingers. I could be embarrassed by how turned on I was. I could feel how hard he was against me. I squirmed in the bed, trying to get him closer to the part of me that was aching and so, so ready.

Rolling back, Andrew pulled me on top of him. His grin was wicked, as he said huskily, "Use me, Tia. Show me what you like."

And I most certainly did.

The next time that I woke up, it was dark and quiet outside. The bedside clock read one o'clock. Nuzzling closer to Andrew, I breathed him in. He smelled like Irish Spring soap, mint, and something wonderfully familiar.

"You ready for round three?"

Laughing lightly, I propped myself up to look at Andrew. "I think I need more recovery time. You wore me out."

A cocky grin covered his face as he kissed me quickly. His hands roamed over my body as if he couldn't get enough. I knew the feeling. If I had energy, I would have totally felt him up too.

"Besides, don't guys need lots of time in between?" I asked.

"Not if there's a sexy, naked woman in their arms and it's been ten years. I could go for a few more rounds."

"You mean ten years since we last had sex?"

Andrew paused for a half-second before answering, "Yeah, something like that."

"What does that mean?" His evasiveness piqued my curiosity.

"Nothing really, it's been ten years."

"What has? Me or sex in general?"

"In general." His tone was guarded, as if he expected me to judge him.

My mouth dropped, as I sat up in bed and stared at him. That couldn't be it. Andrew was hot, in a slightly unapproachable way, and charming, when he wanted to be, and smart. He was a potent combination.

My brain had to send a stern message to my jaw to pick itself up. "What? How? Are people in Chicago blind? There's a Netflix show where couples date without seeing each other at first, and they still manage to hook up once. Stop laughing! Seriously, what repellant did you use?"

Sitting up so we could be eye level, he ran his hands through his hair, clearly uncomfortable with the subject. In a defensive tone, he said, "I was on scholarships in college and law school, so I had to study a lot to maintain my grades. I worked to pay for my living expenses. It didn't leave me a lot of time to date."

"You didn't go to a party and just randomly hook up with someone?"

"After what we had, it felt cheap to use someone's body to get over you. I didn't, I don't ever want to use others. It's not that weird, okay?"

"Okay, okay." My mind was reeling with the fact that I had been his only. In an age of one-night stands and too many options available with a swipe of your finger, Andrew was an anomaly.

My anomaly.

In a surly and slightly angry voice, he said fiercely, "I hate the thought of you being with anyone else but me. Hate it. I don't judge you. You thought you were divorced. But I hate the thought of someone else knowing you physically, of touching you, of—"

"Shhhh." I kissed him again, running my hands gently along his muscly-arms to soothe his pride. Also, because my hands liked his muscles, and it had been a minute since I had touched him. Andrew relaxed a little into my touch. "I haven't … I mean, I've done stuff. Just not, you know, *sex.*"

Shock colored his face. "How is that possible? I know how that's possible for me. You were engaged. And you look like this. And you are amazing."

I laughed. Then I shrugged lightly. "Physically, for a long time, I wasn't ready. Emotionally, I was scared of getting pregnant again. You know how sometimes, if you are scared of something, that fear grows? I became too scared to have sex. Every time someone would try, I freaked out. I assumed that once I married Clayton, I would feel different."

"Huh. Why me, then? Why now?"

I paused, thinking for a moment. "I don't know. For once, I didn't have questions holding me back. It seemed *right*. I imagine it was similar for you. There was…there is something very *right* about us."

"Undeniably." His admission was hot soup on a wintery day.

Smiling broadly, I joked, "I guess we're both kind of prudes. Would have fit right in during the Regency period."

Andrew's lips quirked. "Would I be the rake that wasn't actually a rake? Do I get to be a duke and have a butler too?"

"As long as I have a lady's maid to bring me hot chocolate in the morning and light my fire," I teased back.

His voice dropping into a deep baritone, Andrew said, "I thought lighting fires was my job." His hands crept dangerously close to my still-naked breasts.

"I accept your offer, sir."

Before his hands reached their destination, he stopped. Pensively, with a tight smile, he asked, "I'd like to not talk about other guys while we're naked in bed together. However, I'm curious—how do you feel about officially cancelling the wedding? Are you okay?"

The conversation with Clayton. Ompf. That felt as if it happened a lifetime ago. In some ways, it had.

"I'm surprisingly okay," I began, swatting his hands away from my breasts. They were too distracting. "I've thought for a while that Clayton wasn't the right choice, even if we didn't work out. I still care about him because he's an awesome guy. But ultimately I chose you, Andrew. You. I have too many feelings for you."

Seeming mollified, Andrew pulled me into his arms and kissed the top of my head. Though I felt bad for breaking up with Clayton, I knew Andrew was absolutely the right decision for me. It had taken a little bit of internal wresting to feel confident in my choice. This time, I didn't want to be in a relationship with Andrew unless I was fully in it. The overwhelming sense of relief mixed with the headiness of being with Andrew only reminded me that I had made the right choice.

In case Andrew wasn't completely convinced how serious I was about starting over with him, I continued, "I've already told the wedding planner, who has cancelled everything. Once I told my parents, they handled all of my Chinese relatives who were planning to use my wedding as an excuse to stockpile US-made purses and vitamins. What, why are you smiling?"

His tentative smile flashed into a big grin, making Andrew's eyes crinkle at the ends. Gah, he was distractingly handsome. And he needed to smile more. He wore smiles very, very well, especially when it was the only thing he was wearing. On a mental Post-it, I added a daily to-do: "Make Andrew smile, or even better—laugh."

"I'm happy," he whispered, his voice dropping, as he framed my face with his big hands. His warm lips sought mine hungrily. It had been too long since he kissed me. He should always be kissing me and smiling. And not wearing clothes.

He pulled away from me, wringing a happy little sigh out of me. His eyes were triumphant and hopeful and something else that I was too scared to define. "I wasn't sure you would tell your parents. I'm glad you did, and I'm happy you're still here."

My answering grin was so wide I could feel my cheeks being squeezed. I said, "Not going to lie, I was terrified. I thought about never telling them. The first night at home, I almost texted Pippa to see if she knew of a casting agent who could hire a Clayton look-alike to go through a fake wedding with me."

Horror shone on Andrew's face, even as one side of his mouth tugged up in the beginnings of a smile.

Giggling at the memory of my late-night frantic googling, I said proudly, "After some major inner dialogue, a fake marriage seemed more work than just telling my parents the truth. So naturally, I did what they used to do to me when they had something serious to discuss. While stuck in a car on the way to a Thanksgiving party, I told them. My mom cried. My dad lectured on my impulsiveness. Then we pretended everything was fine at the party. On the way home, they cried and lectured some more. The next morning, my mom steamed some buns and cut me a pear, and—"

I laughed at the memory of the plate of pears appearing in front of me as I hid in my parents' office. "After that peace offering, I knew everything was going to be okay. They're still confused and upset and have dredged up all of the lectures—poor health, working in a zoo. But at the end of the day, they'll have to deal."

Feeling shy all of a sudden, which was weird since I had been naked in front of Andrew for the past few hours, I whispered, "I had hoped that you would give us a chance. If 'us' was a possibility that you wanted to explore, I had to stand up for us, which I didn't do last time with my parents. I didn't want to *hide* us and have you think I had doubts."

"You're amazing," Andrew said, right before he kissed me again, this time with more urgency. "You're crazy to ever doubt whether I would want another chance." Kiss. "I always want another chance." Kiss. "I'm crazy about you, Tia." Kiss.

Pulling back slightly, Andrew looked at me intently. "Crazy about you, my Ting Ting. You won't regret this." That promise and something infinitely tender in his voice made my heart beat faster.

Words threatened to bubble out, words that I wanted to shout to strangers or add in big caps to my annual, cheesy Christmas e-newsletter. "Merry Christmas! This year, I published a peer-reviewed paper. Oh, by the way, I got the maybe-love-feels for my ex-but-not-really-ex-husband, whom most of you didn't even know about. Surprise!"

Okay, okay, maybe that wouldn't be the best place to make an announcement about Andrew and me. But the thought that Andrew might be in future e-newsletters... filled me with giddy energy.

Ten years ago, both of us were still trying to figure out who we were, beyond who our parents were. Neither of us were comfortable with ourselves. That insecurity had poisoned our relationship. Now, our families and backgrounds were parts of us, not the definition of us.

I was also so very cautious about scaring away Andrew. While he was miles better now at expressing himself, he was not gushy. And all of these unsorted and unspoken words inside of me were full of gush. We were on day one of maybe happily ever after, which meant that I had plenty of time to make him spill his feelings and accept mine. For now, it was enough to just be with him.

Actually, scratch that. I did have one more demand. On that I was much more certain he would accept.

Trying to be sexy, but probably looking funny, I wriggled my eyebrows. "So, how about round three?"

Andrew's laughter burst out. Checkmark making him smile and laugh today. With a small tilt of his head, he drawled out in that sexy, sexy voice of his that made me think of naughty things, "I'm at your service."

CHAPTER TWENTY-ONE

TIA

May 1, 2010 (never sent)
Andrew,
Yesterday, I signed my acceptance letter and sent in the deposit check. I'm off to college in the fall! I want to reinvent myself at college. I'm going to see if "Tia" sticks—she seems like someone confident and happy. No one will ask if my parents own a laundromat or Chinese restaurant (even if my parents technically do, since the ski lodge has a couple of restaurants and laundry service) or ask me how to pronounce my name. I'll go to parties at college, drink while underage, have drunken hookups. Maybe.
But the "Ting" part of me stays with you. It's the part of me that hopes that you are okay. It's even the silly part of me that thinks maybe one day, we'll find our way back to each other. Like I said, silly.
Yours,
Ting, for now

Thursday night, I had my weekly meeting with my teacher's assistants to discuss recitation materials and prep work for finals. Teaching was one of my favorite parts of being a professor. Instead of it taking away from my research, it gave me a much-needed break from hunching over my laptop, three monitors, and cell phone trying to solve the world, one model at a time. And sadly, not the hot-models-with-abs kind.

Modeling and researching the latest AI technologies was a mostly solitary job. Outside of saying hello to coworkers when I went to the bathroom (very brief hellos, because who wants to delay someone from peeing?) or awkward conversations while waiting in line to order food (stop asking me which sandwich I'm getting, because it's always the hot pastrami with mustard), I was locked in my office, with the occasional conference call with my collaborators.

All that to say, I actually enjoyed talking with real humans during class and with TAs during our prep sessions.

Except, not today.

Today, Dave was being his usual indecisive self. Audra had to tell everyone about her Thanksgiving vacation. I couldn't have known more details if I had been binging twenty-four-hour security tapes of her break. Nisha had a five-page typed list of questions and scenarios. I mean, how many times did I need to tell her the probability of a city-wide Internet outage for a week before the final project was exceedingly rare? In fact, students might even be more productive if they couldn't access social media apps with the ability to swap faces or make them sound like chipmunks.

On a normal week, I would have enjoyed the back-and-forth. Today, they were a roadblock to Andrew. After a glorious weekend in Colorado, Andrew had flown back to Chicago for work while I flew to Boston. It had been an exceedingly long four days without seeing him.

Surreptitiously, I glanced at my text messages, trying to hide my smile as I read his last text and wrote back.

Andrew: Getting off the plane now. Can't wait to get you off tonight

Me: Stop it! I'm at school

Andrew: Did I tell you how hot you are when you boss me around? I like a woman on top

Me: I'm going to ignore that comment. What do you want for dinner? I can grab some sushi

Andrew: Nah

Me: Thai?

Andrew: Are you on the menu?

"Professor?"

"Huh?" Face flushed, I looked up, disoriented to see my TAs staring back at me.

"What do you think about assigning groups for the final assignment? I could randomize all of the students and have a list ready tonight." Nisha waited.

"Hmm, that's definitely an option." I gathered my brain cells together, pushing away the lusty thoughts.

Finals. Students. Need to finish ASAP. "I lean toward letting the students pick their own groups though. No matter how randomly you assign them, someone is going to be upset. Let them choose—no need to overengineer."

"Okay." Nisha jotted down some notes and closed her laptop. "That's it for my questions."

"Sounds good. Thanks so much. Email me if you have any more questions. Good night!" Stuffing my laptop in my purse, I practically ran out of the conference room, waving a frantic goodbye over my shoulder.

Even though it was early December, normally I would have walked home and called it my exercise of the day. Tonight, I was too excited to get home. Plus, I could exercise later. Horizontally in bed.

Or vertically. I was not opposed to climbing Andrew.

Ten minutes later, I hopped out of the cab at my apartment building. There, on the sidewalk outside of my apartment building, was Andrew, a suitcase in one hand, and the prettiest gift in the other—takeout.

As if my pants weren't already falling off at the sight of him, his stare heated me up. It was positively inappropriate for public settings.

All of a sudden, I felt overwhelmingly shy. Never mind the flirty texts that we had exchanged for the past few days or the actual sex in Colorado. I was back to being just a girl, standing in front of the boy that I liked. Extremely, extremely liked.

The last time we had talked was a brief, two-minute-thirty-seven-second phone call, where we had talked about logistics of when he would be flying back to Boston. So yeah, seeing him in person after a few days apart was intimidating.

What if Andrew had some sort of epiphany while apart and decided that I was only a booty call? We lived in two different cities with established careers, and had already messed up once. Maybe he thought, *screw it, she's not worth the headache*?

Or what if he met some hot flight attendant on the way here and decided to fly away—

I didn't have time to finish my thought, as Andrew walked over. No, walking was too tame a word. He prowled over, stopping so close that I had to tilt my head up to look at him.

"Hi," he growled, before taking my lips in a needy kiss. His hands framed my face, as his tongue sought mine. This kiss was not gentle. It was dark and heady, as he took possession of me. His hands dropped from my face and pulled my hips firmly against him, showing just how much he missed me.

A low moan echoed in the night air. I pulled back, startled to realize it had originated with me. Against Andrew's chest, I mumbled, "You're not running away with the flight attendant, after all."

"What are you talking about, Tia?" His voice sounded muffled against my hair.

"Oopf, never mind." Waving away his question, I pulled him eagerly into the building.

As soon as the elevator door closed behind us, Andrew pushed me up against one wall, nuzzling my neck. He rumbled, as he sucked gently on a sensitive spot, "I've missed you, Tia."

Warmth pooled low in my body, as I murmured, "I've missed you too. I wasn't sure … Ooh, that feels good. I wasn't sure how … we would be …"

Frowning again, Andrew looked at me. Looking frustrated and a little sad, he asked, "Did you think that we were just fooling around back in the hotel? You're more than a pussy to me."

Inelegant as his confession was, I got the meaning behind his crude words. It was a miniature step forward, and I would take it.

Walking backward out of the elevator and toward my apartment, I teased, "How flattering. I was hoping you'd notice that I had other assets too: boobs, butt, mouth, a torso, face. By golly, did you know that I even have fingers? Ten of them in fact?"

One hand grabbed my wriggling fingers, using that single touch to pull me flush against him. On someone else, it might have seemed aggressive, especially as I didn't love having people in my personal space. When Andrew did it though, I was ready to suggest some silky ropes.

Andrew loosened his grip enough to kiss the palms of my hands, muttering softly, his breath fanning my skin. "Oh, I remember these fingers. In fact, I still have marks on my back from them."

"Shhhh!"

Immediately, I pulled one hand free to fumble for my keys. Andrew was no help and clearly lacked any sort of self-consciousness as he pressed hot, open-mouthed kisses along my neck.

By some miracle, the door opened, as we stumbled inside. Kicking the door shut, Andrew carried me to my bed, his mouth never leaving mine. He stepped away just far enough to strip off both of our clothes, his heated eyes caressing me.

Naked. And he made no move to touch me.

I resisted the urge to cover myself, to cover my flaws. If you asked if I was a confident woman, I would have said yes. Mostly. I knew I was intelligent, a good friend, good at my job, generally nice, occasionally funny. If you called me weird or goofy, I would even agree.

But looks—that was a loaded topic. Physical appearance wasn't something that I talked a lot about as a kid. My parents praised me for good grades. Outside of taking me to the dentist to get braces in high school or making sure that I wore clean clothes, my looks were irrelevant. With guys, outside of Clayton and Andrew, the typical guy who chased after me had some sort of weird East Asian fetish, and their judgment couldn't be trusted.

My brain knew that I wasn't ugly. I was very normal looking. For the most part, I was fine with that. I didn't need to look like a Hollywood star.

However, at this moment, my heart really, really wanted to look like a sexy siren, who could pose confidently on the bedsheets without blushing like a tomato.

A few months ago, in one of those glossy magazines near the supermarket checkout, I read that if you don't point out your flaws, no one would notice. Well, that was bullshit. Unless Andrew's eyesight had soured dramatically in the course of four days, it was impossible for Andrew to miss seeing the not-flat curve of my stomach, or the lack of definition in my arms and legs. Especially when my jiggly parts were next to his tautness. His very swoony abs and that delicious V-shaped tapering pointing straight to—

Averting my eyes, I stared at his shoulder. Ai ya ya, even his shoulders were delicious looking—all smooth muscles. In fact, I was pretty sure that his shoulders possessed muscles that didn't exist in mine. How could shoulders be sexy?

A tortured groan tore from Andrew's lips, as if he was in pain. I chanced a glance at his face. Stark yearning blazed in his eyes as they slowly swept over me. His hands, trembling slightly, touched my body reverently, and he blew out a shaky breath.

Nudging me gently, he turned me over, his hands still tracing invisible paths along my back. My vision was hindered in this position, which only made my other senses hyper focus on his touch.

I wriggled out of discomfort at being displayed like this, and immediately, his hands grabbed at my ass, rougher than before. I tried to make light of this tension-filled situation. "I should have laid off on the milkshake earlier."

Kneading my butt in his strong hands, it took Andrew a moment before he responded, "Why?"

"I eat too many of them, and all of those add up to make my butt too big."

Slap. One hand spanked me, as he admonished, "Stop it, Tia."

I should have been mortified, but it seemed that everything Andrew did made me mortifyingly wet. "Your ass is perfect."

To prove it, Andrew lowered his hips against mine, his dick hard and impossibly large between my cheeks. He chuckled at my soft moan, one hand holding himself up, the other sliding underneath to seek out my center.

"I've missed you too much, Tia. I'm afraid this one will be quick," he growled, kissing the sensitive spot on my neck, as he rocked against me. "I promise, the next one will be better."

"Don't want to wait. Ooh, that's it, right there. Andrew!" My back arched against him, as he slid two fingers, two magical fingers, inside me.

Growling, Andrew lifted my butt, propped a pillow underneath me, and in a swift move, thrust inside of me. It was too deep, and I wanted to weep with pleasure.

He held himself still above me. I could hear him drawing mouthfuls of air to calm himself down. I didn't want him to calm down. I wanted Andrew to lose control. More of the real, needy him, not some restrained version. I wanted quick and hard.

"Move," I pleaded, arching back, and squeezed.

"Fuck!" His whole body stilled. For a moment, I thought he was going to continue to tease me, to tease us. Before I could beg again, Andrew growled, driving into me over and over again, wild and desperate, his fingers finding my center of pleasure. We thundered toward the edge, racing each other to find bliss, our voices rising as pleasure overtook us. There were no soft encouragements or tenderness, only rough promises as he pounded inside of me, shaking what I thought was a sturdy bed. This was madness, and my body welcomed it.

With a scream as I clawed my sheets, I tumbled into mind-warping pleasure. Or did I fly, lifted by bliss? My body was wracked with tremors and wrecked by Andrew, as he spent inside of me.

Le petit mort.

The French had it right. I was floating outside of my body, even as I pulsed with the aftereffects with Andrew still inside of me.

Pulling out gently, Andrew turned us so I lay tucked against his side. "Are you okay?"

I pushed up lethargically to look at him and was surprised to see a shadow of self-consciousness on his face. Whatever I was feeling, Andrew was no more certain of my feelings or us than I was of him.

Tenderness washed over me, as I smiled at him. "Yeah, never better. I missed you since Sunday. And—and for the years before then too."

It took a moment for my confession to sink in. I watched as his expression went from confused, to surprised, to hopeful. Tenderly, Andrew leaned over to kiss me.

Hope wasn't much. It was also a tricky feeling, because it was often misguided and set you up for disappointment. However, at this moment, lying in my bed, with my arms and legs tangled around Andrew, hope was more than enough.

Still groggy from sleep, I opened one eye, squinting in the sunlit room. Instead of spooning me or doing naughty things to my body, Andrew was sitting up in bed, phone in his hands.

Bitterness marred his expression, as he sat there, staring blankly at the screen.

Alarm rose in me, erasing the remnants of sleep. Sitting up, I touched Andrew's shoulder. Startled, he looked at me, quickly clearing away any expression.

He smiled lazily. "Good morning, sleepyhead. How'd you sleep?"

I took his lead, though I was still puzzled. "Tired still. Someone kept me awake last night."

A more genuine smile spread across his face, as he said, "I heard no complaints. In fact, I believe you were loudly enthusiastic."

"Your memory must be failing you. I was not loud."

"Uh-huh, must have been someone else screaming my name, and telling me to go faster and harder."

I blushed as Andrew laughed. It was one thing to be wanton in the heat of it all. It was another, very different thing, to be talking about one's wanton behavior in broad daylight.

"Is everything okay?" I gestured toward the phone still in Andrew's hands.

He turned the phone and placed it on my nightstand, with the screen down. "Everything's fine, just some annoying thing that I have to take care of later. It shouldn't affect us."

"Shouldn't? As in, it might?"

"Won't." His voice was firm, allowing no room for argument.

It was an evasive tactic. On the other hand, he had the right to privacy. I'd only been back in his life for a little bit. Did I really have the right to pry into every facet of his life? There was plenty of time to learn about him. Right now, I needed to trust him.

After a moment, he said, "There's something else I'd like to run by you. I've been thinking. Back in Colorado, we agreed to give our relationship a try. We didn't get into any specifics of how this relationship would work."

"I see. Like where would we live and so forth?"

"Yes." Andrew nodded before getting up. "Hold on. Let me get some paper to write this down. I don't want any misunderstandings."

Comfortable in his skin, Andrew walked butt naked toward his suitcase to grab his notebook. I nearly groaned out loud when he leaned down slightly. His butt had faint red marks from, well, I plead the fifth. But I will say that, my inner muscles were still sore from that *incident*.

"Is this how you win negotiations? By strutting around naked and distracting your opponent?"

Without missing a beat, Andrew bantered, "Only with the special ones."

I threw the nearest pillow at him. Because my arms were weak and the pillow was a dense, memory foam, magical pillow, it landed five feet away from Andrew's feet, drawing his laughter at my lame attempt.

Hesitantly, I asked, even as I hated the thought of us being apart, "Should we date long-distance—"

"No long-distance. We have to be in the same city, as soon as possible. I want to live with you and see you every day, not when we have nothing better to do for a weekend."

His mulish look softened when I nodded enthusiastically. "Okay, which city should we move to? I like my university, but I think I could get another job somewhere. I would need time though to apply and interview."

Looking sheepish, Andrew said, "I spoke to Quinn, my boss, already. He's given the green light for me to relocate, as long as I fly back to Chicago on a regular basis and that I get reciprocity in Massachusetts to practice law, in case he expands Cipher to Boston."

My smile couldn't have been broader, unless my face grew wider. "I like your initiative."

"What can I say? I'm an optimistic guy."

We both cracked up. That feeling of hope was contagious, warming us in our little alcove away from the world. We were in a rose-colored filter where we could blithely arrange our lives as if we were playing with unlimited time, resources, and commitment.

Andrew scribbled a note about living in Boston, his chicken scrawl so familiar and still so hard to read. Tapping his pen against the paper, he said absentmindedly, writing in the margins, "At some point, if we're living in Boston, we'll need a bigger place."

"With bedroom doors so I can slam them if you do something stupid."

"It's inevitable that I'll be an idiot. Until we move, you'll have to contend yourself to slamming your closet doors for now. Now that we'll be in the same city and living in the same place, let's talk about how much time we should spend together."

Confused, I stared at him. "What do you mean? I assume we'll hang out when we're both free."

"How much time? Free time and hanging out are too vague. What does free time mean? Does it mean that you've exhausted all options to do something with someone else? Does getting ready in the morning together or waiting for our coffee to brew check the box for hanging out?" Although Andrew's voice didn't rise, his words were clipped, and I got the feeling that he was trying to hold on to his control.

Ai ya ya. I didn't understand his questions. I mean, I understood the questions literally. I just didn't understand why he was pushing for so many guardrails. Relationships were supposed to be fun, right?

In a light tone to try to diffuse this situation that perplexed me, I teased, "I assume, some days, we'll see more of each other. Some days, we'll probably need more space from each other. Let's not be too prescriptive. Next thing, you'll come up with a schedule for when we have sex."

His voice defiant, he responded, "Maybe we should."

Jumping out of bed, with a blanket to try to cover myself, I stared angrily at him. "Why are you taking the fun out of this? I refuse to let a schedule dictate when I'm in the mood, or set timers for when we are together. 'Oh, it's only been thirty minutes? That doesn't count as hanging out for today.' This is completely irrational."

Arms folded across his unfortunately still distractingly muscly chest, Andrew disputed, "No, this is rational. You don't get a job without signing a contract. Hell, you don't order food online or go on social media without agreeing to some terms and conditions. If this is more important than making sure the right butter chicken was delivered on time, then I fail to see why we wouldn't set parameters for this relationship."

"These aren't parameters. They are prison walls," I pleaded. Was he still so insecure about our relationship and me having doubts that he needed these parameters? I wanted to shake his gorgeous shoulders so he would see how serious I was about us. With or without formal agreements.

Instead, I took a deep breath. And then a couple more. He wouldn't respond to emotional pleas about my feelings. I tried a different route. "As a lawyer, you probably spend most of your time dealing with the gray in a contract. As much as you can lay out conditions on paper, you can never be comprehensive over time. Things change internally within a situation, and things change outside that impact a situation. On top of that, when you have a relationship, as you said, there are too many factors that can't be measured easily. I'd rather have the freedom to figure out our relationship, as things come up, rather than hold ourselves to outdated, indeterminable standards."

Glumly, Andrew looked at me, his jaws clenched as his mouth formed an unhappy line. He stood up from the bed, letting the blankets fall away from his body. "You may want the freedom to figure this out, but I just want to know so I can set my expectations."

Tilting my head to consider him, I took a few more deep breaths. Our relationship was too fragile to survive irrationality and miscommunication. Cautiously, I ventured, "Why do you need to manage your expectations? Why not go into this with high ones?"

After several heartbeats, Andrew sunk back onto the bed, his elbows on his knees, as he looked at the colorful rug underneath his feet. "You've always been more optimistic than me."

"You don't think there's potential here?" My heart was sinking with each word that came out of my mouth. I wasn't an expert at reading people or situations, but I didn't think that I was awful at it either. Who talked about failing at the beginning of a relationship?

"That's not true. I do think there's some potential," said Andrew, still to my rug.

Now, I was getting mad again. What messed-up mixed messages was he sending me? Let's move in together. But oh wait, this relationship is going nowhere. Let's get hopeful. But oh wait, not *that* hopeful—mildly okay is more the speed. One step forward, three steps back, a couple steps sideways, and let's spin around until I'm on my butt looking like a fool.

I glared at the top of Andrew's head in a fit of pique, waiting for him to look up so I could call him out for his heartlessness. But when he did look up, I lost my anger. Because it didn't look as if he was heartless. In fact, he looked as if he had *too* much heart.

Realizing what I was reading in his eyes and looking highly embarrassed, Andrew tried to shrug off the conclusions that I was drawing. Shaking his head, he stood up to pace. He looked cornered, and my heart bled for him…for us.

Tension radiated from him as he walked the length of my studio apartment. Or more like prowled. He seemed furious that I wasn't collapsing at his feet and his so-called contract, but most of all, I could see the heaviness of resignation weighing on him. Andrew was primed to fight or flee, and I was scared he would give up on us.

Equally, I was scared of making the wrong movement, of saying the wrong thing. But when I imagined living another ten years without Andrew, I was terrified of what would happen to me. Can you fall apart twice and still be able to pick up the pieces?

As if the words were torn from him, he said harshly, "I know I have all of these material things now—nice clothes, a car, a house. What if that's not enough? What if you realize that beneath all of that, I'm still the messed-up kid from Colorado whose dad was a criminal? Sometimes, you can't outrun your past."

I stared at him. This new Andrew, whom I had re-met a month ago, was confident, sexy, and used to getting his way. There had been so many positive changes that I hadn't fully seen the prickly, lonely, lost boy that I had met a lifetime ago.

At that moment, I realized how deep his scars were. This wasn't about growing up poor and could be fixed with money. Andrew was still dealing with the emotional trauma inflicted by a dad who made him feel worthless and the judgement that he suffered for years from people in our town who couldn't see beyond his parentage. Maybe he would always have insecurities about his self-worth. *Was I ready to handle this for the rest of my life?*

It was a surprisingly easy decision.

Putting my figurative big-girl panties on, I slowly approached him until we were close enough that our breaths mingled. “Your dad sucks. It would be great if you had a different dad. But, we don’t get to choose our parents. Some people aren’t as lucky.”

Andrew’s eyes sharpened, as incredulity and angry acceptance rippled through his eyes.

My heart threw out the filters and shelters that my brain had built to protect myself, as I spoke without knowing exactly where I was going. “You see, I have really high expectations. The highest. I would like a house in the suburbs with a yard, white fence, and k-kids. I have already put all of my *eggs*-pectations—” I laughed nervously, but Andrew didn’t seem amused. His eyes were still narrowed, as if I were a shady witness on trial. “Um, well, my expectations have already flown, and I can’t tamp them down.”

After a moment of expectant waiting, Andrew spoke slowly and deliberately, his tone unreadable. “I don’t get your analogies. Are you saying that you’ve thrown whatever hopes you have for us away? And who are you looking to buy this house with?”

“Argh!” Exasperated at his stubborn refusal to see the good things in front of him, I threw my flowery blanket at him.

Andrew barely spared a glance at the discarded blanket, though he did take the time to look over my now-naked body, lit up by the morning sunlight streaming through my clearly-not-so-blackout curtains. To his credit, after the brief perusal, he trained his eyes on my face. My eyes were not so disciplined, and even in the midst of a fight, it did not escape me that one part of him was excited for the blanket to fall.

In a raw voice, Andrew asked quietly, “Do I not meet your high expectations?”

“Argh!” Grabbing a nearby pillow off the couch, I threw that at him.

“What are you doing? Stop throwing things at me and explain yourself.”

Another pillow went flying through the air.

“I don’t get it. What am I missing?”

Thump. A third pillow landed against Andrew’s chest. I would have thrown more, but the sight of naked, confused Andrew holding three pink pillows with fringe and pompoms tore laughter from my throat.

Andrew looked as if he had tumbled down a rabbit hole into an upside-down wonderland. He probably thought I was deranged.

Meanwhile, I thought he had never looked cuter or sexier. Which is why I smacked the pillows out of his hand and practically leaped into his arms.

And that was a major mistake. Because it made both of us perfectly aware that we were naked, and that he was pressing up rather urgently against me. Echoing his groan at the deliciously distracting contact, I tried to pull back.

Andrew's arms tightened around me, his head resting against my uncombed hair. It was the sexiest, most comforting hug that I've ever participated in. There was nothing comparable or more intimate than being skin to skin. I could feel his strong heartbeat against my chest, the slight tickling of his chest hair against my soft skin, irritating and arousing me.

"You're blind, you know?" I whispered against Andrew's neck, feeling him shiver where my warm breath touched him.

"No, I'm not. I have twenty-twenty vision."

"The fact that you say that makes you even blinder. I meant, I don't care about your past or who your dad is. I want you." To underline my words, I nipped him on the neck and immediately used my tongue to soothe the little red mark. Andrew stilled beneath me, except for that insistent part that grew impossibly larger against me.

Did I ever think naked hugging was comforting? That was crap. This naked hugging was making me uncomfortably on edge.

Burrowing even deeper against my hair, he said in a hoarse voice, "Ting Ting, I don't want anything to destroy this relationship. I'm scared of losing you. I don't want to get addicted to having you around, only to have you leave me for some white picket fence in the suburbs with another guy. I want reassurances. Because I would choose you every day. If you'll have me."

I leaned back to force him to look at me, to believe my words. "Keep whatever was in your past that made you into this driven, caring, *good* person, and don't let the rest destroy our relationship. Let's not make the same mistakes as before. I promise not to doubt us and not care about what others think, if you don't push me away. Andrew, I want a future with you. All my eggs are in this basket, I've counted all of the chickens, I've milked all of the cows, and made cheese out of the milk, and eaten all of the cheese. All that to say: there's no going back for me. I choose you. Every day, every moment, with every part of me."

My neighbors must be cooking onions right outside the door as punishment for the noise that we made last night, because how else could I explain why my eyes were prickling and we were both blinking rapidly?

In typical, understated Andrew fashion, he muttered, "That's good to know. Couldn't you have just said that earlier?" But the lightness driving out the storm in his eyes severely undermined his restrained words.

"I did tell you. Remember the basket of eggs-pectations floating in the air?"

"Right, right. Completely clear. You should work on your analogies. Baskets, milk turning into cheese. Also, use more pronouns. Like 'I would like to have a house with *you.* I have high expectations for *us.* How did I ever survive without *your* amazing cock?'" he teased, walking us backward toward the bed.

"My fingers are pretty good substitutes."

Andrew stumbled, his eyes blazing. In a guttural voice, he demanded, "Show me."

"Another time," I promised, blushing at the thought of him watching. To hide how much that image turned me on, I grabbed his face to rain frantic kisses wherever I could reach. His lips, his shadow of a beard from not having shaved yet, his earlobe where he was sensitive.

Andrew chased my lips, slowing down the pace, teasing me with passionate yet unhurried kisses. This was a different Andrew, patient as if he had all the time in the world. As if we had all the time in the world to be together.

At the edge of the bed, he slowly lowered us, taking care not to break contact between our bodies. So close that I could feel the movement of his lips, he bargained, "How about a low-maintenance house with a fence, and we'll buy vegetables at a farmer's market? I want to be realistic about how much time we'll have." He sucked the bottom of my lips, drawing out a moan from me. "Because I fully intend to keep you very, very busy doing other things."

True to his word, Andrew proceeded to show me just how he would keep me busy. It turns out, I had lied. My fingers were no substitute whatsoever for his fingers nor his mouth nor that very hard, deep, all-consuming part of him that he used to fill me over and over again.

CHAPTER TWENTY-TWO

TIA

May 10, 2010 (never sent)
Andrew,
I was looking at classes today. There are so many interesting ones that I could take. I'm surprised that I'm excited. I think I'm going to sign up for something impractical, like painting. Who knows? I may turn out to be the next Picasso.
Yours,
Tia

Bliss.

There was no other word to describe those first two weeks of December. Except maybe, unconditional, profound, utter bliss. There was a newfound contentment and *settlement* in my relationship with Andrew. Not "settle for a second choice." No, "settle" as in, we had found our home within each other, surrounded by a bone-deep sense of rightness.

For Andrew, the doubts that he initially felt seemed to fade with each day that we spent together. He lingered over coffee, he teased, he was self-deprecating without being defensive. He seemed finally at ease.

Once a week, Andrew flew to Chicago for work. He would fly on the six a.m. nonstop on Tuesday mornings, and land back at Logan at ten p.m. on Wednesdays, exhausted from the marathon meetings and work that he crammed into those two days. The other days, he worked from my apartment or a local café while I reluctantly headed off to campus.

I never realized how indecisive I was or how inefficient I was at work, until I had Andrew to hurry home to. Instead of worrying about what I would say in an email to my department chair, or second-guessing a model assumption, I zoomed through my day. It was as if being around Andrew had fine-tuned me.

The first Saturday after Andrew had moved in, I dabbed some bright red lipstick on top of my ear, grabbed my easel, art supplies, and giant thermos of chai, and headed out to the Charles River to meet up with Pippa.

It was easy to spot Pippa, as she was wearing a crown of flowers and a bold red scarf, in a sea of black- and gray-clad runners. A giant unibrow had been painted across the middle of her forehead.

"Frida Kahlo?"

She nodded happily, twirling and shaking her flower crown at me. Pippa glanced at my brown, boxy suit and raised an elegant eyebrow. "I thought we agreed the theme this week was famous artists. You look like you're going to work and want everyone to forget you have boobs."

Amused and exasperated, I pointed to my fake bloody ear. "See this?"

"Ohhh, you're van Gogh. I like it!" Costumes out of the way, Pippa gave me a big hug. Normally it took me a couple cups of tea and a glass of wine before I could properly ignore passersby, but today, nothing could get me down.

"I've missed our weekly boozy tea parties, Pippa," I told her as we quickly set up the easels on the grassy area next to the river. "You need to plan your world travels around our tea parties and stay in Boston more."

"Bah, when there's nothing exciting happening in my life, I have to travel to find something amusing," she said, one hand holding a tiny teacup and the other a water bottle that smelled suspiciously like a mimosa. "So tell me, is Andrew great in bed? He looks it, you know. All that dark and handsome broodiness."

"Pippa!"

"Tia! It's been so long that I just want to live vicariously through you. Does he eat you up? Are his hands magical? Does he dirty talk? C'mon, spill, pun sort of intended."

Shaking my head, I bit the inside of my jaw to keep from grinning like a Cheshire Cat. Just remembering how he had spread me like a feast inside the shower this morning was enough to make me discard my scarf. Who knew Boston winters could be so warm?

"Wow, that good, huh? So how long are you planning to keep him?"

Confused, I asked, "What do you mean? I think we have a real chance to make the marriage work this time around."

Incredulous green eyes stared at me. "Really? You think there's a future with Andrew? I know you're married still, but I figured that once you got him out of your system, you'd proceed with the divorce."

"Why does he just have to be someone I use for sex? Why can't I want to be with him for him?" My heart hurt for Andrew. If this kind of belittling and being reduced to his looks was what Andrew faced, no wonder he wanted a pseudo-contract to spell out our expectations. No wonder he had been blind to the fact that I wanted to be with him.

I knew Pippa wasn't intentionally mean, but darn it if I was going to let my best friend write him off. "Andrew is amazing. He has so many great qualities. He's smart and ambitious, he can be funny, he's thoughtful, he feels deeply, and he takes care of his mom."

Face frozen in a seemingly permanent incredulous look, Pippa countered, "There are tons of guys who fit those qualities. Those should not be unicorn traits. Those should be baseline expectations."

Beyond frustrated, I near shouted, "Sure, statistically, those are not rare qualities. I just—I don't know how to describe Andrew's … I love the vulnerability that he tries to hide, and I love that he allows me to peek inside of his walls. I love that he's been able to defy statistics and be what he is today. I love the way that he needs me and is comforted by me, because I think that I'm really good for him. Just as he lifts me up and makes me realize that I am powerful and special. Pippa, he's *it* for me. He's always been it for me. I don't know *why* he's it. I just know that Andrew engages something within me that has nothing to do with sex or surface quality. It's as if my soul recognizes his, and he's able to unlock this scary depth of emotions. Yet, I know that he'll keep me safe."

Eyes softened, Pippa looked at me sympathetically. "You're still in love with him, Tia. Have you told him?"

"Not yet." Smiling tremulously, I laughed, feeling suddenly free. "I've been scared of falling for him again, except I've already fallen. Why are you looking at me like that? You should be happy for me."

Her sympathetic expression turned into a grimace, before she busied herself with chucking her tea, followed by large gulps of mimosa.

"What now, Pippa? Your turn to spill."

Pippa drank the last of her mimosa, her face contorted in misgivings. "Are you sure you want to hear this? You look so happy. Maybe it's better if you go home to Andrew now."

"Yes, I want to know if people are gossiping about me or Andrew."

"You know I'm on your side, whatever you decide to do," Pippa said.

"Tell me, Pippa," I insisted.

"Okay, fine. I was in Chicago for a client meeting. I stayed at the Lenox Hotel. It just opened. Very chic, really dark on the inside—"

"As much as I usually enjoy hearing about your travels, I still don't get why you're telling me this." The sinking feeling in my stomach was swiftly replaced by irritation.

"Okay, okay—here goes." Pippa took a deep breath and plowed ahead, her voice speeding up so fast that I had trouble catching her words. "I saw Andrew leaving the hotel with a brunette. They left before I could react, but it was definitely him."

"Are you sure it was Andrew? You said the lighting was dark. Or even if it was Andrew, maybe he works with her. If she's a celebrity, he might be working on her security contract," I protested. When I told Andrew that I wanted to be with him, I meant it. We wouldn't last if I started falling apart at every rumor that came our way.

Pippa looked as if she felt sorry for me. "Why are they meeting at a hotel? They weren't having a business lunch in the hotel restaurant. They were coming from the elevators that led to the condos on top of the hotel. And, it looked as if they were trying to be discreet. The woman was wearing a baseball cap and sunglasses, inside."

Pippa's arms rose a bit as if she was going to hug me but thought better of it. "I'm so sorry. That's why I was hoping this would just be a fling on both sides. Maybe it's nothing. Has he been acting weird?"

That stopped me. I thought back to the mysterious call a couple weeks ago. Or the multiple times that I had seen him texting someone, only to turn off his phone when I got closer. He said that it was nothing to worry about. I wanted to trust him. Yet, all I could imagine was Andrew with a mysterious brunette.

Did I really know him? Did I really know what his life was like in Chicago? Did he actually go to Chicago for work? This was the age of Zoom and Webex and any number of video conference services. Why couldn't he have his client meetings virtually? Was work an excuse to live a double life? *Maybe it was just Charlie. No, she's blonde. Who the heck was this woman? Remember, his dad was a con man. Maybe it runs in his blood. No, no, no ...*

I sank down to the cold grass. My mind was numb. *Stupid. I am so stupid.* All I knew was that Andrew had lied to me again. He had either outright lied or lied by withholding something. Why couldn't he open up to me? I had been thoroughly conned, while he must have been laughing his ass off at how stupidly naïve I was.

Fudge expectations.

CHAPTER TWENTY-THREE

ANDREW

July 1, 2009
Ting Ting,
You're with me in bed sleeping, so I'm not sure why I'm writing this note to you. Except I guess, I wanted a chance to sign this letter as your official husband. Seeing the ring on your finger doesn't feel real. Having you all to myself doesn't feel real.
I'm scared to sleep, because I know I'll wake up as nobody again. I tell myself that it's okay—we'll make it, despite the odds. How could we not? There is no option but to make this marriage work. Because not having you in my life is not an option.
So sleep, love. I'll join you soon.
Your official husband,
Andrew

My life was too good. My work was going smoothly. Boston was growing on me. Most of all, my relationship with Tia was indescribably amazing.

Fairy-tale endings or miracles didn't happen to regular guys like me. Years away from my father had given me enough confidence that I knew that I deserved better than what I had the first seven years of my life. Education—attainable. Good, steady job—attainable. A home—attainable. Small circle of friends—attainable. Even a nice, steady woman who could offer companionship—on optimistic days, even this was attainable.

This joyful state I was in? No, euphoria and constant smiling were not for me.

I was scared shitless.

My phone dinged to signal a new text. I had barely read the name of the sender when my phone buzzed in my hand. Groaning internally, I accepted.

"Andrew?" The voice was thin and sounded muffled, as if she didn't want anyone to overhear.

"Hi."

"Sorry for calling you. I have to see you."

"I think you should stay in Chicago. We'll figure something out."

"I'm just going crazy over here, Andrew, trying to hide this all from Will." Sigh. I could hear her thinking over the phone.

I hated the lost quality in her voice. Most of all, I hated the secrets we had to keep. "I'll figure something out. Give me a couple more days."

"Okay, I trust you." It was misplaced trust. I had nothing figured out.

"Don't come to Boston. I don't want Tia to know. Okay?"

"Okay. Bye."

"Bye."

The phone beeped off.

This was a fucking mess. I rubbed my forehead with a fist, as I sorted through scenarios and possible solutions. The problem was that there was none.

Lost in thought, I turned away from the floor-to-ceiling window near the bed to make some more coffee in the kitchen. I stopped cold.

There, pressed against her door, face ashen was Tia. *Fuck, how much did she hear?*

She recovered quicker than me, and in a low, robotic voice, she asked, "Who was that? Pippa said that she saw you in Chicago with a woman. Was that her? What don't you want me to know, Andrew?"

For a moment, I debated not saying anything—let Tia think the worst. Once everything was solved, I would confess everything to Tia and hope that she wouldn't run from me again. But, I couldn't stand the hurt look in her eyes, and I didn't want to make the same mistake as ten years ago.

"Tia, it's not like that. I saw Charlie when I was in Chicago this week."

"I thought she was blonde?" Relief and suspicion warred on her face.

"She is," I insisted. "She wore a wig."

"Why?" Suspicion seemed to be winning.

"Her parentage isn't common knowledge. To this day, I'm not even sure if her dad knows. Because of her parents and who she's married to, she gets photographed sometimes."

"Okay. So, what's up with the weird phone calls, then?"

Fuck. "What do you mean?"

"Was that Charlie on the phone? You told her that you didn't want me to know. What's the secret?"

I hesitated. That was the wrong move.

"That's how it's going to be, huh?" Sadness shone in Tia's expressive brown eyes. "You've been furtive about texts too. Sometimes when you get a text, your face gets really dark and angry, and then you go outside. You told me that it's about work, but I don't think so."

She thought for a moment, her nose crinkling. "You have a different look when work texts or calls come in. Also, I've seen you in the middle of the night on your personal laptop, not your work laptop. There's something else you're not telling me. I know you well enough to know when you're hiding something big."

"I will explain."

Her right eyebrow rose a fraction.

"Later," I finished lamely. I knew I should tell her now. *Will she stay if she knew the mess that I was in?* It wasn't a chance that I wanted to take.

"When Pippa told me that she saw you in Chicago with the brunette, I cried like a fool. And then, you know what? I thought, I didn't trust you last time and jumped to conclusions. This time, we're both adults. I'll act like a reasonable, mature person, and come to you first. I appreciate that you told me part of it, but partial truth isn't enough anymore."

"It's not that I don't want to tell you. I promise, I'll tell you the rest after this is—after I handle this." I reached out to her, to close the physical distance.

With every step I took toward her, Tia pressed herself even tighter against the door. As if she pressed hard enough, she'd be able to escape to the other side of the door and out of my life.

There were those tentacles with thorns again crawling and destroying my insides. I could tell Tia. I wanted to tell Tia. It was at the tip of my tongue to tell Tia.

No, she would never stay when she saw how ugly this was. No one would choose to be part of this. Fight for her afterwards.

That thought stopped me. I bit my tongue so hard that I could taste the metallic tang of blood. Still, I kept my mouth firmly pressed shut, lest stupid confessions came out.

Looking sad and with something that looked despicably like pity, Tia said, "I want to trust you. I want to wait for you to tell me whatever is happening, even if it's horrible. But why should I trust you if you refuse to trust me? Why should I put myself out there and look like a fool, if you still refuse to let me in? It's not a real relationship without that foundation."

"This is the realest relationship that I've ever been in." That was the miserable truth. Even as I could feel our relationship crumble before me, Tia had been and was still the bedrock on which I rested.

"I ran away ten years ago because I was too insecure and scared to fight for us. Andrew, I'm walking away today because I'm standing up for us." She held up a hand to stay my words. "I'm walking away to give us time to think. I need to calm down, and you need to decide whether you're all in. I know that I am great and that I have lots to give. It's taken me a long time to realize that, and I won't shortchange myself."

"Tia, stay." My vision blurred with fear. I heard her words, and some part of my brain even understood where she was coming from. It didn't mean that I was any less petrified that I would never see her again. My insides tore with every shake of her head and the resolution in her eyes.

She said, "If you want us to have a real chance together, you need to show both of us that you're ready to fight for us, that you're willing to let me in, and trust that we can work through anything. You stay here for as long as you need. I'm going to head to Pippa's. I'll call you soon."

Before I could unstick myself, Tia slipped out of the door. The click of the latch closing behind her echoed in my head, until I could hear nothing but that final echo and see nothing but the pity and dejection in her eyes. It was worse than straight-out rejection. Pity was just drawn-out rejection, because who wanted to be with someone they felt sorry for?

Frustrated, I threw my phone across the room. It did nothing for the emptiness that was overwhelming me, so I punched the wall. Fucking bad idea. The exposed brick wall did nothing to alleviate my bad mood except give me bloody knuckles on top of it.

Feeling trapped by the walls of the apartment and judged for the mess that I was in, I did the one thing that usually helped—I ran.

CHAPTER TWENTY-FOUR

ANDREW

September 1, 2009 (torn, never sent)
Ting Ting,
Please come back.
Yours forever,
Andrew

That day, I ran ten miles. Afterward, I threw myself into work. Exhausted, I slumped into fitful sleep on Tia's couch. I couldn't bear to sleep in the bed when she was so conspicuously gone. Yet, I couldn't bear to leave the apartment in case she came back.

On Sunday, I ran eight miles, showered, and went to a nearby church service. The peace that service usually gave me lasted only until lunch. I ran another five miles and threw myself into work again. Exhausted once again, I slept on the couch. The couch was just under six feet, which meant that I slept scrunched for the second night in a row, dreaming of Tia's pitying, judging eyes.

On Monday, I got up at four a.m. to fly to Chicago, barked at my colleagues, argued with my clients, and was a general ass. Before heading back to O'Hare to fly back to Boston, I stopped by my colleague Alex Greene's office. Hacker extraordinaire, with a more-than-occasional willingness to stray over lines that he'd claim he didn't know existed. I spent at least twenty percent of my time trying to convince him that he needed to stop doing whatever quasi-law-blurring thing he was working on and bailing him out of whatever trouble he found himself in because he found some clever loophole that still managed to piss people off.

As per usual, I dropped off my cell, laptop, and backpack in the box before his office door. Experience taught me it was either that or have Alex go through my stuff and take out batteries, SIM cards, memory cards, or whatever he deemed was hackable.

Barely sparing me a glance from his multiple monitors, his fingers flew over the keyboard as he said, "You look awful, Parker."

"Thanks."

Eyes narrowed on me for a moment before turning back to rows of code. "You're being sarcastic."

"Did you find anything?"

"No." Alex's fingers paused over the keyboard, brows furrowed.

Dread lodged low in my stomach. Alex was my best shot at getting out of this mess, and if he couldn't find anything, I was fucked.

A moment later, he amended his statement. "Not yet. I'll send a message if I do. When I do."

"You could just text or call me."

One dark brow rose in disbelief. "Risk someone hacking it? No, I prefer the advice column in the *Chattanooga Times* better. Don't forget to use the latest encryption code. It was in last week's *Des Moines Register's* yard sale section. You know what happened when you used the wrong code last year. Anybody could have read your text."

For the first time since Saturday, I laughed. "Duly noted. It was a rookie mistake. Thanks, Alex, for doing this."

"It's what friends do, right? Help each other? At least that's what my wife says."

My flight ended up getting cancelled that night. Winter plus Chicago equaled delayed and cancelled flights. Opting to stay at a hotel overlooking a tarmac, I stayed up until three in the morning working on a particularly tricky contract. Two hours later, I was back in the terminal only to hear that my six o'clock flight had been delayed until eight, then nine forty, then noon, and ultimately one in the afternoon.

Exhausted from the lack of sleep the night before and from waiting in the airport while trying to work with shitty Wi-Fi, I promptly fell asleep as soon as the plane took off.

It was close to four by the time I got back to Tia's apartment. Silence met me, heavy and morose. The absence of Tia followed me like an unwanted shadow. There was no peace to be had here. Only reminders that I had screwed up. The probability of convincing her to forgive me after I solved the mess was diminishing.

"Fuck."

Grabbing my coat, I locked up and headed down the stairs. I walked briskly through the crowds of people heading to subway stations and parking lots, past stalled cars navigating the crooked streets built before city planning was the norm, past joggers on the Harvard Bridge toward Cambridge. It was an ironically named bridge, as it actually led to MIT. As Tia had told me with a laugh, it was 364.4 smoots long, where one smoot equaled the height of some MIT frat guy named Smoot.

It was a stupid way of measuring things.

Yet I loved that Tia had giggled uncontrollably when she described how a bunch of probably not sober frat boys carried one of their brothers along the bridge, armed with measuring tape.

I hated the silliness of women giggling. It reminded me of how kids gossiped about me when I was younger. Yet, I loved Tia's giggles.

I loved that she pointed out every random store from her apartment to the university, as if she had personally visited each one of them, as if each one was important. I loved the way that her fingers wound around mine as we walked around the city after dinner, tightening when she saw something interesting. I loved how she felt, tucked under my shoulders, and the light in her brown eyes as they gazed up at me.

It had been seventy-five hours since Tia had walked out. Seventy-fucking-five hours of limbo hell. Memories of her were starting to feel like unachievable dreams, not reality, and that scared the shit out of me.

It was almost five when I arrived on campus. It was more deserted than I had ever seen, given that this was the last week of finals. There were a few groups of students walking through the long hallways, stress written on their faces. I walked toward the lecture room that Tia taught in. She had mentioned last week that she was planning to hold extra office hours to answer any questions while her students worked on their final project.

Opening the door to the large lecture hall, I spotted Tia immediately. She was shorter than most of the students clustered around her. Despite that, there was a quiet, commanding presence as she held court over the stream of steady questions.

As I watched Tia, who hadn't yet spotted me, one person at the edge of the large room caught my eye. In a room full of young students writing down every single thing that Tia was saying, there was one person who wasn't participating. Like me, he was watching her carefully.

The hairs at the back of my neck prickled. I didn't know why, but I didn't like how he watched her. There was something too still about how he sat, too out of place.

Without a plan, I walked slowly in the man's direction. A few rows away, he turned toward me suddenly, a smirk on his face, as if he were waiting for me. Expecting me.

It couldn't be.

My heart dropped as my eyes flew to Tia. I must have made some sudden movement, for she finally glanced my way, her surprised eyes catching mine, before we both looked at the other man. As if this was the most natural place for him to be at, he winked at me and exited out a side door.

Pushing a couple students to the side, I rushed over to Tia, my hands patting her down. "Are you okay?"

"Andrew, what's going on?" Surprise laced her voice. Surprise, not fear. I forced a deep breath in an attempt to calm down.

"Hey, man, she doesn't keep answer keys on her."

"Yeah, wait your turn if you have questions."

I turned toward the voices. There was more unfounded concern over me getting an unfair advantage on the final project than alarm over the strange man in the lecture hall. Maybe I was the one going crazy.

Whispering low against Tia's ear, I warned, "Stay here," before bolting across the room. The side exit let me into an empty area near some study rooms filled with students cramming for exams. A few stray students and faculty wandered around. There was nothing out of place—just the regular bustle of a university before winter break.

I was the one out of place, searching for that conniving, sly face that resembled mine. I was officially losing it. My fear of my past taking over my present was making me see things. Sleep. I needed more sleep.

Feeling ridiculous, I walked back toward the lecture hall. My phone buzzed and I absentmindedly glanced at it. It was an unknown number, but the message left no doubts who had sent it. "It was easy finding your professor. I can visit again or not. It's up to you."

"Fuck!"

Heart pounding, I raced inside the lecture hall, only to find a few scattered students still debating model assumptions. Tia was nowhere to be seen. Practically shouting at the students, I demanded, "Where is she? Where is Tia?"

"You mean Professor Wang?"

"Dude, chill out."

"She's probably in her office."

"Did she say you can call her Tia? She doesn't allow us to call her that. Do you think it matters for grades?"

Barely hearing the trail of questions behind me, I made a beeline for Tia's office, cursing the lax security on campus. My mind was filled with images of her hurt, her cornered, her scared. My long strides ate up the distance. *Shit, shit, shit.* She would be alone in her office. Unprotected.

Alarm sped up my feet, until I gave up all pretense and sprinted down the hallways toward her office. The door to Tia's office was ajar. I could hear movements inside.

Prepared for the worst, I reached to push the door open, just as it swung wide, revealing a startled Tia. Her pink lips parted into an O, as she stared at me greedily.

I looked behind her, my shoulders drooping with relief at the empty chaos of her office. Not able to resist any longer, I pulled Tia into my arms, breathing in her scent.

Her heavy book bag dropped to the floor, as her arms slowly wound around my neck, stroking my hair as if she instinctively knew I needed comfort. *Her* comfort.

"Are you okay?" Her voice was a balm for my lonely soul.

I was ruined.

I needed her.

I needed to show her how much she meant to me, how critical she was to my existence. So I did, the only way I knew how.

CHAPTER TWENTY-FIVE

ANDREW

September 2, 2009 (torn, never sent)
Ting Ting,
I miss you. Don't hate me. I promise it's better that we're not together. You can be more *without me.*
Still yours forever,
Andrew

My lips found Tia's, desperate for her to respond, elated when she let out a tiny gasp before her hands yanked me by my jacket inside her office, slamming the door behind us. I turned us so Tia's back was against the door, while I pressed my body against hers.

I told myself to slow down, to be gentle, to not scare her. But it was impossible when she moaned against my lips. That little sound scorched my skin. I was frantic for her.

More.

I could never get enough. My heart, my body, my soul were imprinted by her, and wherever she was, I was destined to chase after her.

Minutes, maybe hours later, I gentled the kiss, my initial urgency soothed by Tia's responses. Pulling up for air, I gathered her close to me, holding her gently, a dichotomy to the violent beating of my heart.

Her light laugh sounded muffled against my neck. "This is a nice surprise. Making out isn't very professor-like. My students might actually think that I have a life outside of their grades. Hopefully no one heard us."

I kissed her temple, my lips curving up in a small smile. "You'll know if sign-ups for your class skyrocket next semester."

"Or I get put on probation for inappropriate behavior. Tia's Smoky BBQ might have to become reality, if I get fired. Be prepared to eat all the burnt food and lie to me about how great it is."

"I'd rather save my stomach from your cooking. If you get in trouble, you can blame me and my charm."

"What? You mean the lack of it?"

I laughed. It felt so good to be with her. Kissing her was great, but beyond that, laughing and talking with her was balm for my heart.

Tia's eyes softened as she looked me over, as if re-exploring me. "I'm glad you came to me. I missed you."

"Why didn't you call me?" My voice was teasing, even as my heart balanced on a precipice, waiting for her response.

"Waiting by the telephone anxiously, have you?"

"On pins and needles."

Dropping her half-smile, she sobered. "I wasn't ready. No, that's not right. Actually, I wasn't sure if you were ready, and I couldn't bear it if you told me … Anyways, you're here. I'm so happy you finally decided to come tell me the truth."

There was a sense of expectancy in her tender gaze. I winced internally. I was an ass. Fully prepared for a slap in the face, I tried to put a positive spin on my words. "I'm sorry. I missed you and needed to see you. But I'm still trying to figure out something, and I think, I *know* I can get it under control. Then I'll tell you everything."

If someone had popped a balloon with the words "Tia's hopes" written on it, it wouldn't have been clearer how disappointed she was. Her voice was almost pleading. "Let me help. You don't have to solve everything by yourself. I am strong enough to help you take on the burden."

"No!"

Tia recoiled at the vehemence in my voice, looking hurt and small. I softened my voice. "Sorry. You don't understand. I don't want you involved in this shit."

"Why?" she asked determinedly. "Is it dangerous?"

"Not physically."

"Are you doing anything illegal?"

"I'm not planning to go to jail."

Her eyebrows furrowed. "That's an evasive answer. I don't like it."

"I don't care if you like it or not." I thought of the man in the lecture hall, my anger and fear rising. Not fear for me. I could take care of myself. "I care about keeping you away from this. It's messy and sordid. You shouldn't have to deal or be exposed to this. It's enough that he showed up on campus. I—"

"Who is *he*? Wait, does this have to do with the guy you chased down? He's just a parent whose kid is looking at MIT."

"You talked to him?" My lungs felt too full.

Shrugging, Tia said, "Not really. I did an admissions panel earlier today for prospective students and their families, and he was there. What's going on?"

"Nothing. Forget about it. Trust me to—"

Bitter laughter welled up, as Tia nailed me in place with her disappointment. "Trust you. I do trust you, which is why I'm still talking to you. The problem is that you don't trust me. You don't *trust me* to know myself. You don't *trust me* to make my own decisions about what I want and what I can handle. All my life, I've gone along with decisions other people have made for me because they thought they knew better. And I let them, because it was easier. Well, not anymore. Just like I won't let my parents' opinions of you dictate what I should do, I don't want you to tell me what I should think or do, out of some unnecessary desire to protect me."

Frustrated, Tia sighed. Glumly, she picked her bag from the floor and turned off the office lights. I forced myself to stay still, to let her go.

I was making the right decision. I had to believe that. Once this whole thing was over, Tia would be glad that I had kept her out of it. Then, we could make a proper start to our relationship.

I had never wanted anything more than Tia now, but seeing her disillusion weakened my resolve. Although she didn't say it, she was disappointed in me. I hated letting her down.

However, I didn't claw my way into a top law school and my current job without an eye on the future. And Tia was undeniably my future. Which meant that I had to put my past to rest, before I could present myself to her.

Deal with the mess first—don't bring Tia into it. The refrain ricocheted around my brain, pounding the reminder when my hands started to reach for her.

Buttoned up in her puffy coat, Tia turned to me at the darkened entrance of her office. Looking wounded, her voice wavered as she said, "Andrew, I'm not giving up on us, you know? I'm not fragile. Whenever you're ready to come to your senses, I'll be ready. Until then, I don't think it's a good idea for us to see each other. Physical intimacy isn't a replacement for trust in a relationship."

Tia opened up the door and waved me through.

I was officially dismissed.

The next few days crawled by. I was now well-versed in the sketchy happenings of Des Moines and Chattanooga, after poring through newspaper wanted ads looking for a message from Alex. I found a man looking for a live-in masseuse with big assets, a couple trying to loan out their twin crying babies for anyone who wanted experience with parenthood, and way too many sketchy jobs that promised lifelong fulfillment and great pay.

Still, no message from Alex.

Charlie called daily, despite me telling her to wait. I couldn't blame her. We were in this mess together, tied by our blood to our dad's threats. There was a weird bond that existed between us from these secrets. We brainstormed ways to get out of this and discussed fall-out plans, usually until Charlie's husband came home from work. Then, she would promptly whisper goodbyes and hang up.

These secrets and trying to get out of them unscathed were my obsessions during the day. At night while I slept, my brain forgot that I was trying not to think about Tia. At daybreak, I would wake up, disoriented from vivid dreams of her. Then I would remember that I was alone.

The smell of Tia's fruity lip gloss lingered in bed. The scent lingered as I worked from the apartment, until I missed her so fucking much that I physically ached. To escape, I would flee to a nearby coffee shop to work. Then, I would miss her scent and scurry back to the apartment. It was a vicious, draining cycle.

My resolve to stay away from Tia was threadbare. Every day, the thought of lying at her feet, with my secrets exposed for her to stomp on, gained appeal. Assuming Tia stayed once she knew my secret.

Worthless piece of shit who'll never amount to anything. Memories, I corrected myself. They were only memories. I wanted to hide in a dark corner, like I used to as a kid, instead of facing rejection.

Because that would hurt the most, wouldn't it? It was one thing to have a relationship fall apart because you didn't open up. It was a completely different thing to have your partner reject you for who you really are. Like a stamp that said, "Rotten Core."

For most of my life, fear had driven my decisions. Fear of my father made me be quiet, stay out of sight. Fear of being poor and going without food made me work hard in school. Fear of commitment made me only date women whom I had already mentally crossed off as potential partners.

Fear was a good motivator and had served me well in life. But in this case, fear of Tia walking away kept me from picking up the phone. Fear of her rejection kept me from running to her, even as I was starting to see a glimpse of what a real future for us could be like.

By Friday, I was no longer sure why I had insisted on keeping the secret from Tia in the first place. The stress of the situation was getting to me. I wanted to share my stress and anxiety with my wife, and trust that she would stand by me. I wanted someone to lean on, and in return, I was warming up to the idea of being someone else's rock.

Back in high school, I had once found what looked to me like a dead potted orchid in a dark coat closet in Tia's house. Shrugging as if this was the most natural thing, Tia had explained that taking away sun for a short period was a last-resort way to shock the orchid's system into blooming. I didn't know if that was true or one of the random things that Mrs. Wang made up, but that story stuck with me.

I felt like the orchid that was being shocked. I was deprived of my light. In return, I was undergoing some type of brutal transformation, forced to deal with ugly truths.

I had been given a second chance with Tia, and I was wasting it. I thought keeping her away would protect her and save our relationship, but I was starting to realize what a shadow of a relationship we actually had. Tia had mentioned that she was ready to go all in, which meant that she wasn't yet. Or maybe she was, and I wasn't ready to accept everything she had to offer.

If experiencing only a part of her was the best thing in my life, what would the totality of her be like? What would the totality of *us* be like?

For the first time, I understood her frustrations. Like the smart person she was, Tia could see the potential for something even better. Me being in a figurative closet without the sun was forcing me to see above the "now" and grasp that there might be something even better if we both let ourselves fall.

I sunk down onto Tia's bed and leaned over to smell her pillow. The one that was near the windows, because she wanted to wake up in the mornings with sun on her face. The scent of Lip Smackers and her lavender shampoo were still there. At some point, they would fade away. At some point, I would have to do laundry. But it lingered today.

"Fuck." My curse rebounded, punching me in my senses.

I was a grown-ass man smelling pillows. "Pathetic fool."

My fingers dialed Charlie's number before fear stopped them. "Charlie? When can you get on the next flight?"

CHAPTER TWENTY-SIX

TIA

June 5, 2010 (never sent)
Andrew,
I found out that one of my friends from Beijing will be a sophomore at Harvard. I think you'd find Pippa fascinating. It's funny how small the world is. We were best friends in elementary school across the world but lost touch when I moved to Colorado. Yesterday, out of the blue, she sends me a message on Facebook, and it turns out we'll be at the same school again. So unexpected.
Maybe we'll circle back to each other, even as friends. I miss your friendship.
Yours,
Tia

Andrew: I'm an idiot.

Me: Yup, certified idiot.

Andrew: Can I see you tonight?

Me: What is this, Tinder at midnight? I'm not a booty call. Don't call or text me unless you're ready. I don't do games.

Andrew: No games. I'm ready.

Me: Pippa's address is 351 Beacon Street. I'll be back from dinner at 8.

Andrew: Ok

Andrew: Who are you going to dinner with?

Me: I'll trade you. Your secret for my dinner date's name. If you say sorry, I'll even tell you what I'm eating.

The buzzer at the gate rang harshly in the empty house. Pippa's parents typically kept a staff of five whenever someone was living here. As soon as Pippa had jetted off to Switzerland for the weekend, I had asked the housekeeper, maid, chef, gardener, and a modern-day version of a butler to take time off. I did not need extra eyes to watch me pace the marble floors, waiting for someone whose name rhymed with Handrew Barker to come to his senses.

The kiss in my office had nearly destroyed my self-control. For a moment, I thought about forgiving him. Wasn't half of Andrew better than nothing?

So it was with great relief to get his texts earlier that day. More than relief, it was much welcomed confirmation that I had done the right thing to put my foot down.

I hadn't lied when I told him that I had dinner plans. I also didn't feel the need to mention that I immediately cancelled my very platonic dinner plans so I could try on Pippa's entire closet. I was aiming for one that struck the right balance between "Andrew, you're an idiot" and "Andrew, rip this dress off me."

Surprisingly they all led to a simple red velvet dress that dipped into a V at the front to show my braless boobage. Because let's face it, this night was ending up with me braless and him doing magical things inside of me.

That is, assuming Andrew confessed to whatever ridiculous thing he had felt the need to hide. I was one hundred percent sure he was blowing it out of proportion. I was fully prepared for him to confess to something like getting drunk one night in college, thinking he was going to be like his dad, and consequently signing himself up for AA. It would explain the texting and secrecy.

In my slinky, red dress, I opened up the door, ready to hear Andrew's confession and move on to fantastic make-up sex. Instead, I saw Andrew walking up with a petite woman, her face hidden by a hood. She was clearly not someone random he had run into at the gate.

Despite the questions pounding in my head, my heart leaped at the sight of Andrew's tousled hair and gray, uncertain eyes. There would never be a day when this man didn't have an effect on me.

At the foot of the steps leading up to the front door, Andrew stopped and looked at me warily. Hoping I wasn't inviting a figurative vampire into the house and opening myself up for a blood and cry fest, I answered his unspoken question, "Come on in."

As if just seeing my dress, Andrew stared at me as if I were water in a desert, his eyes smoldering as they leisurely looked me up and down. His eyes widening at the low V. Any other man, I would feel offended at being ogled. With him, it was hard to take offense, when my own eyes were busy checking him out.

Our mutual lusting was interrupted as the woman delicately cleared her throat and removed her trench coat. Long, red hair framed a beautiful, ethereal face, large blue eyes, a pert nose, and tiny freckles.

She reached out a dainty hand as confusion crowded my brain.

Automatically, I shook her soft hand and mentally reminded myself that I needed to be better about moisturizing my own. "Are you Andrew's sobriety coach?"

Her delicate eyebrows arched up in surprise. "No."

Fudge. Ugly jealousy wrapped its tentacles around my lungs, squeezing the air out in an epic letdown. There went my reasonable explanation for this whole situation. My brain was bulldozed by the single fact that this mysterious woman was beautiful.

Yes, she was in sweats and looked exhausted and I was all dolled up. Even in sweats, she looked like a porcelain doll that most men wanted to protect.

Whereas I would be lying if I said that I had no insecurities. They were quiet or easily ignored most days—after all, I was mostly pleased with how I turned out. However in the face of a real-life American doll, doubts came loudly marching in. *Who the heck was she? Did he want to be with her?* What did that make me? A novelty? Someone to slake his lusts with?

"Tia, no." Andrew shook his head, coming slowly to me. "Whatever you're questioning, don't. This is Charlie, my sister."

The woman scratched at her hairline, peeling off a red wig. Sheepishly, she said, "Sometimes, paparazzi follow me. I have a collection of wigs that I use to avoid them. It gives me a chance to try out different hair colors that I wouldn't normally."

I looked back and forth between the two siblings. One tall, broad-shouldered, dark-haired with gray eyes, the other short, willowy, white-blonde hair with blue eyes, holding a red wig.

"Huh, who knew wigs could cause so much confusion? This is not what I was expecting tonight." Mentally, I crossed off all of the delicious horizontal activities that I had planned. "Do you want some tea? This feels like a conversation that needs tea and cookies."

"That would be lovely, thank you." Charlie looked relieved that this wasn't going to turn into a drag-out fight.

Before I headed into the kitchen, I grabbed a shawl from the entryway closet and wrapped it around myself. Shawls were great inventions, perfect if you didn't want to suck in your stomach while standing next to people with no body fat.

It was Andrew who spoke up first, his baritone gruff and apologetic. "Tia, I'm sorry. I should have told you everything when you asked a few days ago. No, I should have told you *before* you asked. I have no excuse except that I was stupid and scared. If you're still open to listening to the *full* story, I'd like to—we'd like to—"

"No, I should be the one apologizing," interjected Charlie, putting down the teacup that she had been drinking. "It's not Andrew's fault. I begged him not to tell anyone. If you want to blame anyone, blame me. Please. He's done everything to protect and help me. I'm the one who's sorry for everything!"

Surprised, I crossed off "uppity" and "cold" from my first impressions of Charlie. "Before we assign blame, I'd like to understand the story first. Andrew told me the sibling portion. But whatever is happening recently, it can't just be about you being half-siblings, right?"

Andrew nodded at Charlie. "You start. It might help for Tia to hear the beginning."

Stopping to take a drink of tea, Charlie gathered her words. "As Andrew told you, I found out in high school that my dad was not my biological father. It was a shock, to say the least, when I found out about Brandon."

"Did you tell your parents what you found out?" Despite the havoc she had unwittingly wreaked on Andrew's and my relationship, I could only feel sympathy. Brandon Parker was a rotten man.

"No. What would I say to my parents? I suspected that my dad knew, but we didn't talk about these things in our family. Moreover, I didn't have the closest relationship with my mom and didn't want to cause an uproar. At the end of the day, their marriage seems to work for them."

"Charlie's parents are both prominent politicians. It would have caused a scandal," said Andrew.

"Yes, I found out during my dad's first campaign for Congress, and my mom was exploring a run for state attorney. Beyond that, my parents are ambitious …" Her voice trailed off, as pink dotted Charlie's cheekbones. She didn't sound as if she was particularly pleased about those ambitions, rather embarrassed.

"To say the least," muttered Andrew quietly.

Looking earnest again, Charlie leaned in closer to me, her manicured hands pressed down on the table. "I hired a PI after I found out about Andrew. When he told me Andrew's address in Colorado, next thing I knew, I was in my car driving to Colorado. When I got to his apartment, I shoved the lab reports at him and begged him to let me in. Andrew told me later that you misunderstood the situation—there was no other woman. I'm sorry for causing trouble in your marriage."

Andrew gave her thin shoulder a gentle, brotherly squeeze, and Charlie turned to him gratefully. Even though Andrew had already told me about Charlie a few weeks ago, faced with the reality of Charlie, I was once again filled with regret. Even if our marriage would have fallen apart eventually, I should have never suspected Andrew of cheating. With what felt like the start of a pounding headache rushing in, I closed my eyes and tried to breathe. Andrew's hands reached out to hold mine tightly, and I held on to them as if they were anchors against the onslaught of sadness.

Acknowledging Charlie's apology, I replied, "It wasn't your fault. Reflecting back, we simply weren't ready to be married back then."

Charlie smiled slightly, and it made her look approachable, more earthy than the golden fairy that she reminded me of. “I’m glad we have a chance to, hopefully, start over. I’d like to be friends with my brother’s wife.”

Her gesture touched me. “As an only child who always wanted siblings, I’ll take you up on that offer.”

Another quick smile, before it faltered. Anxiety blooming on her face, Charlie said, “Tia, you were right earlier about this being more than an affair my mother had twenty-some years ago.”

Andrew’s face darkened at her words. He looked at me carefully, his voice low and urgent. “This is the part that I didn’t want to drag you into. Are you sure you’re ready, Tia?”

“Yes.”

CHAPTER TWENTY-SEVEN

TIA

June 12, 2010 (never sent)
Andrew,
I'm flying to Beijing tomorrow for two months. I haven't been back since the summer after eighth grade. Even though I was born in Beijing and lived there until I was eight, I'm still nervous to go back. My Chinese has atrophied, and while I don't feel one hundred percent American, I'm perceived as such there. I've often complained to you about being Chinese growing up in a small town in the US and not fitting in. I need to remember my privilege that I have two cultures that I can choose from. At least for the next couple of months, I'm committed to enjoying my relatives spoiling and feeding me, even if I have to "pay back" by practicing English with my little cousins.
Yours,
Tia

Was I ready? Probably not. I also knew that if he sensed any hesitation on my part, there was a good chance that Andrew would shut down. Instead, I gave him my best trust-me-really smile and squeezed his hand.

As if reciting homework in front of a class, he started tonelessly, "My dad—our dad—Brandon reached out a couple weeks ago to Charlie."

Ai ya ya. I gasped. I should have suspected, since nothing made Andrew as insecure as his dad.

"It was a complete and, as you can imagine, devastating surprise," Charlie added. "At first I ignored the calls. There's a certain amount of public interest in my life, because of my family, and it's not uncommon to get random calls. Eventually, after getting maybe a dozen calls from the same phone number, I picked up. I actually thought it was Andrew calling as a prank at first—Brandon's voice is very similar to Andrew's. He asked for money."

"It's what he's always after," said Andrew bitterly. "He asked for ten million."

I gasped again.

"I tried telling Brandon that I don't have the money. He insisted that I figure out a way. I mean, my husband's family is well-off, but Will's inheritance is held in trust. If I asked his parents, they'd be more likely to push for a divorce than have a daughter-in-law with 'tainted blood' and scandal attached to her name."

"So what happens if you don't pay the money?"

No longer able to meet my gaze, Charlie looked down at her French manicure. A tiny, random part of me was impressed at how immaculate they looked, even during this time. "That summer when I found out about Brandon, I started drinking. I lost control of the car one night and hit a house. There was a woman inside. I don't think I hit her. I don't remember much. I must have called my dad, my real one, not Brandon, at one point, because I remember him bundling me up into his car and telling me that everything would be okay. The next day, everything was dealt with, as if nothing had happened. I asked my parents, but outside of telling me that the woman was fine, they refused to talk about it. I tried searching for the woman to apologize, but I couldn't find any information. My best guess is that my parents paid her off and pressured the police and DA's office into keeping the entire matter quiet."

Falling silent, Charlie looked lost in thought. This was definitely not what I was expecting. Words failed me. Instead, I popped consecutive cookies into my mouth. Stress was always better handled with a side of dessert.

In a very soft voice, Charlie whispered so low that I almost didn't catch her words. "It'll kill my parents' careers if this gets out. I think I can handle the bad press, but I don't want to hurt my parents or lose my husband when he finds out. I was supposed to be the perfect political wife. Yet, here I am, in the middle of a blackmail scandal."

"There's more, Tia," Andrew said, looking embarrassed. "As soon as I graduated from law school, Brandon found my number and asked for money to 'rebuild his life.' He said that I owed him, that he only went to jail because he was trying to provide for me and my mom."

Bristling, I protested, "The nerve! You can provide without stealing and conning others. You shouldn't blame yourself, Andrew."

His lips tugged to the side at my indignation. "I don't. I ignored him until he showed up in Breckenridge. I didn't want my mom to fall back under his influence again, so I ended up paying him. Eventually, when I saved enough, I convinced my mom to move to Florida to a gated neighborhood. Brandon hasn't bothered her as long as I keep paying him. It's a small price to keep him away. The problem is now he wants ten million, and he's not picky about who gives it to him."

"What is he threatening you with, to get you to pay the ten million? Is he planning to go after your mom?" I asked.

Andrew shook his head. "He seems to have lost interest in my mom recently. He's threatening to go to the police and tell them that I'm money laundering."

"What? How can he do that?" I protested.

Andrew winced. "It was naivety on my part. In the past, I didn't care what Brandon did as long as he left my mom and me alone. When he asked me for ten million, I asked one of my colleagues, Alex, to look into his finances. It turns out that since Brandon left prison, he's convinced a lot of people to invest money with him. We think he creates fake documents to show how the investments are rising and then pockets the money. He combines my monthly payments with what he's embezzled and routes them through a few accounts to make them look legitimate. There's no way to reveal his fraud without the chance of implicating me. Even if a police investigation confirms that I'm innocent, no one is going to trust me. Who would hire a corporate lawyer accused of embezzlement? No firm or client would take that risk. And that's assuming the police find me innocent and don't arrest me. I didn't want you to think that I was guilty, especially when I can't prove definitely that I'm innocent." Taking a controlled breath, Andrew tried to pull his hands away.

I held tight. We were in this together. I needed Andrew to see the visual of our hands linked together. "I don't need proof to know that you're not the next Bernie Madoff. I would have believed you. I do believe you."

He caught my eyes and pressed one hand to his lips. "Thank you."

I nodded in acknowledgement.

"The deadline is tomorrow at five p.m. to pay the money." Charlie's words pulled us back to the urgency of the situation. "I suggested a hitman but Andrew didn't love the idea. I still reserve the idea as a backup. Oh don't worry, I'd hire an extremely good one who would leave no trace. Definitely no subcontractors either."

Charlie's face was calm, showing no sign that she was joking. But of course she was, right? Who talks about hiring assassins in a brightly lit dining room surrounded by teapots and cookies? For goodness' sake, there was a fancy rug under the dining room set as if the thought of wine and food spilling on it was not a big deal, and cabinets that showed off plates that no one ever used.

"We could pay Brandon," I suggested after a long silence.

Both Andrew and Charlie looked at me. Charlie with hope, Andrew with dawning horror.

"No, Tia." Andrew's hands on mine tightened, almost painfully, though I wasn't sure that he even realized it. His mouth was set in a mulish line. "We're not going to your parents for help."

"What's wrong with asking for help? Their philosophy has always been, their money, my money, my money, their money. They're annoying sometimes, but they're good about unconditional support." At that moment, I realized just how true those words were. Yes, my parents were tiger parents and helicopter parents and whatever other new term cropped up in the future. Yes, I probably needed to stand up to them more. But when I had told them that I was with Andrew over Thanksgiving, after the initial protests, they had grown tentatively okay with us being together. Whenever I needed them, as I had during my hospital stay and the long months after, they were my biggest supporters. They fed me, forced me to shower, forced me to go outside and slowly inch back into life.

Instinctively, I knew that no matter their grumbles, they would do everything in their power to protect me, and by extension Andrew and Charlie.

Before Andrew could protest again, I said, "I actually wasn't going to suggest asking them. Um, you know how I wrote my PhD thesis on fraud? After Pippa left that law firm that you were both at, she started a little audit firm and asked me to build a few algorithms to help detect fraud. We sold it last year to E&Y. I could help with the money. It was Pippa who did the legwork in selling the company, but I do have enough for Brandon's blackmail."

Andrew's eyes shone with pride. "You're amazing. However, Tia, this is not your problem. We shouldn't use your money."

Very gently, I placed my hands on his cheeks, holding his face until he glared sullenly back at me. "You silly man. You're my husband." I turned to quickly look at Charlie. "You're my family too. And families support and care for each other—whether blood or chosen families. They may bicker internally, but they protect their own, whatever the cost. So why wouldn't I help you? Think of it as me being selfish. I don't want you to go to jail. Technically, this might even be considered your money too, since we're married, and there was no prenup."

I could practically see the thoughts churning in Andrew's mind and protests forming. Nonetheless, he seemed to be really mulling over this.

"I'm not convinced this is a good option. I don't like the thought of using you for your money. There needs to be a better solution. However, I'm okay keeping this as a backup option," he conceded stoically after a long pause.

Victory. However small the concession.

My heart swelled with bubbling hope. I couldn't have loved Andrew Parker more at that moment. I understood the depth of pride he had swallowed in even *thinking* about letting me help. Not because he liked it or thought it was the easy way out. Instead, because he took my opinions into consideration and put the collective us and our future before pride. Besides the permanent banishment of Brandon Parker to Uranus, what more could I have asked for?

Taking out his phone to check messages quickly, Andrew said, "I've asked Alex to dig into dirt on Brandon, in case there is another way to get rid of him without paying. In the meantime, Charlie, I made a reservation for you at the Four Seasons. Why don't I take you over so you can get some rest?"

I walked both of them to the front door, feeling anxious and unsettled.

Bundled up again in her trench coat and gloves, Charlie smiled tremulously at me. "It's not the circumstances that I imagined officially meeting you. I'm glad you're back in Andrew's life and mine."

"Same." And I did feel glad to know the mysterious Charlie finally. She looked so forlorn that I wanted to pat her head, and tell her it was going to be okay. Because I had enough social awareness to know that patting near-strangers' heads was considered eccentric by society, I settled for just telling her it was going to be okay.

She pretended to agree, though her smile was bracketed by worry lines at the corners.

Andrew came to stand in front of me, his hands framing my face as he bent for a sweet kiss. The touch was too brief. I barely had time to decipher what was happening before he had pulled back. With his hands caressing my cheeks and his lips a breath away from mine, he whispered low enough that only I would hear. "Thank you for believing in me."

I puffed out a breath. "I told you I was different this time. You—you still have to agree to let me help. Your stubbornness might still send us fleeing to a country with lax extradition laws before this is over."

A small smile showed off his single dimple, as I gave in and pressed a kiss right where his lips curved up. "I like the thought of 'us.' I'll think about your offer. Seriously."

I hoped that his pride wouldn't hold him back from saying yes. Especially with Charlie to protect. But I didn't hold my breath. In fact, part of me was pretty sure that by the end of tomorrow, I would be married to an ex-lawyer, under investigation for money laundering, with a half sister who was disowned by her ambitious politician family. Minutes after the news would break, my parents, with their secret Chinese gossip tree, would call to interrogate me. This would devolve into my parents bemoaning the loss of no-skeletons-in-the-closet Clayton and not so secretly asking me if I was sure in my choice of husband. Once they had properly lectured me, they'd fly over to Boston or whatever country we had fled to and make sure that Andrew, Charlie, and I were fed with real food.

Yet, despite the uncertainty, when I thought about a solid, placid life with Clayton versus this mess with Andrew, I knew without hesitation that I preferred this muddled imbroglio.

What did that say about me? I had thought of myself as a feet-on-the-ground, no-drama type of person. Outside of the impulsive marriage to Andrew in the first place, I had followed rules, made pragmatic decisions, avoided hairy things until I chose Andrew again.

So really, I was the epitome of practical, unless it came to Andrew.

Right now, he needed me, and I was resolved not to falter. I was done running away. I was completely, irrevocably with him, for richer or poorer, in sickness and in health, in good times and in blackmail times.

One hand coming up to cradle my cheek, Andrew asked hesitantly, "I'll see you tomorrow, Tia?"

"Sure. Good night."

It wasn't until they were down the stairs and heading toward the gate that I realized that I was disappointed. And disgruntled.

This was our reunion, with all of our secrets on the table?

Logically, I knew that I wasn't in some sweeping romance novel where the hero and heroine had orgas-mazing sex on a tiny boat in the middle of a thunderstorm as they sped away from the villains.

But, gosh, couldn't I get a make-out sesh at least? Or get to second base? I'd settle for some over-the-dress fondling and sexy talk too. Or you know, what I really wanted: promises of a future together. Didn't those promises usually come after the hero spilled his dark secrets?

Before my mind was fully off the logistical questions of how you'd navigate a boat and have sex while waves were soaking you, I heard my voice call out, "Andrew, are you coming back after you drop off Charlie?"

Yeah, that didn't sound desperate at all.

Andrew's head jerked back to me, his expression unreadable in the dark. "Do you want me to come back?" The intensity and yearning in his voice made me want to run over and drag him back.

"I do."

"Then, I'll be back." His tone was husky, and I thought I detected a note of relief.

As far as romantic gestures went, it wasn't much. Yet, my heart danced a jig and my insides warmed at his promise. The unsettled feeling lightened a smidge, because you know, there was still blackmail to get through.

I watched them open the gate and move toward the street. As I was about to press the button to close the gate behind them, I saw movement. Charlie's white-blonde hair caught my eye as she twisted around so quickly that she stumbled.

Squinting, I tried to make out what was happening. All I could see was the shadows of Andrew and Charlie stalled at the gate. I heard the rhythm of low, rapid words, though I couldn't catch anything specific.

"This is a happy coincidence." A new voice cut across the short distance, smooth and sophisticated, and oddly familiar. It reminded me of one of Clayton's parents' acquaintances, though none of those acquaintances had ever caused the icy shiver down my spine or my heart to rev up in fear.

Andrew's angry voice cut through the darkness. "What the fuck are you doing here?"

CHAPTER TWENTY-EIGHT

TIA

June 15, 2010 (never sent)
Andrew,
I just came back from a visit to the Great Wall. To think that people built it without cranes, trucks, and "modern" technology. We talked about going there together one day. There were so many things that I wanted to show you. The Summer Palace, the Forbidden City, the Great Wall. Or just the vibrancy —ren shan ren hai—people on the mountains and people in the water—the amount of people would blow your mind. I would have enjoyed showing you the less touristy things too, like going for walks after dinner, eating lamb kabobs in the street at night, joining the dancing in the squares.
I hope you have a chance to leave Colorado and visit the world someday.
Yours,
Tia

"Tia, go back inside."

I ignored Andrew's warning. Because how could I leave him when something was clearly wrong? Forgetting that this was winter and I only had a shawl, I headed for Andrew. I needed to hold his hand, to reassure him, to get rid of whatever was making him unhappy.

Closer now, I could see Andrew trying to nudge Charlie behind him, as they both stared, with identical horrified expressions, at a shadow hidden by the gates from my view. Shivering in the dark, I padded across to the gate in my pink, fuzzy slippers.

"Tia," Andrew warned again.

"Professor Wang," the cultured voice spoke from a looming, growing shadow. "Good to see you again."

Confused, I stopped in my tracks, letting my eyes adjust to the darkness. "You! I saw you at the admissions panel, and I think later at one of my office hours. You said your son was looking at MIT. What are you doing here?"

"Naïve, little professor, you don't see the resemblance?" the stranger mocked. As if the streetlight was a prop in this farce, he stepped underneath it and doffed his baseball cap.

I gasped. "Brandon Parker."

Now that he was standing feet away from Andrew, I could see the clear resemblance that I should have noticed before. The same dark, dark hair, the same gray eyes, similar height and build. Brandon's gray eyes were cool, calculating, as he smiled.

I shivered. I did not like the machinations and insincerity underlying his smile.

Wrapping one arm around my shoulders and using the other to keep Charlie half hidden behind us, Andrew threw out, "Why are you here, Brandon?"

Eyes widening in mock innocence, Brandon's smile grew broader. "Why, is it a crime for a father to see his *two* children? To make sure they keep up their side of the bargain?"

Behind me, I heard Charlie gasp. I reached for her hand behind me, to offer a tiny measure of solace.

At our non-response, Brandon asked confidentially as if we were at a dinner party with close friends, "Does your dear husband, William, know?"

As tiny and delicate as Charlie looked, her grip on my hand was ferocious. I chanced a glance back. Her face was full of desperation and sadness. I shrugged Andrew's arm off and wrapped Charlie up in a hug. I may have hated this woman for a decade, met her just a couple hours ago, but she was Andrew's sister, and therefore, my sister. And right now, my sister was hurting.

I hated Brandon Parker more than I had ever hated anyone before. Stories of him had swirled around for most of my childhood, though they paled to the actual, physical presence of him. Stalking us. Taunting us.

Nonchalantly, Brandon shrugged. "I never expected either of you to become so useful. Imagine my surprise."

And that was the core of him. He was a user. Of people. Of situations. People like Andrew and Charlie—good and principled people—were endnotes. At least until he wanted something. I hated him with every word he uttered.

Brandon looked down at Charlie. "It's ironic to have you as a daughter. I've been telling people that I'm the misunderstood, discarded half brother of William Parker—Senator Parker's husband—for most of my life."

"I didn't realize you were connected to Senator Parker?" I asked Andrew.

He didn't take his eyes off Brandon, as he replied, "We're not. My grandparents were potato farmers. It's part of his scam."

"No matter." Brandon waved off the word "scam" as if that was as benign as ordering a latte at a coffee shop. "That story garnered more sympathy than a farmer's kid. Your grandparents were useless, small-minded idiots who couldn't recognize the greatness in me and never gave me a damn thing." Voice bitter, Brandon spat at the ground.

He stepped forward, half in the streetlight, half out, looking like some two-faced joker. On the side of his face that I could see, his lips curled up. "Now that I think about it, I might need to change my story. What do you think of the US representative and his state attorney general wife refusing to let me see my own daughter? Or, I know, the golden socialite who refuses to acknowledge her poor, dear daddy?"

"If you used your fake connections to the Parkers to your advantage, why are you blackmailing us now?" asked Charlie tentatively.

The ever-present smile broadened on Brandon's face until it looked almost sinister. "Now, now, kids. Blackmail is such a dirty word. I'm only asking for what I'm due. Sixteen years in prison was a long time. So plain, so boring. Aren't I allowed to want a more luxurious life? Since we're blood, I'll let you in on a secret."

In a conspiratorial whisper, he said, "I'm in love."

"With yourself?" Sarcasm dripped from Andrew's voice. There was a readiness, a tension about him, as if he was baiting his dad.

For the first time, Brandon's smile fell off, as his face twisted in an ugly sneer. For once, his outside reflecting the ugliness of his soul. "No, you fools." Twisting his face back into a smile, he said, "Kids, you should congratulate me. I'm about to be a married man again."

"Who's the unlucky lady?" asked Andrew.

"And what, have you fill her head with lies about me?"

"You being a shitty dad and a shitty person are not lies," said Andrew.

"Silly kids, you still believe that. This conversation is starting to bore me. If you have friends who can live in this mansion"—Brandon pointed at Pippa's house—"then, you can ask them for some paltry change for your poor father. I'll expect to hear from you by five p.m. tomorrow. I do know where to find you."

Still chuckling, he slid away from the streetlight and into the blackness of the night. A few seconds later, I heard the sound of an engine rumbling past us, as I released my breath slowly.

Andrew and Charlie looked equally tense, their mouths set to identical frustrated, bleak lines. I was still holding Charlie, and I could feel her tremble. With fear, with worries, with the cold—I wasn't sure.

This was not a happy family reunion. Even if Charlie had expected a rotten human being, it couldn't have been easy to see how correct she was. If she had any good expectations, Brandon had effectively broken them.

Finally, when Andrew spoke, his voice was decisive. "We should stick together tonight. Brandon's not physically violent, but who knows? Tia, do you think Pippa would mind if Charlie and I stayed here tonight?"

Without hesitation, I said, "You should absolutely stay here. Pippa's parents installed some serious security. There's the gate, cameras, little buttons everywhere to call the police. There's even a bunker in the basement. I'd feel better if the two of you were close by."

Charlie said gratefully, "If you're sure that Pippa won't mind, then yes, I'd prefer to stay here. Hotel rooms seem flimsy to me. Too many people coming in and out."

Once inside the house, I showed Charlie a guest room at one end of the long hallway. Afterwards, Andrew and I walked through the house, checking all of the locks.

I was too aware of how alone we were. While he didn't touch me, I was too aware of his presence, of how close we were.

"Should I show you your room? You can have your pick of the guest rooms. There are ten bedrooms," I asked, my eyes fluttering, unable to meet his intense gaze.

"Where is *your* room?" His voice was low and husky, and it stirred up nerves that were entirely removed from what had happened earlier and served only to remind me just how much I had missed him.

Entirely too aware of how close he followed without touching, I opened the door to the bedroom that I had been using. I looked down at my slippered feet, not able to meet his eyes.

I may have thought a good game when I got dressed in this slinky dress, but at heart, I was just a geeky girl with awkward moves. If I jumped into bed to pose sexily, I'd probably bump my knees along the way.

"I'd prefer to stay in this room tonight, if it's all the same to you." His voice trailed off, leaving the decision to me.

Yes! Come inside of me—my room, I mean.

In a much more normal-sounding voice than the one screaming for joy inside my head, I tried for nonchalance. "Sure, makes sense. It is a very cold night, and I could always use some extra heat. It saves me from having to turn up the heat or make myself a hot water bag or something."

See, I was made to be a seductress. Because sirens compared hot men to hot water bags.

One side of his lips quirking up, Andrew smirked. "I bet I can think of something even warmer than a hot water bag."

"Really?"

"Really. Why don't you strip off this sexy dress that's been driving me fucking nuts all night and let me show you? My method works best skin to skin."

CHAPTER TWENTY-NINE

TIA

July 1, 2010 (never sent)
Andrew,
Today would have been the one-year anniversary of our marriage. Would haves, should haves.
My parents have never brought up therapy, but I think I might need it. Over the past few months, I've started exercising to gain back my physical strength. Why shouldn't I value my mental state the same, or even more?
Except for sleeping, I'm always around my parents, and now, surrounded by my relatives, yet I feel so lonely about the fall of our relationship, about our baby. And I don't want to feel lonely. I don't want to feel out of control. I want to take action of my life.
Yours,
Tia

Confession? Andrew's method, well—methods, worked one hundred percent better than any hot water bag. He was also right that skin to skin was optimal. That seemed to ignite the most … heat.

On Saturday morning, I woke up sated from Andrew's version of keeping warm and finger-tapping-ly anxious. We hadn't spoken much about the events of last night because … we were keeping warm.

As weak winter light flitted through the curtains, the little issue of the five p.m. deadline loomed front and center in my mind. I looked over toward Andrew. He was awake and staring alertly at the ceiling, even as his arm wrapped around my shoulders, tugging me against the length of his body.

Sensing my movement, he turned to look at me, his mouth curving up in a small smile, "Good morning, Tia."

"Good morning." My eyes scanned Andrew's tousled hair, his day-old shadow of a beard, the drama of his dark eyebrows. The storminess in his eyes reflected my same anxieties.

Which brought me back to the deadline.

Illegal dealings with nefarious criminals simply hadn't been part of my education. In addition to learning proper grammar or how to count, kids should be taught practical knowledge, like how to pick a lock when you've forgotten your keys for the umpteenth time, or how to eat chocolate without smearing all over your face. Or, more crucially now, how to deal with blackmail.

"What do you want to do?"

Frown lines appeared on his smooth forehead. "I don't know. After last night's encounter, I texted Alex a few more things to look up."

He shifted his body to turn toward me. "Last night, I don't think I really thanked you for offering to help. Tia, I'm really grateful. If I thought Brandon would leave us alone after giving him the money, I would accept. However, I'm stuck on the question, what's to keep Brandon from asking for more or coming back?"

"We could get him to sign a contract to leave us alone."

Andrew laughed bitterly. "He'll find a way to circumvent that. Contracts are a first line of defense and keep well-meaning folks toeing a line. For someone like Brandon with little to lose, he's not going to worry about something like lawsuits for breach of contract. You know what the problem is?"

"You mean outside of the ten million problem?" I asked cheekily.

"Yeah." His lips quirked up in a hint of a smile. "It's all on Brandon's terms. Regardless of what we do, the secrets will always be there."

"Unless they're not secrets anymore," I said, picking up on his reasoning.

"Exactly." Excitedly, Andrew sat up in bed. For a brief, okay, not-so-brief moment, I admired his broad shoulders and abs, because even sitting, his muscles were still deliciously muscly.

"It will be messy. I mean *really* messy. As in, I might be disbarred, and I might face an investigation or even be charged with the very real possibility of jail time. My firm can do a lot to protect me if they choose to, but there's no guarantee. I need you to know what refusing the blackmail means."

Would I be okay with being married to a criminal? Even if he was innocent, which I completely believed, the world would see otherwise. I had been taught from childhood to present the best "mianzi," to save face, to hide what's broken, and only share what presented our family in the best light. Essentially an Instagram filter before Instagram existed. With that ingrained in me, it would hurt to have colleagues whisper about my "criminal" husband, or have some students question my credentials, even though what my husband did should have no reflection on my résumé.

I wished that I could avoid feeling embarrassed, or uncomfortable. Even though my sense of self-worth had strengthened in the past few years, it was hard to erase years of caring how others perceived me.

As I mulled over my feelings, I could see Andrew's confidence in ignoring the blackmail start to falter. With every beat of hesitation, his eyes grew more stoic, more resigned.

His voice hard, Andrew said, "Forget I said anything. We'll wait for Alex or pay Brandon. That is, you still have the choice to get out of this mess. It's not your mess."

"No!" Throwing my pros and cons aside, I said, "You're mine, so your mess is my mess." I grabbed his face with both of my hands. "There's no getting rid of me. Not." Kiss. "A." Kiss. "Question." Kiss.

"Okay." He sighed happily, pulling me in for a real kiss before tucking me against his still-naked chest.

"When I think about not being together, I panic. Being together isn't a question in my mind," I said to his chest. "Will it suck if you get investigated or go to jail? Yeah. Even though I'll stand by you, it doesn't mean that I won't have doubts sometimes or handle things wrong."

"I wish I could make it easier for you," Andrew said fiercely.

I shrugged. "Me too. But I still pick you. Besides, look on the bright side, if everything falls apart, we can always get a plot of land in Montana and live off the grid. Remember when we used to try to carve bows and arrows or went camping with school? Those skills will come in handy."

"The nonexistent skills that we had? I remember the fish that we never caught because someone didn't have the patience to wait for fish to bite the hook, and all of the complaints about no hot water or electricity."

"Well, then, you'll have to use your prison time wisely and figure out how to magically get us amenities, before we decamp to the wilderness."

Laughing, Andrew wrapped me up in his arms. I took in the happy sound and stored it in a keep-doubts-away mental container.

Suddenly solemn, Andrew captured my eyes with his. "I love you, Tia."

The moment froze as we looked at each other. There were no sounds. There was nothing else except him. Those four little words, eleven letters, floated around us, forcing this moment into clarity. I tried to discern whether he had actually spoken the words, or if I had imagined them.

He repeated, "I love you, Tia."

My lips released a breath of air as the words tumbled out, racing each other to be spoken. "I love you."

We had thrown those words around when we were younger. This time, there was gravity in those promises. These were no longer the impulsive, innocent words spoken in secret. These were words declared in sunlight, with the full understanding of how hard love was and, equally, how rewarding it could be.

Yes, this was a weird time to say those words. So what if we weren't in some romantic setting? Some words couldn't wait.

We smiled shyly at each other, relishing this time. Hopeful and giddy giggles burst out of me, breaking us out of our frozen moment. The world started to move again—this time, with us tied by those little letters carved in our hearts.

Our plan was shot by breakfast.

Face ashen with horror, Charlie said unequivocally no to letting the secrets come out. Without her cooperation, we were back to waiting on the mysterious Alex and preparing to pay.

Inside, I was relieved that we were sticking with paying Brandon off. He might ask for more money in the future. However, I was also okay with removing him from our lives for the short-term and dealing with him later, when I had more time to prepare.

The rest of the day became a waiting game. We forced ourselves to play Monopoly, Catan, Trouble, cards, backgammon, random games that we had never heard of, until there were no more games in Pippa's games closet. No amount of haggling over sheep for wood or Go Fish could distract us from checking the time.

Every now and then, Andrew would get a text or call. Every time, he shook his head. His hacker friend had come up with nothing useful. To my disappointment, hacking and computer magic were not as easy as one-hour TV dramas indicated.

When you're dreading something, time seems to move both painfully slow and whiplash fast. When the grandfather clock in the foyer chimed three times, I was shocked that it was only three o'clock when I had already lived a lifetime that day, and shocked that we only had two hours until the deadline.

"Fuck." Andrew scrubbed his hands over his face, before fisting them in his hair, causing his hair to stick up in random places. "Fuck, fuck. I should be able to take care of both of you. What kind of man am I that I can't protect you two?"

"What kind of man are you?" I yelled, startling Andrew as I stood up. Yelling was always more effective when standing up. "You're an incredible man trying to make the best out of a sucky situation."

Still angry, I dropped into his lap. Because I needed to touch him. And even in my frustration, I wanted to offer comfort.

"I love you, Tia." His gray eyes were untamed and fiery. The love in them reached into my heart and fought back any doubts that I had about picking him, leaving behind a raw, vulnerable heart that beat for him.

"I love you, Andrew," I mouthed, for my voice was stuck in the sting behind my eyes. Blinking rapidly—*why were my onion-cutting-punishing-neighbors following us*—I repeated the statement again, my voice barely above a whisper.

"Andrew!" Charlie cried out. "Alex is calling!"

Andrew grabbed his vibrating phone. Without preamble, he asked, "You got any news?"

Even though I was sitting on his lap, I couldn't make out any words on the other end of the call, except that the voice sounded butter smooth and dark. Andrew didn't say much except a few murmurs of agreements and the very odd statement of, "I don't want to go read yard sale posts on a South Dakotan Facebook group, or dig for a comment on a Banana Cake Queen Instagram post. Text it to me." A few seconds later, he hung up and stared at his phone intently.

"Did Alex find anything?" asked Charlie.

"I'm not sure if it'll turn out useful," he said vaguely, as his phone buzzed with incoming messages. His fingers scrolled through the images, before he stood up so abruptly that I nearly toppled to the floor. "Last night, Brandon mentioned that he was getting married. I asked Alex to look into Brandon's fiancée and see if there was something that we could use. Alex thinks he's found the woman."

"What's her name?" I asked.

"Sarah Anne Esposito. She lives in Boston. Alex is confirming and pulling some more info—"

"I think I know her," said Charlie, her face animated. "She had an affair with the last Chicago mayor. Rumor had it that she wanted the mayor to leave his wife, which he never did. There was a huge amount of gossip a few years ago. I didn't realize she had moved to Boston."

At that moment, Andrew's phone buzzed. He scrolled through the incoming messages, his expression unreadable. Not able to contain my questions or impatience, I huddled near him, standing on my tippy-toes to read the texts.

His lips curved up in a quick smile before he turned over his phone to me, his eyes gleaming triumphantly. "Here."

My heart beating, I read the texts from Alex, calling out the highlights for Charlie to hear. "'Esposito just filed for divorce from Jack O'Toole, who's an enforcer for the Flanagan family. O'Toole is suspected in at least four murder investigations.' Yikes."

"Listen. I think our best bet is for me to go talk with her. I'd like for you two to stay here."

"Andrew, I want to come."

He turned to me, pinning me with the intensity of his gaze. "This is not about me not trusting you. I need you to stay here with Charlie and help her, in case Brandon calls. If he does, tell him that we're planning to wire the money to him today. Don't admit anything else."

"I'm scared for you," I croaked out past the lump in my throat. That statement lingered in the air. Worries and fears in my head were just that. Spoken out loud, they felt real. Possible. Probable.

"I'll give Dan a call to come with me, okay? He's good to have in a fight. I'll come back to you. Promise." Andrew enveloped me in his arms. We were so close that the only sounds that I heard were the thundering beats of his heart against my cheek. I could feel the tension in his shoulders and the almost-painful way he held on to me.

I didn't know if Andrew's nervousness made me even more anxious or calmer. Either way, I had to be strong for him. I would not be another worry for him. "Good luck. Whatever happens, I love you," I whispered against his shirt.

"I love you, Tia." Barely had the words tumbled out of him, when he pulled back and rushed for the door.

I turned to look at Charlie and smiled sheepishly. "Should we finish the puzzle?"

"Can we drink wine instead?"

Surprised laughter burst from me as I linked my arm with hers. "Oh yes. Let me show you Pippa's wine cellar. You know, if you're ever in Boston in the future, hopefully not on something as exciting as this trip, you should join Pippa and me for a boozy tea party."

"I would love to. What's involved in a boozy tea party?" Her face retained that pinched, worried look, even as Charlie tried to continue my line of distraction.

"Anything goes. Years ago in college, when Pippa and I took an art class together, we would do our assignments by the Charles River. We've kept up the tradition since and spruced it up with drinks."

"I'm no great talent."

"That's not a problem. Painting is not the point. It's dedicated time to hang out and be silly, because sometimes when life gets busy, as it seems to always, you need to schedule in fun."

Wistfully, Charlie sighed. "I'll take you up on the offer. Lately, my life has seemed too serious and regimented."

From some of her offhanded comments in the past twenty-four hours, I had a suspicion why. I bit my tongue to avoid snooping further.

For the next couple of hours, we kept our conversation light and drank rosé in the kitchen. I told funny stories of our boozy tea parties, of teaching, of growing up as the only Chinese-American family in a small town in Colorado. I didn't mention people asking where I was "really" from, of ignorant kids doing squinty eyes, or being asked at lunch in middle and high school why I was eating "weird" food instead of pizza. I didn't share how kids would tell me that they like General Tso's chicken, in an attempt to relate to me. Instead, I told of how my parents prohibited television the whole of my junior and senior year of high school so I could study, until I found out that my parents were secretly watching Chinese dramas after I went to bed. Then the rule became no TV except for Chinese dramas. I told of the time when my five-year-old cousin came to visit during July Fourth and informed me that the holiday was to celebrate the liberation of the US from dinosaurs.

No matter how hard I tried to distract us, both of us stared at our phones. Finally, giving up pretenses, Charlie asked, "What do you think is happening now? It's past five, and I haven't gotten any messages saying that my world has fallen apart. Do you think Andrew and Dan have convinced Brandon to back off?"

That question loomed in the room. I looked at Charlie's hopeful and anxious face, likely reflecting the same mixture of emotions as mine. "I don't know. They might still be talking."

"Yeah."

We fell into deeper silence.

Eventually, Charlie pulled out a rolled-up magazine from her purse and pretended to read. I opened my work laptop, staring at some code for a project, not making heads or tails of the language in front of me, even though I had been the one to write it.

The only sound in the too-large, too-silent house was the rhythm of us checking our phones every few minutes. My phone stayed silent, and I didn't know if I should be thankful or frightened. Charlie's phone buzzed a few times. Whoever the person was, Charlie ignored him or her.

After a series of insistent buzzes, I chanced a question. "Do you need to get that? I don't mind. If you want to take the call, I have my phone here and can let you know if Andrew calls or texts."

With a deep, unhappy frown, she shook her head. "It's my husband, Will. I told him that I was visiting my dad for the weekend in DC, and apparently, he saw both my mom and dad on TV at a rally in California."

"Ai ya ya. Would he be so upset if you told him the truth? It's not your fault who your biological dad is, and the drunk driving incident happened so long ago. Everyone makes mistakes."

Shaking her head adamantly, Charlie said, "He married me for my bloodlines and my pristine reputation. He had run me through a full background check before he even asked me out on our first date. What good am I, if I'm ruined socially?"

"I'm sure he married you for reasons beyond who your parents are and that you are a goody-two shoes. You're still his wife. You see how damaging secrets have been in Andrew's and my relationship—don't make the same mistakes as us," I protested, feeling a surge of protectiveness.

"You're different. You love each other. In my case, Will and I are clear that our marriage is of convenience and mutual benefits. I'm his political partner first. His future hostess for fundraising dinners and his surrogate to attend luncheons at a retirement home or with the firefighters' wives association. I'm a trophy for his future career in politics, because some voters still like seeing their government officials with a partner, kids, and a dog or two. Somewhere far down the line, I'm his wife. And I'm okay with that. I knew what I had gotten myself into when I married him. As Will's wife, I lead a very privileged life. Don't feel bad for me. Not everyone can have a love story like yours."

Despite Charlie telling me not to feel bad, I felt bad. Her marriage was too reminiscent of my relationship with Clayton. Never to her extent, though there had been expectations, some put on by myself and some hinted at by Clayton's family, that I needed to conduct myself a certain way. Looking back, I realized just how "on" I was around Clayton, his family, and his friends.

In our relationship, Clayton had never seen me without makeup or in sweat pants. Even though we had gotten engaged, like a storyline on some TV show, I had never tooted in his presence or pooped in his apartment or anywhere he might be soon after. As far as I knew that he knew, I peed roses.

Maybe because Andrew had known me since I was eight or maybe because I knew his faults, for whatever reason, I was myself around him. I would say it's a miracle that he loved me for myself, except that I knew that I was pretty awesome. The wonder was not that we loved each other. The wonder was that we found each other twice.

"Tia, do you hear that?"

Startled out of my reverie, I looked over my shoulder, trying to tune my ears to the sounds outside. Low male voices, on the other side of the front door.

Alarmed, we looked around for potential weapons. I made a quick dash into the kitchen to get a couple of knives. Charlie grabbed my laptop as…a shield? As a way to bonk someone in the head? For a quick second, I almost asked her to get a different weapon because I couldn't remember if I saved my work. Then I remembered that I had done nothing but stare at the screen. Plus, ai ya ya, lives were at stake!

I turned off the light in the foyer. We waited in the darkness, one of us on either side of the door. From Andrew's stories and what, thankfully, little I had observed in person, Brandon didn't seem like a physically dangerous guy. But desperation was a powerful feeling.

The voices outside the door stopped.

The door opened slowly.

CHAPTER THIRTY

TIA

August 21, 2010 (never sent)
Andrew,
When I ran off with you to Vegas, I was a sheltered, very possibly spoiled girl who had never made any big decisions for myself. I had been content to drift in life, letting others tell me what to do, to shape myself to others' expectations of me.
I want to change and own my future. I'm not quite there yet ... however, I feel stronger today. Just by making the decision to get a therapist, I feel more in control. Watch out, world.
I'm heading to college tomorrow. A whole new world in front of me. This will be the last letter that I write (and not send) to you. I don't want to forget you, but for my own sanity, I need to move on and focus on what's possible.
Saying goodbye to fictional you is almost as hard as saying goodbye to the real you. I don't know why I'm crying...
Yours always,
Tia

As much as I loved British detective shows, I realized that mysterious private investigator was not my future calling. Not with the drums beating within my heart or shivers coursing through my body.

Across from me, I could see the light bouncing off Charlie's huge eyes. I'd venture a guess to say she was not going to turn from political wife to covert spy anytime soon either.

The door opened as one of the men stepped through. I could hear his quiet, controlled breathing before I could see his face. He blocked the weak light from the street. The foyer was pitch black. I squeezed my eyes shut for a moment in terror, before remembering that, how was I supposed to use a knife on an intruder if I couldn't see?

I opened my eyes just as I heard, "Tia? Charlie?"

"Oh, thank God!" I hurtled myself at Andrew as Charlie turned on the lights.

"Whoa!" He backed up, his eyes wide in alarm. "Did you have a change of heart while I was gone?"

I braked a couple feet in front of Andrew to look at the forgotten knives in my hands. "Oh, these?" I waved my hands innocently. Except when you're holding knives, even common kitchen knives, people around you still flinched in alarm.

Gingerly, Andrew took them from me and handed them to the man behind him. Nodding a brief greeting to his sister, Andrew turned to look at me, drinking the sight of me in, as if he needed to replenish his visual memories of me. Then, he grabbed me and enveloped me in … him. I ran my hands all over him, relieved not to find any bloodstains or noticeable broken bones.

I peeped over Andrew's shoulder and smiled sheepishly at the second man. "Hi, Dan. How's Kat feeling?"

"Hey, Tia. Fucking tired all the time. This baby better give fucking awesome Mother's Day presents for the rest of his or her life—no half-assed doodles. I expect some fucking Picasso-level handprint paintings."

Dan paused and noticed Charlie for the first time. Ignoring the laptop she still held as a shield against her body, he said, "You must be Charlie. I'd shake your hand but …" He nodded toward the knives Andrew had transferred to him.

"You must be Dan. Andrew's mentioned you before."

“Has he? Good things?”

“The best fucking things,” said Charlie, with a shy smile. I stared at her in surprise, as Dan burst out laughing.

I had a million and one questions. With my nerves shot and my thoughts running every which way, I didn’t know if I should be shouting for joy or helping Andrew pack his suitcase for a getaway car. So I did what I usually do when I’m stressed: eat and drink tea.

A few minutes later, we were gathered by the kitchen island. Andrew started, “Brandon had used Esposito to get her ex-husband’s account information. They were planning to transfer O’Toole’s money into an offshore account and leave the country. Once we told her that Brandon had nothing to his name and was using her to get access to O’Toole’s funds, she was pissed and scared of O’Toole’s reaction if he found out she was involved. She thought he had funds of his own and believed his spiel about being connected to Senator Parker and her billionaire in-laws, the Sandekes. When Brandon showed up, we told him that we’d tell O’Toole about his plans if he ever came near us again. It helped that Esposito was ready to shoot Brandon on the spot. She’s sketchy but not stupid enough to stay with Brandon.”

“You don’t mess with the fucking mob’s hitman. Or his ex-wife. That should be a life lesson.” Dan nodded emphatically.

“So… this is over?” Hope shone on Charlie’s face, as she gripped her once-again buzzing phone.

The crooked grin widened on Andrew’s face. “Yeah. I think Brandon is genuinely afraid of O’Toole. He’ll probably disappear for a long time.”

Relief had me bouncing out of my seat and into Andrew’s lap. From the corner of my eyes, I saw Charlie slump inelegantly in her chair as Dan patted her back.

Andrew’s eyes looked tired, with shadows underneath them. I realized that I had never loved him more. I looked forward to years, nay, decades of helping him remove those shadows with lines at the corners of his eyes and mouth from smiling and laughing too much.

As if just remembering, Andrew asked, “By the way, what were you doing with the knives earlier, Tia?”

"Charlie and I thought you were intruders. Why were you so sketchy?" I accused, as I snuggled in closer.

"Sketchy? We used keys to open the gate and the door. It wasn't as if we were breaking windows and jumping over gates. Actually, I was concerned that something had happened when the lights went off inside the house."

"Oh, I thought it would make it harder for any intruders to see."

"Fucking scary to see knives being wielded by a ninja in the dark," Dan added, grinning, as he stuffed a cookie in his mouth. "Remind me not to be on your bad side."

Companionably, we chatted around the kitchen table. In the space of a few hours, this kitchen had turned from a somber waiting room to a mini-party. In high spirits, Dan and Andrew excitedly discussed details of the confrontation with Esposito and Brandon. It was hard not to get caught up and find confetti to throw around.

In the midst of the excitement, I looked over at Charlie, who was still staring morosely at her phone. I asked gently, "Are you okay?"

Hesitantly, as if she was making the decision as she spoke, Charlie said, "I don't know. This is all I've been thinking about for the past few weeks. It's a huge relief for it to be over—it feels surreal. Now that it's over…I should probably head back home."

"Are you sure?" Andrew asked.

Hands gripping her phone even tighter, Charlie shook her head. "I think it's best if I leave as soon as possible. There's a ten o'clock flight tonight that I'd like to get on. I've been away from home too long."

I had an inkling why she needed to go home, and I didn't like it one bit. It was one thing to be dedicated to your marriage and *want* to be with your husband. It was a completely different thing to rush to him because he demanded it. I opened my mouth to join Andrew's protest, when Charlie looked at me pointedly. Frowning, I kept my mouth closed.

Instead, I gave Charlie a big hug, as Andrew awkwardly patted her shoulder. With a tickle in my throat, I said, "This is the weirdest way to hang out with my not-so-new-sister. I mean it, Charlie, I hope you do visit us again in Boston. There's always more room for another easel at our tea parties. Or we could visit you in Chicago. And I expect you to stay in touch with me and reach out if you ever need to talk about you-know-who."

"Who is you-know-who?" said Andrew, in confusion.

Charlie ignored him and smiled at me. "I will. Next time will hopefully be less exciting. I don't think I'm cut out for real-life intrigue."

Two hours later, we had said goodbyes to Dan and dropped Charlie off at the airport. In unspoken agreement, we headed back to my apartment, or rather, our apartment, instead of Pippa's house. There was an intimacy and coziness in our home, and after the past day of suspense and our week apart, I needed to cocoon myself in a safe, familiar place with Andrew. Always with Andrew.

"How are you feeling?" I asked as we entered the apartment.

"How are *you* feeling?" Andrew asked, his eyes probing.

"Glad to have everything behind us. I'm so excited to focus on the future now," I told him, wrapping my arms around his neck.

"Yeah, the future," he repeated grimly.

Before I could question his dark mood, he swept me into his arms. If Andrew seemed reticent, I ignored it. If he kissed me with a hint of desperation, I chalked it up to the stress of the past couple of days. After all, he was here with me now, and there was nothing that could mask his need for me. We tumbled into the pleasure-filled chaos, and back down into each other's arms.

CHAPTER THIRTY-ONE

ANDREW

September 21, 2018 (torn, never sent)
Ting Ting,
I thought about you today.
Do you want to hear a confession? I think about you every day. Sometimes in passing, like, I'll hear a joke and want to share it with you.
Today, I thought I saw you at work. It's ridiculous. What reason could you have for being at my law firm in NY? You don't work here.
One of my former classmates and coworkers, Pippa (you'd like her, by the way), hosted dinner on her parents' yacht tonight and invited me to come. She said that one of her childhood friends was visiting and that I might like her.
The truth is, I don't feel like dating anyone unless it's you. Instead, here I am, still at the office on a Friday night, checking our client files to see if your name showed up in one of our cases, and therefore, might have actually been at the office.
It's a strange line to walk. I've forced myself not to google you or search for you on social media. Yet, as far as I've moved away from the past, part of me will always look for you.
Still yours forever,
Andrew

Tia: Where are you?

I stared hungrily at my phone as the message popped up. It was 11 a.m. on Sunday and my first message from Tia that day. Running my hand through my already messy hair, I turned over my phone as I forced myself to stare at my laptop.

At 12:05 p.m., my phone rang. I ignored it.

It rang again at 2:30.

Again at 5:17.

Again at 6:10.

Each time, I ignored it. Each time, a part of me was sliced open, the pain so acute I wondered if I was having physical manifestations of heartbreak.

"Sir, can I help you again?"

Stepping up to the counter, I asked, "Hi, I seem to have missed my flight. Could I reschedule and get on the waiting list for the eight p.m. to Chicago?"

The once-patient attendant at the Delta counter sighed and looked at me suspiciously. "Sir, are you sure you want to go? You seem to be missing a lot of flights today."

"I promise, I'll make this one."

"Okay, I'll put you on the standby list."

"Thank you."

That morning, it hadn't taken long before the inkling of anxiety from yesterday had blown into full panic. What a fucking mess my life was. Even though Brandon was gone, I wasn't naïve enough to think that he was gone for good. It may take him a few years to regroup and create a new scam. However, I was confident that he wouldn't have learned his lesson.

I had been fucking selfish to try to keep Tia in my life. My focus had been on how she made me feel and how much I needed her. It was time I thought about her instead of my needs.

The first flight that I booked was for 8 that morning. I missed that one and rebooked to nine o'clock. I missed that one.

Then the ten a.m.

Then the noon.

And all the other flights that afternoon and evening.

My frequent flyer status helped me get off the standby list every time. And every time, I missed the flight.

At 8:45 p.m., I finally managed to get on the plane that had originally been scheduled to leave at eight. This time, I made it past the lines, put my small suitcase in the cabinets above me and buckled in.

At 8:57, as the flight attendants checked the plane to prepare for takeoff, I stared out of the dark window, my reflection staring back at me. I had never felt worse in my life. This was worse than Tia leaving me ten years ago, worse than finding out she had a fiancé. I couldn't quite put my finger on why this time felt different.

All I knew was the blinding, gut-wrenching panic that had taken over me. *This is the only way to protect Tia. She deserves more.* It would hurt her for a short time before she realized she was better off without me.

But this breakup would devastate me for the rest of my life. She was my world. She gave color and flavor to my life. How bleak my life would become without even the *hope* of her.

As the flight attendants locked the door and the plane started to move, my heart reacted viscerally to the motion. Once I left this time, there was no going back. She wouldn't give me another chance. This was the final chapter, the back cover. With every uneven bump as the plane started to back away from the gate, I felt suffocated by the weight of the cover slamming shut.

"No!" Quickly, I unbuckled as I called out to the flight attendants who were getting ready to tell us about the importance of seat belts. "Stop!"

"Sir, please sit down, the plane is about to take off." The flight attendant nearest me rushed over with her hands stretched out.

"You don't understand. I have to get off." Apologizing to the guy next to me, I stepped past him and into the aisle. I could see the other flight attendant coming up behind me.

Since I was in first class, I didn't have that much distance to go to get to the door. But then what? Figure out a way to open the plane door and leap off a moving airplane? Coming out of this alive was rather critical for what I wanted to do next.

"Sir," the second flight attendant said in a calm voice, as the first one reached for a wall speaker. "Please sit down. Would you like some snacks or a drink?"

"Not unless those were some magical peanuts," I retorted. *Fuck.* "Haven't you ever made a mistake?"

"What?"

"I made a huge mistake and need to fix it."

"We can help you make a return reservation back to Boston. *After* you sit and we land in Chicago," the first attendant insisted.

"No, that's too late. I have to go back, or it'll be too late. I really fucked up with my wife, and I have to try."

"Just let the guy go back. We're still near the gates, and we're already delayed anyway," came a voice from my back. I looked at the disgruntled teenager two rows down. The whole plane was staring at me, some with curiosity, others with alarm.

Another voice chimed in. This time a man in a rumpled suit. "He's clearly deranged. He's been sitting at the same gate since this morning when I arrived from Chicago."

"Yeah, let him go. What if he's dangerous?"

"What if he's sick?"

"Please," I begged.

The attendants looked at each other. One of them sighed and reached for the intercom. "Captain? We have an emergency here. One of the passengers is sick and needs to get off the plane."

Minutes later, as soon as the plane door opened, I sprinted through the jetway back to the terminal. Behind me, I heard one of the pilots asking, "Carol, I thought you said he needed medical attention?"

"Must have found a miraculous cure. Want some peanuts?"

With a shaking hand, I reached to knock on the door. It had seemed natural to use my set of keys on the building, but for some reason, it was important that I be invited inside.

Before I could knock again, the door flung open.

"Hi, Tia."

Her lovely mouth dropped into a surprised circle. I soaked in the sight, the smell, the essence of Tia. I longed to touch her, to pull her into my arms. If she would allow it. Regardless of what happened, it was the right decision to come back.

The beige of the manila folder against the black of her coat caught my eyes. I stared at it, with dawning resignation. I was too late.

"Going somewhere?" My voice came out accusatory. I was a fool in every way. And it was my fault.

"Did you forget something?" Tia demanded defensively, pointing to the forgotten suitcase that I still gripped. "Come back to step on my heart again? I heard you. Maybe not as quickly as you wanted me to, but I got there. You. Don't. Want. Me. I get it now."

What the fuck? Confused, I asked, "Not want you?" This was not a confrontation I wanted to have in the middle of the hallway, so I walked Tia back into her apartment.

Closing the door behind me, I asked again, certain that I had misheard. "Not want you? What are you talking about?"

"Isn't that why you are running from us? You'd rather go back to Chicago than fight for us."

I was furious at myself that I had made her doubt herself. "Not want you, Tia? All I do is want you. All I've ever wanted is you. All I've ever needed is you. I fell in love with you the day you told Joe Abbot to go to hell when he spit on my shoes in elementary school. I've wanted and needed and loved you every single day since then, not even daring to admit to myself how much. I was happy being whatever you wanted me, as long as I stayed in your life. *Never* did I think you would ever want something more than friendship. Losing you the first time broke me, yet I knew it would happen. Why would someone as warm, as good, as caring and thoughtful ever want to stay with someone like me? I had nothing to offer. I could only *take*. I *took* you away from your family. I *took* you away from college. And I didn't have anything to fucking *give* you. So when you left, I didn't bother to correct your mistaken assumptions and chase you, because what did I have to give you in return? I had already been selfish enough to keep you with me for two months."

I swallowed hard. I didn't have gentle words of love to offer Tia. "In the decade since, I thought about you every day. I wanted you every day, needed you, loved you. I think I tried so hard, because I wanted to prove to myself that I could be better, that if ever our paths crossed, maybe you could deem me worthy of your attentions. When you showed up at my doorstep in Chicago, I knew that it was my chance."

Backing up against the couch, Tia sank into the cushions. Without giving it any thought, I knelt in front of her. But I didn't touch her. I didn't want her rejection. Not before I told her everything.

"If you've always wanted me, why did you leave today? I don't understand—there's nothing in our way anymore," she whispered.

"I panicked."

How could I put into words what I didn't understand? How could I make her understand that I was scared to death of screwing up? "Life with me will never be smooth. I have no family wealth or connections. I have a regular job, not some fancy job that comes with private planes or payouts that would allow us to retire at thirty-five. I am prickly. I need space. I get frustrated and defensive easily. I'm insecure at times, I'm overconfident at other times. I'm stubborn. I don't buy flowers, because they're impractical and don't last. I think horse-drawn carriages aren't romantic because I don't want a horse's ass three feet from my face. I don't know which spoon to use at fancy parties. I don't know how to be a good husband to you, and I certainly don't know how to be a dad to our kids. You *shouldn't* want to be with me. The thought of screwing up terrifies me. I've seen how much Brandon can hurt the people around him, and I don't want to hurt you like he hurt my mom. It's not rational, but it's how I felt. So I packed and booked a flight back to Chicago to make it easier for both of us."

"Yet, you're here with me."

"So I am. I sat in the airport all day and tried to leave. But I couldn't. I don't want to leave you. I know what it was like without you, and I know what it was like with you. I *can't* be without you. I *can't* give you up. For however long you want me, I am yours." I had nothing else. My heart was open, and it was hers.

When she didn't speak, I felt that back book cover start to drop on me again. So this was it. She had given me chances, told me that she just wanted me, and I had not trusted her to know her mind. "Am I too late?"

With tears streaming down her face, Tia looked at the folder still in her hands. As my heart pounded against the finality of this, she reached inside and pulled out the papers. When she asked me to sign this time, I promised myself that I would. I would do whatever she wanted me to do.

"I was going to fly to Chicago tonight and demand that you sign these divorce papers."

I nodded wearily. The book was closing. Beyond that, I could see nothing but an empty wasteland.

Tia started, her voice halting, "I was so elated last night, that we had solved one giant problem together. I'm not deluded thinking that our future will be all smooth-sailing. However, I thought we would face whatever challenges came together. I had been so proud, so excited, so hopeful that you put us first. Then today when I woke up to find that you had packed up your stuff, I decided that I couldn't put myself in this emotional turmoil anymore. It's too much back and forth—this uncertainty is driving me nuts."

My heart shattered at the pain that I had put her through. "I wanted to call you that I was leaving, but I thought that as long as I delayed the conversation, we were still together…and I desperately wanted to avoid reality. It was stupid of me. I'm sorry."

I looked into her brown eyes. *One last Hail Mary.* "Tia, please. I know I'm a project. It's also not on you to fix my problems for me. The only thing that I want from you is another chance. I'm all in this time. I won't run again. Tia, please, rip up those papers. I don't want a divorce from you…I'm on my knees… begging you… give me one more chance. I will spend the rest of my life doing everything I can to make you happy. *Please*."

More tears welled up in her eyes, as I felt my heart sink. Violent sadness drummed inside my head, pulling me down, pulling me under the waves.

Then, like a lifeline, her words stopped my freefall.

"I only need…you to love me, Andrew. I need you to take a chance on us and choose us every single day. I need you to believe in us. When you're scared that you're screwing up or when we're fighting or when whatever random situation is thrown at us, I need you to still believe that we are strong enough to get through it. *Together*. I need you to believe that you can lean on me, as I will lean on you."

How could ordinary letters strung into simple words have the power to rescue me? Demolishing all of the remaining walls and excuses within me, I promised, "I will try, as long as you're with me."

With hope soaring in me, I pulled Tia, my Tia, into my arms. When her arms wrapped around my neck, relief flooded my body, drawing out the remaining tension. Pulling back just far enough to look at her, I vowed solemnly, "I want you. I need you. I love you, Tia. I love you so much."

A huge smile spread across her beautiful face, as she whispered back, "I want you. I need you. I love you, Andrew. Thank you for loving me *more* than you are scared of us."

Laughter bubbled up. "I might be slow on the uptake, but after twenty years of loving you, I think I'm finally ready for us."

Reaching for the pocket on the inside of my jacket, I pulled out a small box. "The last time I was in Chicago, I grabbed something that I had been holding on to for a while. I'd like to return one of them to you."

"Are those—"

I stared at the thin, white gold band in my palm, next to a wider, larger band. "Ten and a half years ago, we got married with these rings and proceeded to make a muck of it the first round. I'd like to start anew. Tia, will you please be my wife again?"

"Yes!" Eagerly, without waiting for me, Tia grabbed her ring and slid it onto her finger. It still fit. It was a simple, understated ring with no diamonds. I had used up all of my savings to buy her that ring and had carried shame that I couldn't get her anything fancier. Yet, seeing the thin band on her finger, there was a rightness to it. And this time, I didn't let myself wonder if it was enough.

"I love you, Andrew," Tia said, leaning in to kiss me.

I savored the feel of her. The softness of her lips, the intensity of feeling as if I had come home. Finally. "I love you, Tia."

"Do we start our happily ever after now?" she whispered between kisses that soothed over past pain and carried us kiss by kiss forward.

"What will we do with ourselves now?" I teased. "What do people do after they get everything they've ever wanted?"

"Enjoy themselves," Tia said firmly. Smiling at my wife, I scooped her up and carried her to start our happily ever after.

EPILOGUE—6 YEARS LATER

ANDREW

October 4, 1999
Hi,
I'm Andrew. What's your name?
Andrew

October 5, 1999
Hi Andrew,
My name is Ting. Do you want to be my friend? You'll be my first friend in the US. I like letters, but tomorrow, we can also talk during lunch or play during recess.
Ting

"Congratulations! Today is your day. You're off to Great Places! You're off and away! You have brains in your head—"

"Daddy, Daddy, what are brains?"

"It's an organ in your head that helps you think and tells your body what to do. Let's see, 'You have feet in your shoes. You can steer yourself any direction you choose. You're on your own. And you know what you know. And YOU are the guy who'll decide where to go. You'll look up and down streets. Look 'em over with care. About some you will say—"

"Daddy, Daddy, why does Mickey Mouse wear gloves? Does he have teeth? Goofy has teeth."

"Hmm, good questions. Um … Mickey has cold hands—"

"Daddy, why does he have cold hands? Maybe he should wear a sweater."

"That's a good idea, Cecelia. Should we read a different book?"

My four-year-old daughter ruffled through the pile of books on her bed and delightedly pulled out a thin book with kids playing and Chinese characters on the cover.

I was tired from work and from convincing a charming, outrageous toddler that broccoli was indeed healthy despite it looking like a tree. Now, we were about to start book number six. Which wouldn't be so bad, except despite having read the books multiple times before, each page still generated questions, and each answer generated more questions.

Yet, as I looked at the adoring brown eyes of my daughter as she valiantly tried to hide a yawn, I had never felt this lucky. Batting away my own yawn, I opened up the book. "Cong qian, cun zi li you ge lao ren, ta ji shi nian lai, kao zhe ti ren…"

"Daddy, why does your Chinese sound so silly? It doesn't sound like when Mama talks. Or when Yeye or Nainai talks. Did you forget to practice your Chinese today? Mama says you need to practice more," Cecelia's little voice reminded me.

I smiled. Even at this young age, she had a clear grasp of who was boss in this house. It wasn't me. And I was completely okay with being wrapped around Tia and Cecelia, and soon, my baby son's fingers.

"How about I read it instead?" Tia's voice came from the doorway. She was two weeks away from her due date, and it still amazed me that her body was growing our son.

She had been scared and anxious, and anxious about being too anxious, throughout the pregnancy with Cecelia and now this one. I didn't like feeling helpless, and I didn't want to add myself as another burden for her to worry about. So I did my best to supply her with an endless amount of lemon squares at all hours of the day, doing chores, and taking Cecelia on field trips to give Tia time to nap. I hoped it was enough.

"Yay! Mama, snuggle with me." Cecelia shoved aside two frilly pillows, one of her five blankets, and expectantly patted a little space next to her.

Smiling, Tia shook her head. "Your baby brother is getting too big for me to lie down. I might not be able to sit up again."

Pouting slightly, Cecelia asked, "When is he going to come? It's been soooo long. Why is he soooo slow?"

"Soon, darling," I said, as I patted her shiny, dark brown hair. "When he is born, you'll be a big sister. You'll have to look out for him and protect him."

"Just like my sister, Joy?" Yawning, Cecelia rubbed her eyes, as she pointed vaguely above her head.

"Yes, darling."

"Can you rub my back, please? I don't think I'm tired. But I'm going to rest a little bit. Just a little bit?"

"Sure," Tia whispered, turning off the lights in our daughter's room.

We sat there in the dark, with me patting Cecelia's back as her breath deepened, my other hand reaching out to hold Tia's, as her head came to rest on my shoulder.

In the past six years, Tia and I had our share of fights, disagreements, hurt feelings, and miscommunications. But there were many, many more moments of happiness. Vacations, reading and drinking tea together over rainy days, laughter bordering on sleep-deprived hysterics the first few months after Cecelia was born, and taking family walks after dinners.

I had turned out not to be a crappy husband (I was still happily married, right?). To my bigger surprise, I had turned out not to be a crappy dad. No amount of books could have prepared me for Cecelia, but we quickly learned that she didn't need much. She didn't seem to mind when my attempt at pigtails was a lopsided disaster, or that I fed her too many chicken nuggets. Cecelia simply needed my love…and that I had an overabundance to shower on her.

There were so many big, joyful moments and so many little, mundane moments of happiness that had brought peace for me. There were also moments when I was so happy that I became terrified that something would happen, that I would screw up. But those moments were becoming increasingly infrequent, with the help of therapy as I learned to process my past. And every day, Tia and Cecelia patiently showed me that love wasn't about loving perfection, but rather loving the whole of someone, including the weirdness and flaws.

So, no, our happily ever after didn't consist of a castle or the serenity that movie and book characters floated off into. Our happily ever after was a work in progress, sometimes messy, often wondrous, but always the one in which we chose each other, we believed in each other, and we loved each other.

THE END

ACKNOWLEDGMENTS

Thank you for reading this! I'm so thankful that you chose to spend some time with Tia and Andrew. Hopefully, you enjoyed them, as much as I adore them.

I've had stories running around in my head for years. I even "published" an illustrated book of poetry when I was in fourth grade. It was really bad, and hopefully has disappeared to the same place that socks go.

However, when I thought about writing a "real" story, that thought scared me. I procrastinated by writing an endlessly long outline, googling random facts, and thinking that I *can't*. In early 2018, while on maternity leave, I thought I'd give this writing a real shot, especially since my baby was a great daytime sleeper (note the word "daytime"). I wrote the first couple of chapters of the best Regency novel ever and even managed to have an agent take a look.

Turns out, it was not meant to be the best Regency novel ever. It sucked.

But, one thing that I learned, just by writing those chapters (which will also never see the light of day), was that it wasn't the story that *I* was meant to write. Instead, Tia and Andrew are who I was supposed to write about. In contemporary times …

I'm still holding out hope that someone will eventually write that best Regency novel ever. Because I spent a lot of time, coffee, and avocado toast on the world's longest outline.

This story wouldn't have happened without some amazing people. To Penny, Fiona, and Brooke for taking this chance on me, telling me not to panic, and working through the story with me. To Sarah M. Anderson and Maria Vale for your feedback and being reader #1 of a partially written story and reader #2 of the full story. To Michelle and Judy, thank you for your thoughtful suggestions to help make this book so much better than what it started as. To all of my fellow Smartypants Romance authors for your support, reading my story, and late-night questions—I feel privileged to be part of the sisterhood.

To my husband for playing endless rounds of catch-me-as-I-jump-off-the-couch with the kids while I wrote, making me coffee while I typed at night, and not judging me when I fell asleep before the kids.

To my kiddos, yes, I'm sorry, this book took a really long time and has no pictures. But in seriousness, despite whatever guilt I felt whenever you caught me writing, I believe so strongly in following your dreams. So I hope, my little Baozi and my little Jiaozi, that you will chase after your dreams too.

ABOUT THE AUTHOR

Nanxi Wen thought she was going to write the greatest historical novel. Turns out, her characters decided that they want to be in the 21st century with modern plumbing, online shopping, and reality TV shows. Her first book comes out in February 2021 – Give Love a Chai.

She lives in New England with her husband and two clingy monkeys (aka toddlers). When she is not despairing over word count, she enjoys reading, snacking, drinking coffee, sitting by the fireplace, hanging out with friends (far apart and with masks) and daydreaming.

Sign up for Nanxi Wen's newsletter!

Find Nanxi Wen online:
Website: https://nanxiwen.com/
Facebook: http://bit.ly/3jdMerD
Goodreads: http://bit.ly/3o9oDKs
Facebook Reader Group: http://bit.ly/3nb3Kxp
Instagram: https://bit.ly/3rfjtO5

Find Smartypants Romance online:
Website: www.smartypantsromance.com
Facebook: www.facebook.com/smartypantsromance/
Goodreads: www.goodreads.com/smartypantsromance
Twitter: @smartypantsrom
Instagram: @smartypantsromance
Newsletter: https://smartypantsromance.com/newsletter/

ALSO BY SMARTYPANTS ROMANCE

Green Valley Chronicles

The Love at First Sight Series

Baking Me Crazy by Karla Sorensen (#1)

Batter of Wits by Karla Sorensen (#2)

Steal My Magnolia by Karla Sorensen(#3)

Fighting For Love Series

Stud Muffin by Jiffy Kate (#1)

Beef Cake by Jiffy Kate (#2)

Eye Candy by Jiffy Kate (#3)

The Donner Bakery Series

No Whisk, No Reward by Ellie Kay (#1)

The Green Valley Library Series

Love in Due Time by L.B. Dunbar (#1)

Crime and Periodicals by Nora Everly (#2)

Prose Before Bros by Cathy Yardley (#3)

Shelf Awareness by Katie Ashley (#4)

Carpentry and Cocktails by Nora Everly (#5)

Love in Deed by L.B. Dunbar (#6)

Scorned Women's Society Series

My Bare Lady by Piper Sheldon (#1)

The Treble with Men by Piper Sheldon (#2)

The One That I Want by Piper Sheldon (#3)

Park Ranger Series

Happy Trail by Daisy Prescott (#1)

Stranger Ranger by Daisy Prescott (#2)

The Leffersbee Series

Been There Done That by Hope Ellis (#1)

The Higher Learning Series

Upsy Daisy by Chelsie Edwards (#1)

Seduction in the City

Cipher Security Series

Code of Conduct by April White (#1)

Code of Honor by April White (#2)

Cipher Office Series

Weight Expectations by M.E. Carter (#1)

Sticking to the Script by Stella Weaver (#2)

Cutie and the Beast by M.E. Carter (#3)

Weights of Wrath by M.E. Carter (#4)

Common Threads Series

Mad About Ewe by Susannah Nix (#1)

Give Love a Chai by Nanxi Wen (#2)

Educated Romance

Work For It Series

Street Smart by Aly Stiles (#1)

Heart Smart by Emma Lee Jayne (#2)

Lessons Learned Series

Under Pressure by Allie Winters (#1)

CPSIA information can be obtained
at www.ICGtesting.com
Printed in the USA
LVHW031527060521
686701LV00004B/930

9 781949 202755